Dear A

by Katie Blanchard

Dear Anna

ISBN: 978-1733664004

Editor: Traci Finlay
Proofreader: Bex Kettner at Editing Ninja
Cover Designer: Teddi Black

To my husband, Brian,
for believing in me, and for your obsession with Forensic Files.

Medeia's Journal

DEAR ANNA,

    I was the perfect wife.

    You were his whore.

    You plotted against me with the devil, himself.

    Will God let you repent for your sin?

    I WON'T.

One

"ARE YOU OKAY, MISS?"

"Huh?" I turn my attention to the old man standing three feet from me. The smell of rain mixing with asphalt rises and clogs my lungs. My shirt clings to my body from the assault of raindrops. I push my wet hair back with the hand that's not holding a shopping bag.

"Are you okay, miss?" the stranger repeats. "We saw that you were standing here and we, my wife and I —" he points back toward his van where a worried woman sits staring out the window at me— "wanted to check on you." His smile is a gentle reminder of a time back when strangers didn't just pass by without a kind word.

"Yes. Sorry, I thought I saw someone I know." Embarrassment constricts my chest.

He follows the direction of my eyes. "That couple in there?" He enquires, as he is involved now in solving my dilemma.

I wish he'd leave. "No, they've already walked away." I turn my head again to find my vehicle. "Thank you, though."

"Sure thing, honey. Take it easy." He bids me farewell as he walks back to join his wife in their minivan. The rain exposes his body's hunchback form.

"You, too." I rush to my Mercedes, senses now returning. I feel the coldness of the weather stain my skin, but it's not what penetrates my bones and makes my blood retreat into frozen icicles.

I stare back at the restaurant, pushing my wiper blades to their limit to clear the scene. There before me is my worst fear. Even with my vision blurred by the weather, I still see my husband of ten years dining with a woman who looks like more than just a business associate as he smooths a stray hair away from her face.

My eyes betray me as I watch him kiss the lady on the lips after they place their order with the waitress. There's familiarity in the curve of her face and the way she holds herself—the angle of her chin and the dip at the end of it. I've seen her before. She flicks her hair away, revealing her profile.

Anna.

I'm great with names. They stick with me instantaneously upon meeting a person. Anna is the secretary whose voice floods my ears whenever I call John's office. She's the perky blonde behind the desk whenever I drop something off for him when he is in a business meeting. Now she is the one leaning across the table in rapt attention as John, *my* husband, regales her with a story.

You got to keep a man interested, Medeia, or he'll stray.

My mother's mantra comes flooding back in my memory, and I wish I could call her up and tell her all about this. She would know how to fix the damage, but she's dead — gone not even a year now. I'm left to deal with the ease of John's hand in Anna's telling me this isn't the first time they've held onto each other, alone.

Their fingers aren't hesitant to be conjoined. Instead, they flock to each other, taking comfort in the familiarity they find hiding in the nooks of each finger. My eyes stay glued to them as they begin to enjoy their meals, close to the window. It's as if God is on my side and wants them to be observed by me. I take note of how they don't even care, how John, in particular, doesn't care. My husband is not concerned with the fact that he is on display in a restaurant window with a woman who is not his wife. Let the people stare. I search for any trace of a guilty conscience, maybe just a glimpse of him looking over his shoulder to survey the restaurant inhabitants, but I look on in vain. What would he say if I told him someone saw him? Would he lie or fess up? If I were anyone else looking in, I would easily assume they were another couple—not a married man and his whore.

I came to the shopping center this afternoon to buy some things for his birthday. Talk about irony. John consumes this day. I had no idea when a familiar sports jacket caught my peripheral vision, that I would find this scene.

They don't see me because they're too busy laughing and staring at each other like fresh new lovers with no problems. They took no notice of the paralyzed figure in the middle of the parking lot, staring after them. He never looked for my car to make sure the coast was clear. That's even more terrifying than the act itself — the blatant disregard.

Inside I am frozen, but at the surface, my skin begins to warm from the heat of my emotions. My throat is suffocating me as it tightens with the force of infidelity being lodged there and refusing to move. My jaw rigidly locks in a solid clench of anger. The adrenaline shifts the icicles in my veins to move. He texted me this morning that he couldn't meet me for lunch because he had to work through it to catch up.

He chose her over me. After what I did for him, this is my payment? He doesn't even try to hide his whore from the world, but he is sure not to flaunt his wife in it.

And what am I to make of his mistress? No doubt that she is young. My thirty-six-year-old body can still compete, though. I'm an attractive woman, just as she is. Except we are opposites, clear as day. I don't have to look hard to find what my husband sees in her over me. Her shiny blonde hair falls in curls around her porcelain face. My flat brown straight hair envelopes my olive skin tone. You can tell she is a bubbly person from the way she is bouncing as she talks to him. I have never been one to bounce. Bubbly is for the secretaries, which is what Anna is. John's secretary.

She giggles and touches his arm. What could be so funny? My husband is not a comedic guy. He doesn't have a sense of humor. He can stretch out a joke for ten minutes, never reaching the punchline. He's the type of guy who will explain why something is considered funny and ruin the essence of the joke itself. So, what is making Anna laugh? A joke about his wife who doesn't suspect a thing, perhaps?

Medeia Moore — his dedicated wife that does it all for him. I am everything John needs or wants; I make sure of it. I have done everything to keep John's attention through the years. Am I the reason that they are giving themselves over to fits of laughter?

I bow my head, peering at my outfit. The rain has soaked me to the bone, but that's not what makes me look frumpy. Lately, I've been choosing comfort over style when I go out during the day, yoga pants instead of hip-hugging jeans that express the curves beneath. The things that I hide from John when he isn't there. I wouldn't dare wear this when he is around. I gaze back at Anna, and she's shimmering in a tight bodice dress that I would consider too risqué for the office, but she wears it with confidence oozing from the scarlet color.

She's the woman that unfortunately ends up making the rest of us intimidated and small-feeling. We could arrive as done-up as possible, and she would still knock us down in a pair of sweatpants and a t-shirt. Her poise allows her to be a knockout in a potato sack bag.

On our wedding day, I encompassed that very feeling. I was the spitting image of a princess, with my hair curled and makeup better than a supermodel. Ten pounds lighter and much more svelte, and on that day, John stood before God, family, and friends and swore to forsake all others. And since that day, I have worked to remain the perfect image of a rich man's wife: perfect manicure, expensive clothing, heels, hair maintained. It's a strict grooming regimen to give me the bonus appearance of money. It's tiresome, and I do let myself go at times when John isn't home, but I have tried to take his comments into action. I am the perfect woman for John, straight from his design. So, why am I watching him smile at a blonde with spaghetti sauce on her chin? This whorish pig threatens the stability I have dedicated my life to maintain. I feel my shelter slipping through my fingers.

I felt like a million dollars on the day that I married him, and today, I feel like a cheap penny dropped on the ground and not worthy enough to be picked back up. That's not fair. I am worth something as well. My pity party gives way to the righteous anger coursing through my body.

My hand lingers on the door handle, ready to confront him, to tell him what an enormous asshole he is. For all that I have done for him in ten years, that he would dare end it like this. For what I sacrificed to save him. I'll throw the spaghetti plate in Anna's face, smear what I imagine is perfect makeup, like her pristine hair. That's what I'll do. I yank the handle toward me and jump back into the rain. I feel the adrenaline pumping through me, causing my teeth to chatter.

I stomp my way to the first line of cars, looking left and right to cross. This will be my moment. I can't believe after what I have sacrificed for John; it hasn't afforded me fidelity. I've turned my whole life over to John's rules. Why? Then it smacks me in the face like a puddle splashing up from a car. John has all of the money. I came into the marriage with nothing, and that's why I never strayed from the straight line that I needed to walk to be the perfect wife. If I go in there now and let myself be known, I'll put myself in a worse position.

I'll be penniless. John has made it legal, thanks to the prenup, that I will never have any of his money to my name if I leave him. He knows it's my weakness, coming from such a poor family. It's what we had constructed our lives to be, a safety net so that I don't end up like my family, and so that we don't put ourselves in a position similar to the one ten years ago. Oh, god. I turn and run back to the car, leaning into the steering wheel to hide my tears from shoppers running back to the shelter of their vehicles. I can't escape my marriage and be better off—he's designed it that way. Terror shocks my system. I need to get out of here.

I pull the car out of the parking lot, no longer wanting to risk being seen by my husband. If he notices me here now, it will be my demise instead of my triumph. I wipe the tears off my face. He can't get away with this. I will find a way out. In the quiet of my car, I promise myself that. It's not time to confront him, not until I've come up with a plan.

I'll be damned if I go back to the shack of my childhood without a fight.

Two

JOHN IS A CPA, OR AT least that was the career that got him to where he is now. After years of proving his talent in the accounting world, John began his company and now runs a multi-million-dollar business by providing people in the Pittsburgh vicinity with their own personal finance team. He has financial advisors, accountants, and others all under his belt now. He's not anyone's accountant anymore, now he runs the business and oversees everything.

To ensure that he runs the company efficiently, my husband stores a copy of all the employees' files at home so that he can use the information to better delegate assignments and be able to handle an internal problem amongst coworkers with the advantage of knowing each of the involved party's history. It has proved beneficial for him to give slack to an employee who has a daughter sick at home. It shows faith in the boss and helps grow loyalty to the company on the employee's part. John is no doubt an excellent businessman, and a now an equally fantastic liar.

Anna Trayor, however, is not a significant employee or person. She is a twenty-three-year-old girl who was hired on as a temp and then promoted to fulltime when John's senior secretary retired. She lucked into the position; she didn't earn it. How cliché and ridiculous it is to start an affair with your secretary. For his power and wealth, my husband is not even aspiring to be something more than a twenty-five-cent smut novel in the back of a clearance rack at a used book store.

There are several chicken-scratch notes by my husband in her file. *Skirt too short, bent over the desk at me today and I saw her red panties. I must remember to tell her to buy some black ones.* Why would he be so hurtful and careless to leave a paper trail of evidence for me to find? That note shall remain a deep scar in my mind for all eternity.

For some reason or other, my husband has written it down so that he doesn't forget. My underwear is nothing of significance. I am the ball and chain, the same old thing he comes home to every day, the one whom John refuses to let work because he doesn't want that kind of wife. He finds it insulting that I should like to work when he can clearly provide for us.

I note that his former secretary, who was older than dirt as he put so lovingly on her file, didn't get any notes about the color of her panties. I search through a few other records from his department to find that not only is my husband a closeted pervert, but on paper, he appears to be a lousy human being and boss. The personal notes for the employees would be enough to get him sued.

Smells like fish, tell her to wash her unused cooter.

Doesn't have a brain cell, but the clients like him. Attempt to transfer his charm on to someone else and then let him go.

Dumbest bitch ever but has wealthy friends.

Nothing more about Anna. I will have to dig deeper. Know thy enemy. I lug myself up from the floor and move to continue my day in its regular routine.

John has a set of rules for me, something he created for my benefit.

"You don't have the wealthy upbringing that I do. Let me show you some shortcuts and steer you away from this poor life. You want to be rich; I can help with that."

The list became a Bible for my life. I rid myself of friends who were involved in crimes big and small. That narrowed me down to being friendless. Any new friends were screened by John first, and he rarely approved of my picks. I began to dress rich; the clothes provided by John. I stopped working in an area overrun with thugs and the poor. It led me to not working at all. John loved this. He cleared my parents' mortgage for me and my brother's fines. I hadn't anything left to work for anyway. We married, and grooming routines like manicures, facials, botox, and haircuts were added — all to keep me on the straight and narrow to leave my old life of bad choices behind.

I hear the front door slam and look up to the ceiling. Every time John does it, it sets my nerves on edge. I have never vocalized my annoyance because I know it's his way of venting out a tough day.

"Good evening, Medeia." His voice coos around each word as he enters the room. I'm a little taken aback at his ease into our night when his day was rotting from dishonesty. But, little does he know, that tonight will consist of both of us lying to each other. It is in my best interest right now to continue to play my role of the perfect wife. I don't know enough about the situation to plot my move.

"The first thing you have to learn, Medeia, is that you never act on emotion. That's when things get sloppy."

My father's words send shivers up my spine. He acted with emotions one morning and left our whole world in ruins. I won't take after him. I've worked too hard maintaining these rules to end up just like my father. There is no way that I intend to lose this security or go back to a life of meager portions that left me with nothing but desperation to commit crimes. Ten years in a marriage deserves to earn me money.

"Hi, honey." It's barely an utter, as I pour him a glass of wine just like I do every night, serving my master. I choke back the feeling. "How was work?"

"Same as usual. Making money." He smiles. "How was your day?"

I sip my wine and try to act casual. "Oh, dull and uneventful."

"Perhaps you should pick up a hobby. Lori said you gave her the cold shoulder when she mentioned joining their book club." He sips his wine and starts walking toward the dining room. "These are the people we need to keep in good graces with, you know. That's your duty as my wife."

"I don't feel like participating in the book club, John." I sit in my seat at the table as my husband takes his place at the opposite end.

"Honey," he rests his hand on mine, "Is it because of your depression? Is it worsening?" John's mouth ticks upward on one corner, it's a hitch he can't hide, almost like he is happy at the possibility.

"No, I feel fine. I think that the book club isn't the place for me, and I'd be much better served elsewhere. Maybe a job of some sort."

"Honey. You've just started making progress in therapy. Let's not overwhelm you." He dives into his duck and ends the conversation. Checkmate. That was John's new favorite move—therapy.

When my mother passed away, I suffered a mental breakdown. I searched for her everywhere on the streets, not wanting to believe that she had gone. John had me admitted to a hospital for a week.

"Speaking of that, honey, there is something I wanted to mention to you this evening. I called Dr. Janson and scheduled you an appointment tomorrow at two." My husband moans into the bite of duck he's chewing. My therapy is discussed in a passing way, never sincere, and never with a troubled face.

I nearly drop my fork onto the porcelain dinner plate adorned with tiny cherubs. John made me an appointment. Why? I am indeed capable of doing that task myself; I'm not a child. And shouldn't my mental health and progress be in my hands?

"Why did you do that?" I ask.

"Well, I heard you crying again this morning in the bathroom. I'm not sure the new medication is working for you. Perhaps you should ask for something stronger tomorrow." His eyes hold me, and I watch the wetness behind them. He is worried, and the only thing that will erase it from his mind is me handing over control. "Don't you trust me? I'm only trying to help you."

"Of course, I trust you." The words leave my lips before the reality of them sink in. How could I offer up the words to him so quickly when I caught him cheating today? Was I a robot?

I bob my head and try to smile back. I cried in the bathroom this morning because today was scheduled to be the day I took my mother to a play she always wanted to see. Othello. I didn't bother doing anything with the tickets. Instead, I threw on some lousy clothes and pushed myself to run errands and ended up finding John's dirty secret.

"I'm only thinking of your well-being, Medeia," he justifies himself. *Sure, you are, John.*

"No, honey. I know you are, I'm not arguing that point. I'll go. Two o'clock, right?" I do my best to ease his mind. With the discovery of his infidelity this morning, I can't risk angering John and upsetting the system. Not until I can put a plan in action to stop the affair or get myself away with more than a dollar to my name.

I sink my teeth into the duck, longing for the taste of revenge instead.

Three

"GOODBYE, DARLING, HAVE a good day." I kiss John's lips, and I swallow down the revolting lump in my throat.

"Goodbye, dear. Try to forget that nonsense of a career today. I love taking care of you. This is where I want you to be. At home." He kisses my forehead. A move meant to be protecting and loving, but it feels like a mark for a sniper to shoot me.

I hold the front door open, draped in a real silk robe around a matching nightgown, and wave as John's BMW fades from our development. When he's out of sight, I launch myself into the mission for today—find out everything I can about Anna Trayor. Her file didn't provide much insight, aside from the color of her undergarments, so I need to branch out further than what John's employee files can provide.

As I lay in our California King bed last night, I debated what my next steps should be, and without a doubt, I need to become a level-one detective and familiarize myself with the enemy. I can do as John did with the employee files and use it to benefit the choosing of my next move better. If I know what Anna is like, perhaps I can find the meaning behind John's obsession with her and use the information against him along with what we hid a long time ago. It's my ticket to this house. Where do I start, though?

Social media.

I have heard tales from a few wives and girlfriends at the boring social events that John drags me to of how they looked up a former lover of their significant other on the internet. I will follow their lead. Those hours locked at a table of the "wives" will be useful for something.

I lounge on the velvet chaise in the sitting area of my large walk-in closet and peruse the internet for anything it can spit out about Anna Trayor. Her social media pages are the ones ripe with information. For Anna, the most advantageous was proving to be her Facebook page. She hasn't bothered to set it to private or block posts from being seen by strangers, so all the status updates are ripe for the picking. She wants to let the world in and make herself the center-stage attraction. She's an attention whore. She writes everything down, and I mean *everything*.

Whether it's posting about the day's activities or checking in to locations to show off her lifestyle, Anna doesn't miss a day of keeping people informed, never missing a beat for the past 567 days. And the day she did miss, she apologized profusely for in her next update. The funny part is that there's only ever a handful of comments on her statuses, typically from the same people. Her actual audience is minuscule compared to the grand scale she believes she's projecting her views on. I note that she didn't post about her lunch with John yesterday. Nothing about a love interest anywhere, not even a thinly veiled tacky meme.

Her Instagram is harder to suffer through. It doesn't show me much, aside from her perfect boobs and her idea of stylish dressing in cheap garments from the mall. Instagram is her vanity, Facebook her desperation, and Twitter is filled with rants about what she considers to be the injustices of the world. Her favorite restaurant discontinued a meal so obscure that I'm sure she only called it her favorite because it set her apart from the crowd. I don't believe for a second that she ate and enjoyed it — still, no mention of John. Anna makes sure to keep her dating life private on a place that she posted about her menstrual cycle at least three times.

She doesn't cross-post though, something about her I notice straight away. I don't have to sift through a redundancy of posts on the separate social media pages. Anna plays to a different audience on each platform, making it hard to get a depiction of her true self. I can only judge on the part that she is willing to offer up to the world, and boy is it ugly.

On the surface, I see hypocrisy and contradictions in her posts ranging from giggly nasal videos of her dancing at the club singing with a group to her self-proclaimed "homebody" photos of skimpy pajamas she "wore all day." There's no way a person wore that without freezing their asses off in the wintertime. And alone. Why?

My favorites are the back to back postings checking herself in at a gym with the caption of *laughing at the fatties this morning* next to her "love everyone" memes about body positivity. Anna doesn't have one lick of personality that she came up with herself. She is something fit for the modern world, a shifter who drifts in and out of trends claiming them as life.

I scroll through thousands, *thousands,* of selfies before finding one unflattering photograph that Anna let seep through the wormhole. A picture was taken on her phone of an old picture lying on the floor of her bedroom. It's from high school, and it tells a lot. Anna was not that popular in her school; I instantly pick that up from the lack of grooming on the girl of old versus her now. She is surrounded by only two friends, gripping them tightly in each arm as she finds herself in the center. The need for the attention to fall upon her alone seems built-in long before the ability to put on makeup came together. There's a bulletin behind them, indicating that this photo of them was at the school itself. The corkboard is enclosed in a glass case protecting itself from the juveniles and their unoriginal pranks. There is a faint mirror image captured in the glass that upon zooming in I notice a boy walking past looking on the happy three-some with disgust. An older lady is taking the photo for them, no doubt a teacher instead of another classmate.

Anna had been disliked.

The photo also tells a different story of the girl in all those selfies. There has been work done. Her teeth have become straighter than her sixteen-year-old self possessed, and either puberty hit her late or Anna has had a boob job. That's the option that explains the consistent pictures involving her cleavage. For the amount that I'm sure they cost, she wants to gain mileage flaunting them off. I notice that Anna once wore glasses, a style that's coming back. She switched to contacts as soon as she could, but in recent postings, I've caught her wearing black-rimmed spectacles proclaiming to be a geek at heart.

Which one is it, Anna? Are you a geek or a cool girl?

She checks in at a gym not five miles from my house every morning at five. From the pictures she has of herself there, it's more crowded than I thought it would be. Less of a chance that she would notice me. Perhaps, it's time I get myself a membership and find out which social media posts are the real Anna Trayor and which aren't.

Medeia's Journal

DEAR ANNA,

I found out about your affair with my husband. The posts on your social media pages ranting about sister solidarity feel like a slap in the face. Who are you to pick and choose which female you support and which you ruin by screwing her husband?

Your posts are nearly all selfies. I bet you don't practice what you preach in friendships these days. Do you have any friends?

Four

I USED TO MEET MY MOTHER somewhere of her choosing every single day. Never at the shack, and never at my mansion. There was unspoken shame in both of those locations. My mother regretted not being able to provide the type of life for me that I had now, and she felt guilty that she didn't raise me to be humble in my upbringing. My house possessed the devil of change she loathed seeing in me, hers the devil of the past I didn't long to see. That's why we remained on neutral ground.

"You don't have to wipe your seat down, Medeia, the restaurant is clean enough."

"This is Versace, Mom."

"That's not how I raised you."

'That's not how I raised you' was a favorite saying of hers whenever I would dare to remind her of the cost of things. She wanted me to forget the money and what it was worth in life, but how could I? It consumed me from birth — fighting and scraping to have a little, to finally have more than enough. It gave me a chance at life. Without John's money, I might have turned out like my brother Hank and his run-ins with theft. Or, my father and his angry outbursts leading to more than one arrest and more than one victim. John's rules, teaching me to be of his world, saved me.

Despite the difference, my mother was my best friend. I confided in her about everything—John's dislike for having children to my anxiety over not having a job for a sense of security that John couldn't take away. She knew he scolded me in his side-handed comments. I watched the guilt color her face pink with embarrassment when I would recant a story about him. She told me it was wrong for him to speak to me that way. Even when I comforted her that he didn't mean it the way she took it, she wouldn't relent.

When she didn't meet me that day for lunch, I went back there, back to the dilapidated structure that raised me. The medical team surrounding the rotting wood spoke the words my drunk father couldn't utter when he saw me. She was gone. And so, went a part of me—and my mind, according to my husband.

Therapy was placed on the roster after my stint in the hospital. I don't recall those days, only scenes of arm restraints and needles. The screams echo deep in a dark place inside of me. The attending doctor on the first lucid day explained that I had a breakdown of sorts. Rest was needed, and therapy. Their outlook for my recovery was positive. I, however, knew that a suffering heart never mends.

That's how I found Dr. Janson, renowned grief counselor and famous for his work with the wealthy class of the area. He was the best of the best, and if John was going to have a wife in therapy, it better be someone that had stars around his name. Dr. Janson is a warm and inviting person, and I have become fond of him.

His sharp mind and proper manner of speaking seemed a proven tactic to gain the confidence of his patients. The first day that I came here, I remember feeling at ease by how knowledgeable and professional he sounded. We've grown from there, and he's let his guard down some, switching his tools to adapt to a more appropriate plan for my "recovery."

Except for today— today he is pouting.

The dead air between Dr. Janson and I feels more like a duel rather than an awkward pause of disagreement. His eyes have locked and held mine for at least ten minutes now. I finally break contact and become the first to speak again.

"I *have* been more sad than usual lately, and I think this medication is not helping. All I'm asking for is a different anti-depressant than I'm currently on or a higher dose. I'm not a drug addict, and I'm not trying to suck medication from your prescription pad to get high. I want to get better." I run my hands through the sleek sides of my ponytail, bracing my elbows on my knees. Panic rises inside; if I can't convince Dr. Janson to do either of these options, John will think I didn't bother to ask. I can't risk an argument with a prenup like ours.

Dr. Janson sighs. "Medeia, all I'm saying is that you suffer from situational depression. Medication is not a long-term goal for you." He grits his teeth. "Despite what John may think."

My entire body deflates, and I push hard on the space between my eyebrows. "Les, I just made mention of his suggestion. I'm here on my own accord." I smooth down my dress. Versace again. I wasn't raised like this, but the material did feel different. A little worthier.

"Perhaps we should switch up techniques. There are other methods used to help treat situational depression." He reaches back to his desk where brochures sit perched and ready.

"Yeah. I've Googled them." I slap my knees and lean farther forward. "Can you honestly look me in the eye and think that I haven't tried everything possible? No one wants a broken person."

"Is this about John or your mother? Or your father's awful expectations of you as a child that you could never meet?" His face is stern but softens with his finding of an ah-ha moment. "We discussed this Medeia; I feel like you aren't addressing the real issue. You're blanketing it under stress from your mother's passing."

"Look." I push a stray hair back out of my face. "Striving for perfection isn't wrong to me. It gives me focus. I wasn't on medication before my mother's death, so I don't see how you can say that I am blanketing these feelings under that. You're hunting ghosts, Les, and I'm not about to dig them up with you."

"Yeah, cause people with mental health problems are all on medication and not walking around pretending it's okay." He scrubs his face in irritation. "Medeia, I like you. Enough to be on a first-name basis with you and talk so candidly. This is not the standard repertoire, but I know it helps your progress. That is a breakthrough for you. You're less guarded, but you're allowing that to be your top tier and not pushing for advancement and shattering that glass ceiling. You need to keep working at this depression from all angles. Become familiar with it, raise those ghosts and demons then confront them. I have been doing this for decades now; I think I know a thing or two."

"Well, I've lived with myself all my life, so I think I know me a bit better than you do from your professional book typecasting," I slam back, crossing my arms. I click my heels off the floor in protest.

"I have never once typecast you into a category of mental health issues." He shakes his head vigorously.

"I'm sorry, Les." I sink farther into the couch. "I don't mean to be a bitch. I just had a hard day yesterday."

"Would it help to tell me about it?" He pushes himself upright, giving me rapt attention.

I debate about opening up and having someone else help me digest the situation at home. Another ear to bend and help me plot my way out of this hole. But something stops me, telling me that this is a secret I need to keep to myself for now if I want to benefit from John's affair instead of being demolished by it.

"Tell me about yesterday, Medeia." Les's voice is soothing.

"Yesterday, I had tickets to take my mother to see Othello." I roll my bottom lip inside my mouth to protect it from quivering. Les nods his understanding.

"I like to wake up in bed these days and keep my eyes shut so that I can pretend I'm a teenager again in my old bedroom. I'm lying in bed at my old house, waiting for my mother to wake me even though I'm already awake, listening to the noises she makes about the house as she gets ready for the day. If I concentrate hard enough, I hear her footsteps in the hallway, going back and forth from her room, collecting her clothes and putting on her makeup, in between refilling her coffee mug in the kitchen. Then I hear her tiptoe into my room, pausing at my doorway every single time without fail. She told me once that she took me in in the morning during the quiet moments. She stood mesmerized as she remembered that she carried me in her body and that I was a great miracle to her. Then she eventually resigns herself to the task of getting me up for the day and walks to the bed and kisses my forehead. I can feel her lips on my head when I think about it, but every time I open my eyes, I'm thrown into reality. I'm an adult, not a teenager, and my mother is dead. So, how do I stop it, Les? Do I forget about her?"

"No," he whispers, perhaps remembering his own usual daydream that keeps him going in life. He sighs. "I'll prescribe a higher dosage. Perhaps it will help relax your mind right now."

"Thank you, Doctor. I'm grateful for you." I mean it. He's brought me back from the dark side. With him helping me turn around and face my demons head-on, I comfortably live alongside them instead of wrestling them.

He scrubs down his worrisome face. Something is troubling Les, and he doesn't want to say it out loud for some reason. He's about to do the doctor thing where they say it in a way that makes you come up with the answer that they already know, but don't want to tell you straight out because you would become offended. Also, giving you the answers doesn't aid in your growth—those you are supposed to come up with on your own. I brace myself. I feel it coming. He always does this at the close of our sessions.

"How is the relationship between John and you?"

I don't know how to handle that question. It is vague compared to the other ones that Dr. Janson usually leaves me with to ponder.

"Oh, good. Normal, I suppose. We are married, so it has its battles like any couple. We fight over the standard things like dinner and cleaning up." I smile to hide any dead give-aways in my demeanor. My teeth are fake, so every smile since they got put in has been fake, anyway.

"Mmm." He jots down a few more notes, and I'd give anything to read one of those entries on me, or even his most psychotic patient. Wouldn't that be the world's most interesting read? Inside the mind of a man that gets inside the minds of the craziest people, losing their minds. "Well, I'd love to chat more and discover this issue, but unfortunately we are at the end of our time today. I want you to schedule a follow-up with the front desk. Sooner than our regular appointment. I need to know if this increase in medication is working for you or not." He stands and wanders over to his desk and leans over to retrieve the small prescription pad in his top center drawer.

With that, my body instinctively rises from the couch. I hate this part. I am leaving, not knowing if I'm in a better place or not. I'm thankful for the doctor because he has helped me in the grief process of losing my mother, but I always leave feeling like I gave up the power and conviction of my disease that I walked in the doors holding. I think the session will go one way, and he steers it in the opposite direction, and I end up losing control.

"Of course, Doctor. Thank you." I reach for the prescription when he hands it over; he holds it tight until I force myself to look into his eyes.

"If you need anything, Medeia, do call." His face is what I imagine a good father to look like—worrisome eyes that hold love and not hatred, wrinkles that scream of life rather than an addiction.

"I will."

He lets go of the prescription, so I move to the door and make the next appointment with the receptionist up in the front. When I step into the sunlight, I debate about stopping the medicine cold turkey and allowing myself to feel the grief, but I know it will put my body into shock. For now, my husband will believe that I'm on a higher dosage, but I didn't ask for it, so I'll hold off on the increase.

The sunlight warms my face, but something inside grows cold.

Medeia's Journal

DEAR ANNA,

Why is he so obsessed with you?

Five

"I DON'T KNOW WHAT I can do for you, Mrs. Moore."

"What do you mean?" Across from the lawyer's desk, I clutch my purse firmly in my lap. I bet it costs more than his entire cheap suit.

"If you have a prenup that you say guarantees you nothing, then that's what you'll get." He shrugs. He's the only lawyer I could get to meet with me on such short notice that didn't work anywhere near our home or John's company. I should have done more digging.

"What about his infidelity?" This seems ridiculous. There's no way that a prenup to your marriage allows you to hump whoever you want.

The baby-faced lawyer stretches his arms up above his head. "Do you have proof?"

"I saw him in the restaurant with her." I screech.

"That's hearsay. You have no pictures, no video, no emails, no notes, no texts. Nada. This is a no-fault state, so it doesn't hold as much weight as you're hoping."

"What am I supposed to do?"

"Get proof."

"Will that cancel out the prenup?"

"Not in my opinion." He raises his eyebrows at me and points to the door. "It was nice meeting you, Macy."

"Medeia!" I shout. "I can't say the same about you." I bolt out of the chair and rush out of his office. I slam the door with finite on his slimy smirk. What a jerk. Is that all I get? I never signed a deal with the devil, so why is my soul being taken from me?

Shit. I slam the car door and lock myself inside. Shit. Shit. Shit. I repeatedly bang my hands off the steering wheel. I bounce my head off the horn, and it scares a couple walking past. I get nothing. Nothing. Not a dime. I'll have to sell my clothes. I'll have to get a job.

I groan in the space — a job. Now, how in the hell am I going to manage that when John doesn't want me working?

LATER AT DINNER, THE mere mention of a job sends John's need for control in overdrive. My knife digs into my tender, medium-rare steak much harder than it needs to, and the scrape of the plate causes John to stir at his end of the table.

"I know you're mad, dear," he coos.

"No, no, I'm not mad." I obscenely smile to let my husband know that yes, he has ticked me off, but I don't wish to talk about it because I will spit obscenities. On top of the lawyer this morning, I feel trapped.

"I told you, I don't think that now is the best time for you to begin a career. The therapist just upped your medication." *Because of you, John. He upped it because of you.* I almost pout, but I suck in my bottom lip in with defiance. I won't beg him.

I wish I hadn't told him about the therapy session today; I wish I had lied and said that tears were a sign of happiness or made up some bullshit in medical speak. However, I can't lie as well as John can. His whore passes through my mind wearing a white wedding gown. I slam my knife down again as my teeth tear into the piece I just stuffed inside my mouth.

John exhales.

"Honey. I hate to see you so upset Medeia. I don't want to risk your health. It was so terrifying for me when you were in the hospital." He chokes up on cue.

My body sags, and I set my knife down. But the Post-it note in Anna's file blares into my vision, and I jam my fork into the next piece. Fuck him. That trick of acting worried would have sent me straight into submission before, but not now. I long to scream and throw shit in a tantrum just like my father would. My blood runs cold at the thought. I take a breath and count my chews so that I can afford myself some time to calm down. I will address this with my head about me; emotion will get me nowhere. It got my father nowhere, and my mother became the worst victim of his tantrums.

"I understand," I say after I've calmed down. I channel it out of my body. "I just...well, I wanted to have a hobby. I feel I've mastered the tasks around the household, and lately, I've been feeling bored and unchallenged." A professional tone always strikes a better nerve with John. He can't stand when I speak what he deems to be hick or uneducated talk. "I thought that a career would be a preferable option because it had the extra incentive of cash flow coming in. You're always saying we can't ever have enough money." I raise an eyebrow. He nods the agreement that it is a true statement.

I watch my words work on my husband. He scratches his head with the butt of his fork and hums into his steak. He sees my point; perhaps this will go my way after all. It would be easier to find work with my husband on board rather than sneaking around, although the thought of entering the workforce again disturbs me. I've become accustomed to my lifestyle.

"Plus, Dr. Janson didn't think it was such a bad idea." John loves therapy, maybe this was the lie I needed to fake, but to my surprise, John laughs.

"Honey, he would think that. If you have a mental breakdown, it's more money for him. Trust me; I have your best interests at heart here. He spends an hour with you here and there; I pledged my life to you. Remember what happened the last time you were working?" I feel slapped, even though John hasn't touched me.

Tears sting my eyes. I try to brush them off as I put a green bean in my mouth, but the sniffle gives me away. "That was you, too."

"I'll make a deal with you," he ignores my comment. "If you can maintain some hobby outside of the house, we will discuss it again at a later point." He's confident that he's come up with the perfect solution and strikes his fork into the air like the dot of a period—end of subject. "I should have been a therapist. No one can help you like I know how to."

What am I, John? A child? You don't want children, but you want to treat me like one? I'm getting a job.

I bite my tongue until I taste blood mix in with the Kobe steak. This will be the hardest time of my life. I no longer find redeeming qualities in my husband; in fact, my stomach hardly tolerates being around him. But, I'm not an idiot; my corner is empty. And until I fill it, I need to play this game.

"Now that you've mentioned it, I was thinking of joining a gym. Would that suffice as a good launching pad? That is, however, in the opposite direction of making money, but you had made mention a week ago that my thighs were jiggling more when I walk, so two birds in one stone." I want to tell him to fuck off and choke on his expensive steak, the rare delicacy that he entrusted to our mediocre twenty-something chef. When I have money, I won't be so foolish to hire a lousy cook.

"You know what? I think that might be perfect." He raises his glass of some expensive wine that has always tasted like it should be named 'piss' to me. I imitate him immediately. *Cheers, asshole.*

Medeia's Journal

DEAR ANNA,

One thing: five in the morning to workout is fucking ridiculous. I want to hit you with a dumbbell. Choke on your protein shake, whore. This better be worth it.

Six

I STUMBLE INTO THE local 24-hour fitness joint in town, knowing damn well it's the one Anna occupies because of her Facebook check-in locations. Last night, John was all on board with having a trim wife; he even called down and set up my membership over the phone, something only accomplished by the snobbiest of wealthy people. I attempt to be gracious to the front desk when I enter; I'm sure 'bitch' is stamped on my file somewhere because of him. My brand-new outfit, never having seen workout equipment before, already places me in that category.

"Hello, how may I help you?" There's an older lady behind the counter, and I take comfort that she's gripping a Styrofoam cup while addressing me. Perhaps she understands my lack of caffeine from a husband who said it wasn't the best idea to drink that before I worked out this morning. I almost slit his throat; however, orange never was a flattering color on me.

"Hi, I do apologize, I'm a bit embarrassed, but I believe my husband said he purchased a membership for me over the phone last night. Under the name of John Moore, my name is Medeia." The first rule of not having a bad reputation preceding you in a place: blame someone who isn't there.

"Oh, yes. Your husband said you would be here this morning." She smiles and does a cute little shrug I wish I could add to my movements, but I don't think I'd pull it off as well as she does. Hook, line, and sinker, Claudia—as I read on her name tag—will be erasing the bitch stamp on my file now. I need to keep a low profile here, can't risk gym gossip getting to Anna. I don't know how well acquainted she is with the staff, considering she checks in daily.

I smile back. "He's a pain in the butt sometimes, too thorough." I giggle on cue to entice her to join in comradery with me. She falls for it.

"I understand, Mia." Shit.

"I love that nickname." Please take the bait; please take the bait.

"Oh, I apologize. I haven't finished my morning coffee." She raises her cup toward me. "Your name is the most unique I've ever heard. How do you say it again?"

Thank you, Jesus. I hate when people don't listen the first time, though. Thanks, Mom, for a weird name.

"Ma-day-ah," I pronounce it slowly enough to help her out, but not too intense that I hit a nerve.

"Your name is so pretty." She sighs into her body. "My mother sadly named me Claudia, sounds more like a horse's name." She rolls her eyes.

"Nonsense. You have a beautiful name." As I smile back, I notice a familiar blonde breeze past the quick entryway on the side. One of the workers even shouts out a good-morning greeting to her.

Anna.

Oh, you don't disappoint, do you, Anna, dear?

Claudia attempts to conceal her eye roll at the mention of Anna's name, but I catch it. So, she's not a favorite with my new buddy, Claudia.

"You're all set, Medeia." This time Claudia pronounces it correctly. "You have to sign here, and the floor is all yours. I will go over some simple gym rules with you as I show you around."

"Oh, I do apologize, but a tour won't be necessary. I came here before I was married, and it doesn't seem like the place has changed too much." A lie. I had to get to the top floor before Anna could notice me. She would be on the bottom floor, lifting weights as her social media pictures indicate. I can view her better from the open walkway area upstairs housing the treadmills. "Plus, I don't want to take you away from your morning coffee, if I already know everything. My husband didn't allow me my coffee this morning, and I don't want to do the same thing to someone else."

"How awful of him." She gasps. "Well, thank you. You go on and scoot. I'd hate to keep you from your workout. We both win. Besides, you'll be that much closer to getting coffee" She winks at me. *See, John, I can make friends. I'm not as awkward as you make me sound in social interactions.*

I head straight to my destination, not stopping at the lockers to put things away. I didn't bring anything but bottled water with me, anyway. I take the stairs two at a time, the thrill of watching Anna fueling my high. I might not need the coffee this morning after all. I take control of a machine I had my eyes on since first walking in; it has the allure of location. A wall nearby that can aid in the covering of my appearance should Anna glance up.

I doubt she will. According to her posts on Instagram of her workout sessions, she hardly ever leaves the bottom floor. That's where she can scope out the man-candy as she so whorishly put it in a post that was dated three months ago. Perhaps John and Anna weren't together then, or maybe I should have myself checked for diseases from Anna's multitude of partners.

"Can I help you with that? You know these machines are, uh, a bit tricky at first." Leaning against the treadmill beside me stands a man old enough to be my father, smiling a creepy grin.

"I'm good; thank you." I make sure to flash my left hand as I wave him off. Married to an asshole, but still married.

"I'll be down at that end if you need me. Name's Rob, by the way." He winks.

"See ya later, Rob." I don't offer my name, and he takes the hint and walks away. *See, John. I have options. I could cheat. I'm not as immoral as you, though.*

I jump on the treadmill. I set to work choosing my incline of the day. I'm walking a damn steep hill in life metaphorically, why not make it physically, as well? Maybe a fitter lifestyle will prepare me for the workforce that I still plan on joining despite my husband's issues.

I'm two minutes in before the slutty blonde makes her appearance from the locker room. She's in no hurry to make her way to a station, saying hello to all the patrons in the gym. I watch closely to the interactions; more than half of the men stare after her ass but end up shaking their heads instead of reaching out to talk to her. Why won't they take the bait?

"Oh, that's our town trollop in the gym. She'll fuck anything that walks, and spends more time taking selfies on the workbench than actually pressing something." I slam the stop button on the treadmill to avoid falling off from the shock of the stranger talking next to me.

"Excuse me?" I pant out. I look to the right at the woman around my age punching the buttons on her treadmill in deep concentration. Built like an avid runner, and her grimace at the machine tells me she'd much rather be outside running. Her black hair is held up in a high ponytail, enunciating her strong jaw.

"That blonde." She nods in the direction of Anna. "I saw the disgust on your face, shared your sentiments, saw you were new and figured I'd welcome you to the gym. She won't try to be your friend; she's harmless to the vaginas in here. Unless your husband is here." She laughs until she takes in the shock of my face. "I'm sorry; I was just kidding."

"I just—" I wave my hands around trying to catch my words, but everything fails as I try to decipher whether my heart is thumping out of control because of the treadmill or this stranger's confession. "I'm Medeia." I hold out my hand. She instantly takes it.

"Jane. I'm here only on Thursday mornings. Other than that, unless you're a night owl, you won't see me." She starts her machine up, and I punch mine, as well.

"No, I like the mornings." I stare down toward Anna. "More productive this way."

"I usually do forty minutes. You're welcome to join me at the local coffee shop after this if you want." I watch as Jane pops her earbuds in one by one, all the while making it look effortless to accomplish while running at a fast pace.

"Coffee sounds delicious." Did I just make a friend? I smile down at the screen on the treadmill. Someone John didn't approve of first; it feels like a sin and something freeing all at once.

Medeia's Journal

DEAR ANNA,

You spent twenty minutes in the gym and left looking fresh and ready for the day. What the hell do you go for? I did forty minutes of hardcore running for you, bitch, just to see your whore face again. That's okay, Jane is cool, so it wasn't all a loss. Maybe I'll end up with a friend from all of this.

Seven

"YOU KNOW, YOU DIDN'T have to keep up with me the whole forty minutes, but I do commend the effort." Jane pushes the creamer across the table to my side where I'm rubbing my shaky thighs, praying for relief.

"Thanks." I take the creamer with gratitude and shift my weight to sit up straighter with a groan.

"Going too hard on your first day. Rookie mistake." She shakes her head into the cup she's pouring an obscene amount of sugar inside.

"Oh, thank God, you aren't one of those people who eat uber-healthy, as well. I won't have to pretend." I blurt it before I can stop myself.

Jane laughs. "Hell, no. I run forty minutes so I can put sugar in my cup."

"I would say that entitles me to at least two sugar-laden coffees this morning." I rub down on my thighs and wince in pain.

"At the very least, my dear." She waves to the girl behind the counter and shouts for two more for our table. Her crass attitude would send John running for the hills and stamping her inadmissible to our lives, but I like her already. A lot.

"So, what's your story?" She blows on her coffee, trying to will it to a tolerable temperature while I ponder her question.

"Housewife. Bored. Over thirty, so gym. Yea!" I mock cheer over my coffee cup.

"Divorcee. No kids. Wake up angry and run on Thursdays," she responds.

"I have no kids, either," I admit—more to the java in front of me than my new breakfast mate.

"Yo," she hollers. "We will need two huge bear claws, as well." Instead of being annoyed with her, the lady behind the counter smiles and throws a thumbs-up. They must know Jane here.

"You want to talk about it?" She sips her liquid and moans with delight.

"Nah. You couldn't fix it anyway, so what's the point?" I begin to sip my beverage, as well. My companion becomes quiet, so I use the time to take her in. The hands gripping her cup are rough and calloused, and her clothes scream that she works for a living and doesn't have stuff handed to her. I almost feel embarrassed by my new athletic shoes bumping into her worn ones. She's thin but muscular, the running she does hasn't taken away her leg muscles. Instead, they've reacted oppositely and bulked up. My favorite feature on Jane, though, are her eyes, sad and wise. They are deep brown with tiny flecks of gold near the top edges of the pupils.

"My ex-husband cheated on me. Some blonde cunt he met on the internet. I thought running would help me cope, you know?"

I nod.

"Thursdays were when they would meet for a morning snuggle. I found that I was still pissed off even afterward, so much for endorphins, but my body was looking good, better than his fat mistress at the time. He still stole a freaking day of the week from me."

"I'm sorry." It's a dumb thing to say, but it's what's expected when someone tells you their sob story.

"I confessed. Now, you go."

I sigh. What can I confess to my new friend? That my husband is screwing the gym trollop she pointed and laughed at, or that I am not allowed to have a job or a life? That a lawyer is making me the butt of his lunchtime jokes? That the friendship I believe we are starting is strictly forbidden, and she is already a secret?

"Come on. It feels good to get it off your chest. What's bugging you that you needed to join a gym?" Jane coaxes. "Because I hate to tell you this, you aren't there for exercise. You can tell the difference between the people who go for the fitness and the ones who go to physically abuse their bodies to have an actual reason to live in pain."

"I'm not allowed a job," I settle.

"What?" She looks confused and irritated all at once.

"My husband wants me just to be a housewife." I slam my face down on top of the table. "Is that not the dumbest thing to have to hide in a marriage? If I want a job, I have to sneak around like a rebellious teenager." I don't know if I'm talking to the table, myself, or Jane, but she's the only one who answers.

"Not the worst thing I've had to hide. I think you could pull it off." The waiter delivers our bear claws, and I lift my head from the table.

"I'm sorry." I apologize to the waiter, but he doesn't seem to care.

"Yeah. Maybe I can pull it off." I say to Jane. Her simple solution renews me.

"Let's go put in some applications after these delicious treats." She holds her bear claw up, waiting for my decision. If I go with her, I'm defying John's orders, and possibly putting myself in jeopardy of him finding out. But, on the other end, I need a job to start securing financial freedom from my husband, even if it puts me back into contact with people that John feels will assist in my downfall.

"Okay." I slam my bear claw into hers, and the action incites giggles from deep within her belly to erupt. "Let's give it a shot." I laugh as well.

IT'S BEEN TEN YEARS since I worked, and I never had to put in a traditional application for any of the jobs I've held. I was too young at the time to be registered as an employee, so I was paid under the table until I became of age. Now, at thirty-six, the application process is proving to be a bit mind-boggling, but Jane sticks by me the rest of the afternoon while I shuffle from place to place hoping for a job to keep on the low. My hours are unappealing to some because I need to come in after John leaves for work and be back home before him. The rest of the employers find me unattractive for the fact that I haven't held a job in ten years.

Jane had me purchase what she deemed a burner phone, something my husband couldn't trace on the cell phone account we share. She told me it would allow the businesses to call me when I got the job and that John wouldn't know. When I got the job? Jane sure was positive.

I'm losing hope, but I keep smiling. I have nothing but the slim chance that someone will call me and let me work for them. Even if it's for minimum wage, I have to get money in my name. As the lawyer so boldly told me, I gain nothing leaving John.

I may not have secured a job today, but I think there's a good chance that I've made a friend. Jane is the opposite—loud and feisty. After a decade of being John's wife, I have assumed an alter ego of poise and prudishness from my younger days. The fact that Jane doesn't whisper her curse words makes me flinch a little each time I hear her bellow one out. By mid-afternoon, though, I've become accustomed to it.

We are standing on the sidewalk about to get into our respective vehicles and part ways for the day. She treated me to lunch considering I don't have a job, and in her mind, we needed to celebrate the fact that I may wake up tomorrow with one. "Jane, I just want to say..."

"No sweat, girl." She waves me off and steps forward to embrace me — something I don't recall the other wives ever doing when we parted ways. Jane isn't a light hugger; I feel her arms wrap around me and hold on like she's hoping to glue a little bit of me back together. It's warm and all-encompassing, and I didn't realize until now that no one in my life aside from my mother ever hugged me this way. The tears form behind my eyes; Jane senses the shift.

"Hey, it's all right. We all have shit we have to go through. You have a friend now. I'm not going away. I'll help you." Her voice is sincere, and it's the first time today that Jane doesn't feel like anyone around us needs to be able to hear her words as she whispers them in my ear.

"Thank you." I'm the first to let go in the embrace, not because I want to cut off contact, but because I know Jane intends to hold me until I decide to let go, allowing me to determine how much affection I need.

"You know? You're all right, Medeia. I almost slept in today and skipped the gym. Glad I didn't." With that, she waves goodbye and gets into her black SUV. It isn't as lovely as the Mercedes I'm driving around, but I wish more than anything to be as wealthy as Jane.

I pull into my driveway thirty minutes later and sit in the vehicle, staring at the house. It is a two-story colonial, complete with obscene columns that scale the entire structure. It was love at first sight when John brought me here during our engagement. I recall clapping and happily jumping up and down on the driveway like a damn yo-yo. It was the one I wanted. I remember looking over to see John's face lighting up at my reaction, he wanted me to have everything I desired back then, and I was so enamored with it that I didn't realize I would be giving parts of my soul away as payment.

When I take in the grand view of my home, with my fresh eyes, it looks more like a prison. A place that I have spent most of my days cooped up inside with the list of what I could do shortened and dictated by my husband. This was my solace at one time. I used to believe that I would miss this house should I ever have to leave. John talked about moving and buying something else, and the idea caused me great sadness. Looking up at the grandeur of the red brick, I'm terri-fied to go in and be swallowed whole.

I stopped at the store on my way home, grabbed a few groceries, and I did something today that I had never done before. I got cash back at the cash register. My aunt told me in my teenage years that she would do it to have mad mon-ey saved away from my uncle. He couldn't see it because it didn't show on the bank statement, it just made the grocery bill look a little larger. It wasn't a trick I used in my life before John, but it felt just as dishonest and like a slippery slope. It felt dirty and cheap.

I fold the twenty-dollar bill up and slid it into my bra. I would have to hide it. Not only that, I would need to get more. Dirty feeling or not, money was what I needed and would do anything to get it.

Wherever I end up when the shit hits the fan, I know I won't ever choose a development again. Neighbors are not my cup of tea, at least not the kind I have here. They are nosey, and they want to one-up everyone's landscaping and remind you of the Homeowner's Association rules if you dare to do something on your own. I am even imprisoned by the neighborhood's standards of what I can and can't do.

I peer down at my fingers, my manicure is tomorrow, and I have to get my hair trimmed. I like the way money makes me look. In the rearview mirror, I don't see the ratty, pim-ple-faced girl begging the electric company for an extension. She's long gone, back in the past, where I want her to stay.

I climb out of the car and give a curt wave to the neigh-borhood gossip, Susan, who has taken to staring at me through her front window. *Hello, you nosey, bitch.* The curtains suddenly close, no wave. Rude.

I step through the front door, and even my sneakers on the floor create an echo in this vast space. The living room alone matches the size of my childhood home. Also, the apartment I rented at eighteen could fit inside the kitchen. I deserve this space. I've paid my dues. I covered up John's crimes for this.

"Oh, God, Medeia. What am I going to do?" I watch as John panics and begins pacing back and forth in the alley. I note the blood that's soiling his knuckles and cuffs of his button-up shirt. I am calm. This is nothing.

"Don't worry," I say. I bend down and look on the problem.

"How can you say that? Look!" He points down at the mess he's made, the one I'm already looking at. The event has made him hysterical, and hysteric people do not do well in this type of situation.

"I've done this before. They won't find you; leave it to me." I hand him my purse and start to strip off my coat, preparing for what needs to be done. The fear in John's eyes mixes with gratefulness as he rushes to kiss my face.

"Medeia, get me out of this."

Eight

MY THIGHS ACHE WITH each step on the stairs. Another morning at the gym proved fruitless of knowledge aside from telling me that I was ill of shape and that Anna didn't bother to do any work at the gym but take selfies. How did she keep so fit? Was my body that decrepit with age already in my thirties? I shed the layer of spandex and stand before my bathroom mirror, examining the dips and curves of time marked on my naked flesh.

Parts have dropped and taken residence further down than the lycra was holding them up during my time at the gym. My stomach is not nearly as flat as I recall it being the last time that I examined myself so thoroughly, and my butt bears dimples of a few too many stolen candy bars under my husband's radar. Was this the reason Anna gained John's attention? Were these few flaws, brought on by time and the earth's gravitational pull, that revolting to a man who swore to love me for better or for worse? The unshaven spots and untoned areas scream of my negligence, but I never pushed before this moment to see, with open eyes, the effects of my grief.

I had let myself go and lowered my standards when my mother passed away. Who gave a shit about makeup when I would just be crying it off? I look now at the expression lines deepening in my face. I had Botox done a couple of times, and it appeared it was time for some more. I liked the way that money kept me from aging, but in turn, it made me hate my natural self. What was so wrong with these lines? The real problem was that they were frown lines instead of laughter ones.

I slam my hand on the mirror to disguise my reflection; I won't find the answer there. I turn the shower to a scalding temperature to burn my muscles free of their ache. What happens when my body gets toned? Do I get to stay in John's good graces? No, I know why he has kept me around. That night when I made sure his deeds were hidden from the world. He owes me his reputation; it was my key to the house and the money by proxy. Now, I want the money and lifestyle with no John.

As I'm putting on my makeup for the day, John stumbles in yawning and rubbing his eyes.

"Good morning, John."

"Morning." He relieves his bladder and cranks the shower over to a moderate degree of heat, then he shuffles back over to kiss the top of my head. It feels like a twenty-pound weight pushing against me rather a touch of adoration.

"Did you put on concealer?" He tilts his head to one side, studying my reflection in the vanity.

"Yes." I venture.

"Oh."

"Why?"

"Nothing, dear. You look tired is all." He kisses the top of my head again. "Just looking out for you." With that, he pulls the shower curtain closed.

I narrow my eyes at his vicinity. How could I have missed these underhanded comments all these years? The way he cut up my appearance but managed to save his soul with a simple line of how it was all in my best interest. It never was. I can't even retaliate in words considering I was in here not many moments before criticizing myself with worse vocabulary than he dares using.

Weakness is a filthy layer on my body that I am dying to shed. I share my bed with a man who is cheating on me, and I stay. Something I swore I would never do. I'm finding now that it's never that easy. Not as simple as packing a bag and walking. There are knots to detangle before you can leave a marriage. I watched my mother choose to stay every single morning of her life when my father would crawl out of bed and instantly reach for the nearest alcohol bottle.

Meanwhile, she was scrounging up some breakfast to feed her three children who lived most of their lives starving so that my father could fill his need of the drink. Only he never got full, he was insatiable, and she stayed. It angered me as a teenager when I was old enough to understand the world a little better, and I asked her why she stayed.

"Where would I go, Medeia?" She sighed into her coffee cup and reached for my hand.

And so in my mind, I echo those words. Where would I go? I can't call up my siblings because they'd rather not speak to me, and I have no friends aside from Jane, and we just met. So, where would I go?

"I'll be late tonight." I shift my view toward John.

"Oh?" I want to spill my guts here, tell him that I know precisely why he'll be late this evening, but I bite my tongue.

"Don't wait up." He kisses my forehead. "And don't forget your pills." He leaves to the closet, and I listen to him dressing in one of his finer suits. I wonder what suit Anna prefers to see on John? Hope not the light gray pinstripe that I adore — adored.

He doesn't call out a goodbye as he leaves the closet, and I abandon all hope in the mirror of correcting my face. I slide on a simple Dolce and Gabbana sweater dress for today and slither through our bedroom, listening to the sounds of John's breakfast preparation echoing up the stairs.

I hear the front door slam when I come to the top of the stairs. I glide down and wait for the garage door to signal the exit of my husband. When his car's headlights shine through the glass front door as he pulls down the street, I take off for his office. Breakfast can wait.

I miss breakfast and lunch. I don't know what I expected to find, but if I'm going to set myself up to leave John, then I need to know everything I can get my hands on. I'm elbow-deep, sifting through files in the bottom cabinet of my husband's office when I hear ringing. It takes me a little bit to realize it's my phone. I forgot I purchased the burner phone at Jane's insistence.

"Hello," I balance the phone on the tip of my shoulder while tearing through folders.

"Hello, is this Medeia Moore?" a female's voice asks.

"Yes, it is."

"Hi, this is Maggie from Books & Mugs, you applied for a job here." She sounds older than me, and I can hear the wrinkles of time in her voice.

"Yes." I grab the phone in my hand and sit up straight.

"I wanted to ask if Monday was a good day to start?" She keeps her voice soft.

"Oh, my gosh. Yes, that will be fantastic." I beam.

"Okay. I apologize for cutting this call short. I have to go into a meeting right now, but I will shoot you an email with all the details of the job, and you are more than welcome to send me any questions you have back."

"Certainly. I look forward to reading the email." I can't help but grin like an idiot.

"I'll see you on Monday, Medeia." She says it correctly, too.

"I'll see you on Monday," I repeat. I end the call and fist-bump the air. I have a job. Yes, step one complete. I laugh in the dead silence of the house. I should put some music on to celebrate this moment.

I'm still laughing when I grab the untitled manila folder in the back of the bottom drawer. It slips from my fingers, and the contents spill onto my lap.

It stops being funny.

Prenuptial Agreement spread in calligraphy across the top. The one piece of paper I was foolish enough to sign with my heart and not drop the pen with my mind's logic. This paper states that I get nothing in the event of a divorce. I remember the day so well.

"I know this sounds a little harsh, but it's not. My father wants to see this done to protect his assets. The prenup has nothing to do with the money we make together. I swear." John pushes my chin up so that I look away from the paper and into his eyes. "I promise, Medeia, I will always take care of you. There's

no need in this paper because we are never getting divorced. It's only a formality."

"I trust you." I smile back, and his face eases into a relaxed grin, and he breathes a sigh of relief.

"I was so nervous about showing you this because my father can be so mean at times, and I didn't want you to think less of me for it."

"Of course not." I run my hand over his cheek and kiss the spot where my thumb resided only seconds earlier. *"Give me a pen. I'll sign it."*

I jam the paper back into the folder and shove it behind everything else; then I kick the drawer shut with my Prada loafer. John's father never once besmirched his mother in their divorce. He gave her half of everything without a single hesitation. He wasn't the mastermind behind my prenup. John lied to cover his ass.

I hated my father-in-law for years because of my husband's cruel words on his character how he locked him in a closet when he was younger. He told me tales about the many affairs that his father had while his mother was in the house. Little did I know his father never once did the things that John led me to believe. By the time I discovered the hypocrisy, his father had decided I was worthless in his eyes. Our relationship never bettered, and he hates me still to this day.

I can't say I blame him. Everything is on me for not having a spine of my own. I trusted John to be the truth in my life, but he became determined to be the person casting stones and placing the blame upon me. My standoff attitude became famous on his side of the family, with very few of them accepting me or trying to converse with me during family get-togethers. John had perfectly designed a world where I was alone.

I look about the room. I'm still alone.

I pick up my phone and dial Jane.

"Hey, girl," she answers cheerily.

"I got a job," I rush.

"Oh, my god. That is amazing!" she squeals. "I'd ask if you want to go out and celebrate, but I'm at work myself right now."

"That's okay." I'm sad at the prospect of hanging out being diminished. "I have some things I need to work on today, anyway." I look at the drawer I just closed. "Maybe lunch tomorrow?" I hold my breath. I'm desperate for a friend, and hoping Thursday wasn't a fluke of some sort with Jane. It has yet to be seen in my life if I possess the ability to retain a friendship.

"I'll text you. My boss is coming. Have to go. Bye," she whispers.

"Bye," I whisper back and hang up. I don't know why I lowered my voice; it sends me into a bubbly giggle. Girls used to be so mean to me in school, it's my only memory of girl power interaction outside of my protective shell of my sister, and it stung.

The first filing cabinet proved to be nothing but cruel and cold with the prenup tucked away inside. The next filing cabinet is a lot more varied from work documents. There's a copy of John's arrest record from college. He told me about it once. He said it was a simple bar fight. Just a quick arrest and everyone was sent home with no charges pressed, but it made him adamant that night that he would be in severe trouble should someone find out what happened. I go to shut the folder when a title jumps out at me on the page.

Fayette County Probation Office.

"What?" The word echoes off the walls decorated in honor plaques from various schools John has attended. His highest moments while I had one of the lowest.

I flip the folder wide open again and pull the letter sitting behind the mugshot printout. John had to be on probation? I thought he said no files were charged against him. I take out my burner phone and Google John's name. His business and social media pages are the first things to pop up, so I touch the search bar again and add the word "arrest." There is a link to a tiny article in the Police Beat of that time. That's it. Hidden away, out of the public eye, just like his rich father would want it to be.

I read the other papers in the file. John was arrested for beating a man into a coma. He spent months in jail—thanks to his father it wasn't years—and sentenced to three years on probation. Not a simple bar fight at all; in fact, this was at the man's house. John hunted him down after an altercation earlier in the day.

Oh, my god. Chills run down my body. I've been living with this man for ten years. We were dating when this happened. How did I not know? How was he in jail? My mind skips back to that time. I scatter the papers in the folder to find the date. Oh, my god. He said he was on a trip to Ireland, a gift from his parents for graduation. A three-month tour. I thought the life of a wealthy family was so privileged when I heard him go on about such a long trip; now I see it's even more so because he should have gotten years in prison, but his father's money kept him out.

I search for the man's name on the phone. His face has healed in the years past, but there are scars that my husband put there for the world to see for the rest of time. Every day this man wakes up to face the mirror and see the damage John has caused him. His scars are visible on his face; the ones John gave me are hidden from the world. Oh, God.

Why would he lie about this? How could he keep this a secret? We were around so many other people during this time — wouldn't someone have informed me? What about that night? Why didn't he come clean then?

I slam my head back into the other filing cabinet. I am in some deep shit, now. My husband is not only a liar but prone to violence.

Medeia's Journal

DEAR ANNA,

Does he lie to you?

Have you ever caught him in a lie? How does it feel for you, being one of his dirty lies yourself?

You know about me. You don't care. Were your years in school so rot with bullying from the other females that you broke off a feeling of kinship to other women? Is this the pay-back they get? Am I to bear the cross of being your scape-goat?

Nine

"I DON'T THINK THE PILLS are working." John's voice breaks through and drags me from the window of the sunroom where I'm watching an early snowfall.

"What?" I shift my head out of my hand and shake my wrist free from the ache of the weight it held.

"You seem different now. I don't know how to explain it, but ever since that therapy visit, you are off." He fumbles with something in the front pocket of his slacks.

"Is there something you need?" It was bold of me, to not initially agree.

"What?" My husband removes his hands from his pockets, crosses his arms over each other, and leans into the doorway of the sunroom.

"Sorry. I don't understand what you mean by me being different. Have I not accomplished a chore or an errand? Everything is done in the house; I'm bored. I told you before that I wanted to work because of this feeling."

He sighs and kicks his foot off the doorway frame, finally crossing over into the room. "You know how I feel about that, Medeia." He sits down at the table across from me and takes my hand. I feel burnt by his touch. I suppress the urge to tug away.

"I know." I flick a piece of lint from my jeans.

"I thought the gym was going to be your hobby?" He perks up, thinking he's won the argument if I tell him that I didn't go.

"I go at five in the morning, John. That's done for today."

"Oh." He swirls circles on the table with his other hand.

"Medeia. I feel like you're saying this isn't enough for you. Don't I give you the world?"

"Of course, you do, John. It's not a slight against you, my wanting to work. It's simply molding myself into being a more productive and worthy wife."

"I'd rather you fix your appearance to gain the title of a worthy wife. You seem to have forgotten your brush today, dear." He nods toward the unruly mane on top of my head.

"I braided it this morning when it was wet. Don't you like it?" I knew he didn't like it, that's why I did it.

"If you're sure you like it." He shakes his head.

"I do." I don't want to play his games or let the berating of my body take over the conversation tonight.

"I'm not sure your attitude is one that I want an employer to know about and gossip around town over. Besides, it looks tacky. Do you know what everyone will think if you got a job? They'll think that I'm not doing my job as your husband and providing for our family."

"What family? You don't want children," I spit.

"Come on, Medeia. Not this again. Look at how having children drained your parents and separated mine. The lengths your mother had to go to to keep food on the table. Do you want to be them?"

It hurt in a familiar way — my mother being the target of ridicule. "I don't think you're too far from my family's actions. Don't you remember the night my skills of being poor benefitted you?"

"You can go back to that shack in the woods. I'm sure your father will be happy to do to you what he did to your mother. Here you have a chance not to turn into him, or your seedy brother."

I drop his hand and wish him death with my stares. "Do you mean the mother whose funeral you couldn't be bothered with attending because it wasn't your thing?"

He reaches forward and squeezes the hand I removed from his, tight enough to cause pain. "Look. I don't like this new attitude you've developed, so you better stop it, or I'll have to smack it out of you."

I flinch. I think about the mugshot and the guy who is still dealing with medical issues because of my husband's temper. He's never threatened to strike me before, but I haven't spoken against him in our marriage.

"Now, I don't want to hurt you, Medeia, but it seems to me like you've forgotten all the things I do for you. You're becoming entitled."

"My apologies, John. I spoke with emotion." There's an edge to my voice that he doesn't appreciate.

"Don't do it again." He squeezes my left hand again, and I feel the diamond of my engagement ring cut the side of my middle finger. A solid "fuck you" of our marriage. I wish I could hurt him back.

"John, you're hurting me."

"I'm reminding you." His tone is low and warning. I feel my insides grow hot with terror. A flash of John's hands that night covered in blood plays in my mind. He releases my hand and digs into his front pocket.

"Don't forget to take your medicine." His eyes have grown black.

"I did this morning." I swallow hard on the lump inside my throat, but it refuses to move. My body is signaling that I'm not safe just yet. Fight or flight.

"Remember the doctor upped your dosage." He slides the small pill container over and points to my glass of water. I put the pills in my mouth but place them in between my back molar and cheek before sipping my water.

"Open up." He commands, and I do as I'm told. "Good girl."

John leaves me alone in the sunroom, whistling on his way. I yank the pills out of my mouth and toss them into my water, letting them disintegrate inside. I lick the blood from my finger, and the copper taste is more of a victory than a defeat to me. I want more blood but not my own. I hate my husband.

I start work tomorrow. I can hardly wait to leave this man.

Medeia's Journal

DEAR ANNA,

I wanted children. Does he tell you that? When you're with him, is it all sex or does he mention the plans he had with his wife, with me? He promised me a more fulfilled life.

Do you even bother to imagine me as a woman? Maybe even someone who could be your friend? I'm not a terrible person. I'm not entirely sure why he went off and found you. What kind of hold do you have? I'm dying to know.

Ten

MY FIRST DAY OF WORK is a series of blunders with tiny redeeming moments that allow me to believe that Maggie won't be asking me back for a repeat. Dammit. I see her coming toward me with thirty minutes left of my shift, and I hold my breath.

"Medeia, can we talk?" My heart drops. She was the only employer out of thousands that gave me a chance, and now I've blown it.

"Yes." I feel small.

"In my office." She points toward the door, and I nod.

"Of course." I take the apron off from around my neck and hand it to the other lady working at the tea station. I have fucked up orders and burnt myself with more chai tea lattes than I care to remember. The apron I hand over is a mess of stains from today alone.

We cross over the threshold to her office, and she shuts the door behind us. I take up space in one of the chairs at the front of her desk; she chooses to sit next to me, versus the traditional power move of sitting behind the desk.

"I'm so sorry Maggie. Please don't fire me. I'll learn; I swear I will." I grab her hand, begging her.

"Medeia. I'm not firing you. Although those books damaged today will be coming out of your paycheck, it's not enough for me to let you go." She pats my hand.

I breathe a small sigh of relief.

"I realized hiring you was going to be a big chance considering the lack of experience you've had in recent years."

I shamefully bow my head. "I realize you've taken a great leap of faith on me. I promise I will learn. I won't let you down. I want to be able to do this."

She holds her hand up to stop me. "You can save all that speech-making for another day, right now I want to inform you that I'll be putting you on stocking duty tomorrow. It was my fault to put you behind the counter on the tea and coffee considering the amount of time that has passed since you were in the food industry. They aren't the same thing, not with how fancy drinks have gotten these days. I think you'll be best in reshelving, and we will do some training on the register. Do you think you can handle it, dear?" Her gentle touch, on my hand, grazes the Band-Aid I am forced to wear over the visible wound created by John.

"Yes, thank you. I think that is more my pace for now. I am a fast learner. It's going to be a small bumpy ride for me, but don't give up, Maggie. I am a perfectionist. I can't stand not being good at a job so I can assure you that I will master what you throw at me."

"You have a few more chances, Medeia. Prove to me that you can figure out one of these other jobs better than you can a cup of tea." I want to forgive her for being a bitch, for coming down hard on me just because of my status and manicured hands, but I knew the type. I was on her playing level now, needing to work. She had a run in somewhere with a bitch who looked like me, and I embodied all the things that annoyed her about that moment.

"Now, go home. Your shift is done. I'll see you tomorrow."

I shake her hand and stand. "Thank you, Maggie. I'll see you tomorrow." I don't say any more. I don't want to dig my hole deeper or look weak trying to dig my way out. I fucked up today, and I own it. It wasn't my cup of tea, pun intended, but I'm going to make tomorrow better. I have no other choice but to learn this job and accomplish it.

When I get home, I have two hours to spare before my lying husband graces me with his presence. I've changed clothes in the car and stuffed the work clothing into a covert shopping bag, so our chef doesn't bother to comment on it. It's not odd to see a rich woman carrying a shopping bag, but it is strange to see her wearing a polo work uniform.

"Hello, Hannah. Whatever you're cooking this evening smells delicious." I feel a little lighter in my step—even with a lousy day in the books, I'm coming home having achieved the keeping of a secret, one that was going to get me a new life.

"It's chicken noodle soup, ma'am. I made it a little fancier for Mr. Moore's tastes." I want to join in with her constant jokes about John's uppity preference, but I know her to be a gossip. I won't hand over anything.

"I'm going to go upstairs and freshen up before Mr. Moore comes home." With that, I turn on my high heel and march upstairs where I will scrub the smell of books and odd café drinks off my person and reapply my old life so that no one is the wiser.

"Good evening, darling. How was your day?" I greet John with his usual glass of wine and a smile. Only this time it isn't hard to fake because I'm thinking of the money that I made today instead of trying to conjure up one for him from scratch.

"Well, someone's feeling better. My day at work was good. How about your day here?" He accepts the glass from me and holds his elbow to me. I force myself to take it.

"Oh, much better. I found lots to do. I took myself on a walk in the fresh air. Cleared my head." I watch him sit in his chair across from me.

"Good. It sounds like those pills are helping. Isn't your follow-up appointment tomorrow?" John asks as he dips his spoon into the chicken noodle soup before him.

"Yes, it's at night actually, so I won't be home to have my evening with you." I fake a pouty face, to not lead on that I intentionally made the appointment late so that I could have an excuse not to be cooped up in this house with John all night. It hasn't been very long since finding out his dirty secret, but it's been incredibly exhausting to play along, and I need a break.

"Oh, that's all right, honey. I have a few late business meetings tomorrow. I won't be home for dinner. I told Hannah not to worry about making our stuff tomorrow." *Thanks for making sure that I eat dinner, John.*

"You work so hard, my dear." I bite into the chicken noodle soup. Hannah has added some turnips and other odd vegetables, making the simple food tolerable to the rich. It's nauseating.

"Well, someone has to fund our family." He challenges.

I grip my spoon longing for it to be a knife.

Medeia's Journal

DEAR ANNA,

Where does he meet you?

Eleven

I WALK THE HALLWAY to my husband's office and lean on the doorframe. The drawers on the desk are locked to the outside world unless you have the key. I paid close attention to where John put it last night. Now, it weighs a ton in my palm. We keep what's precious but also what's most damaging to us under lock and key. The lawyer did tell me to get proof.

I open the middle drawer and find the usual writing utensils and some highlighters. A few business cards, no one of importance, so I close it. The side drawer holds only gin and Twinkies. Funny, he's allowed Twinkies and I can't even eat a single cookie without a disgusted look thrown my direction. The next drawer down has a few scattered folders; I dig through and find that most are just business proposals from companies. There is one folder buried deep and not haphazardly thrown inside. I carefully extract it from underneath the pile.

It says "A" on it, the only indication of what's inside. I feel my throat closing. I open it to find polaroid pictures of Anna straddling John's desk in suggestive positions and barely-there lingerie.

"Yuck." I throw the folder back in the drawer, longing to scrub my eyes with bleach.

John's iPad sits on top of the paper in the next drawer. I know the code, so it's easy to access the secrets inside. This is his personal one, not meant for work, so why would he lock it away. I quickly punch in the lock screen pin and open the emails. I don't want to risk clicking on photos after what I have just seen.

A few emails to therapists asking about several mental illnesses catch my eye. Why would John feel the need to write these doctors and ask about so many illnesses in great detail? There's nothing more in the inbox, but when I scan the folders, I find another one titled "A." I gulp down a bit of John's gin before I open the first one.

Dear John,

That sounds silly, doesn't it? Because I'm not writing to break anything off with you but to invite you to a hotel later. I'd invite you to my apartment but my roommate is so nosey, and I don't plan on being quiet. xoxo Anna

Dear John,

If I were your wife, you'd never be bored with sex positions. ;) xoxo Anna

Dear John,

Last night was amazing. Please don't worry about the space, and the warehouse was beautiful. It is something that is only ours now. Imagine the number of people who have used those same hotel rooms. Not as romantic as having our own place. Just you and I, as it should be. See you tonight, babe. xoxo Anna

Warehouse? I throw the iPad on the desk and scratch my head. Warehouse? What warehouse?

No. No. No. No.

John Moore, you took your slut to the place you bought me as a wedding present? I punch the top of the desk and close everything up. I bolt from the seat, fetching the keys off the foyer table as I slam the front door closed. I put the car into reverse and peel out of the driveway, heading to a place I know well but don't go to anymore because it symbolizes lost dreams to me.

On the street in an old part of town sits a gorgeous steel building set back from all the others. It has an invitation-only feel to it. Something that makes you take a second look when driving by, and long for access to see inside. It did when I first saw it. Back then I was taking classes to become a real estate agent. When I wanted John to buy the warehouse for me to open a business inside, he agreed without hesitation.

A pretty picture of a devoted fiancé doing the most for his future bride. We were already married when I went to take the final exam and graduated from my courses, and that's when he pulled the trick that he felt I was saying he couldn't provide for us, that I was taking away his right as a man to take care of me. I swooned like an idiot. I was raised on the streets, fighting for survival because my father didn't think it was his job to feed us, then there was a man saying he wanted to do it for me. Swooned. I allowed the dream of having my own business be ripped out of my hands. The warehouse key consistently felt like a dead weight on my keyring from then on.

I slow the car down to pull into the parking lot and dodge the potholes. Like the haunted voices of forgotten dreams, the building brings the memories crashing around me.

"It's perfect, John. I'll put a receptionist area in here. A large L-shaped desk." I point out the area near the front entrance, and John laughs. "What?"

"Nothing, you're just so cute when you're excited. I can't see your vision, but I know you will do great." He comes up behind me, wraps his arms around my middle and lays his chin on my shoulder. "So, do you like it?"

"I love it!" I squeal and lean back into him.

"Happy wedding present." He kisses the side of my face. "To you and me, forever." He tickles my middle, and I run off with him trailing behind.

My key turns the lock, and I walk inside, no longer seeing that imaginary L-shaped receptionist desk. In its place are boxes piled up for John's company. This has become his storage space, and his crap is sitting in something that was mine.

The bottom floor is a section saved only for John; there isn't a trace of me left in here. Even my certificate of completion on the wall is unseen due to the boxes stacked in front of it. There's a second floor that only takes up half the space. Instead of a loft-like feeling, there are walls closing it off to view from down here. It was meant to be my office. I climb the stairs.

On the final step, I smell the cheap perfume and deceit. Dammit, I'm right. I bow my head. There are boxes along the windows, lining the space like a tunnel so that it isn't viewable from the outside. And as I walk around the bend of the first wall of boxes, I see it. A mattress laid out on the floor, disheveled covers tossed about, and the fitted sheet is only on three corners. I walk closer and see condom wrappers strewn about — *classy, John.* There are empty bottles of wine everywhere; a forgotten bra hangs from the corner of one of the highest boxes— *classy, Anna.*

A piece of paper juts out from under a cardboard box serving as a makeshift table. It's the only one that doesn't have two others stacked on top of it, maybe because there is only a wall behind and no windows to see the lovers through here. I squat down to view the drawing on it.

A heart with the initials A.T. & J.M. Cute. I pull myself up and feel lightheaded. I want to puke. I dart down the stairs and out the front door, then to the back of the building where a small patch of woods lays before the river. I bend my body in half and take deep breaths until the feeling passes.

We were once in love, John and I, I still felt it in those rare times when we smile at each other and share a secret moment. It's not farfetched to believe that there was once a human underneath his cold and calculating mannerisms.

"I love you, Medeia."

"What do you love most about me?" We're lying on his bed *after making love. He strokes my hair back away from my face.*

"I love how moldable you are."

"What?" I scrunch up my nose.

"No. No. It's not a bad thing. I think it's a strength of yours. You are willing to change and adapt for this better life. You're better than where you came from."

What a load of crap. He traded my strength and made it my weakness.

Love isn't enough. I thought it when I was younger that my teenage years were filled with the notion. Love doesn't mean you need to stay. Love doesn't always mean it's right. If love is without respect, if you are trading in parts of yourself to fit in alongside the person that you're in love with, then it isn't true love. It's merely an affection of the heart, not a love for the soul.

I lock the front door and gaze upon the building that once held such a promising future. It contains the part of my old life's demise now. I put the car in drive and head to my job, my new life, and drive away from the past that holds nothing for me.

Twelve

"AND THEY'RE COMPLETELY wireless?" I ask the man behind the counter. He looks so unkept and much like the kind of creeper who would install these cameras inside a lady's shower.

"Yeah. You need to make sure they're either charged or have batteries; then they're good to go." He holds a box up to double check and does an overindulgent head-bob when he is satisfied that the information that he gave me is correct.

"I'll take them, and I'm going to need some batteries, too." I stopped on my way home and bought some wireless cameras that I found in one of the books I was stocking today. They should work perfectly for catching my husband's show, and proof of the affair for the lawyer. I was going to come with substantial evidence next time.

I head straight to the warehouse to install them. I can't wait until tomorrow, even if this is cutting it close to the time that John leaves work. I want to see them tonight. I need to see this with my own two eyes. There are so many ways that John could talk himself out of the restaurant scene, but naked on top of his secretary is a hard corner to get out of.

Parking my car a street away, I use the walk to the warehouse to settle my nerves. I come around the back of the building and come in through the back-door entrance. Boxes are stacked everywhere, and it's a tight squeeze to shuffle past, but these boxes are going to make excellent hiding spaces for my cameras. I dart up the stairs and start unpackaging the cameras and putting the batteries in. I place the first one near their love nest, prime number one spot.

I use my phone to sync the camera with the app. Perfect. I throw the trash back into the shopping bag and take out the next camera, pointing it toward the staircase. I want to be able to see them coming and going. I find a stack of boxes near the small railing, and I sneak the penny-sized camera in the cracks.

After syncing it up, I throw the trash into the bag. I'm on the third step when I hear the front door opening.

"Shit." I hiss. I dart back to the top of the stairs and squeeze my body between the boxes surrounding their love nest and the windows outside. I push myself back into the corner and out of sight.

Anna's giggling echoes up the stairs and floods the landing.

"John. Stop."

"You know you don't want me to stop." He growls, and I hear them fumbling up the steps in between sloppy, slurpy kisses. *Gross.*

The heat escalates up my neck, and I yank at the collar of my shirt threatening to strangle my breath. Fuck. How did I get myself stuck here? What am I going to do? I click my cell phone to silent because I can't afford to make any noises. I hit the camera app open and choose the one facing the mattress.

They're stripping their clothes off in front of each other and smiling. I screenshot the picture. That should be enough. Except, I don't close the app — I can't look away. Anna moans loudly and begs for John to open the wine. He pops the cork on the wine bottle between them, pouring the contents into glasses he brought, and they drink while laughing.

"I wanted to fuck you all day. What did I tell you about that lacy underwear of yours?"

"Hmm, I don't recall." She's playing coy and willing him to come to her.

"When you wear them, you're going to get fucked." He dominates over her, pushing his forehead against hers. "Hard." My throat closes, and the room starts growing small around me. Oh god. I'm going to have a panic attack right now, next to my husband and his mistress screwing. No. No.

The anxiety does nothing to stop the attack, and I squeeze myself tight, wrapping my arms around my body as hard as I can. I need to try and calm my central nervous system down. Tight pressure. Tight pressure.

"Oh, Anna. You're so tight." A tear rolls down my cheek as I squeeze my body tight in an embrace. No. Make it stop.

Someone hears my prayers because the grunts end in a climax to rival the worst porno movies. John and Anna lay together cuddling for another half hour before they leave and I'm free to do the same. I stumble out of the back of the building and hit my knees.

How could he do this to me?

Thirteen

MAGGIE HAS ME SEARCHING for a few titles that are new clearance today; it feels like a bogus mission. They're nowhere to be found. Still, I welcome the distraction from the hell that was my evening yesterday playing over in my mind. I texted John and told him I wouldn't be home for dinner because I needed to get a manicure. He bought it. I strolled along the shops aimlessly not wanting to go home and face the liar that shares my bed.

The store is dead quiet today and not having to deal with customers is a welcome blessing: nothing but a low alternative rock song playing over the speakers drowning out my thoughts.

"Tommy, I don't want to be here." I hear the whining of a girl as soon as the front door opens.

"Okay, Annie." The man has an edge to his voice, and I wonder if they'll be choosing the store for their fight today. I hear their feet around the L-shaped aisleway that I'm in. I'm stuck in the corner, and I keep my back to them, hoping to hear someone else's drama for once.

"I hate that name." She bites back and stomps out of the aisle.

"I hate being called Tommy." He quips back.

"Fine." She pouts from the next aisle. "I still don't want to be here."

"We'll be quick. I promise, Anna." He leaves the aisle as the hairs on my neck rise at the name he mentioned. It can't be. I made sure that this job was an hour away so that John couldn't find me. And Anna at a bookstore? Impossible.

I move closer to the end of the aisle and wait until the exit the aisle they're in before I risk a look at her.

Shit.

Another day of hiding from Anna and her — wait a second. Does Anna have a boyfriend? That slut! They're in the middle of the floor ducking through the middle aisles and looking intently for something.

"Jesus, Thomas. Just ask someone." I watch through the endcap display as Anna points my way. Shit. He doesn't listen to her and heads off for another aisle. She trails behind reluctantly.

I beat it across the sales floor as fast as I can to the cookbooks where I can easily make my exit to the bathrooms and come out when the coast is clear.

"Oh Medeia, I need your help."

"Shh. Shh. Carol, don't say my name?" I hold my finger to my mouth and grab Carol's shoulder with the other.

"What? Why?" I'll give her points for knowing to keep her voice low.

"There's someone who works here over there, Thomas. I heard them say her name." Anna shouts.

"Just switch me nametags. Quick." I tell Carol as I yank my lanyard up over my hand and shove it at her.

"What?" She's confused.

"I'll buy you whatever you want; just take my name tag."

"Uhh — okay." Carol glides her lanyard up around her head as I motion with my hands for her to hurry up. I put it on over my head and take off behind Carol to the little nook of books near the bathroom.

"Be me," I whisper back at her baffled reflection before I duck behind the books for safety.

"I swear I heard someone's name I know." The volume in Anna's voice grows as she moves in on Carol. Please, don't fail me, Carol.

"Hello, may I help you?"

"What's your name?" Anna demands.

"Medeia." A sigh of relief leaves my body when my ears hear Carol's sweet lie past her lips.

"Medeia? That's a unique name." Anna is grilling her.

"Not really. You'd be surprised. Is there something I can help you find today?"

"My boyfriend is looking for a Julia something cookbook. It's supposed to be famous or something."

"Julia Child." Thomas and Carol both correct her at the same time.

"Whatever." Anna sounds annoyed.

"It's right back this way on the back shelf I believe." Carol is raising her voice a slight octave, signaling to me that she is walking my way. I move around to the next aisle.

"Perfect. Thank you so much." Thomas exclaims.

"No problem. Is there anything else that I can help you find today?"

"No. This book is what I wanted. Thank you." Thomas sounds polite. What is he doing with Anna?

"Let's go, Thomas." Anna stomps off toward the registers.

"Thanks for your help. I'm sorry about her mood. She's upset today."

"Understood." Carol waves him off.

I hear Maggie greeting Anna at the registers so I know I'm almost in the clear. Carol rounds the bend looking for me.

"Boy, that blonde had a hard-on looking for you. She wouldn't keep her head still." Carol chuckles as she pulls my lanyard off her neck to give back to me. I mirror the same movement.

"I owe you my life, Carol." I grab her hands.

"No sweat, sweetie. That was fun." She rubs my hands together to comfort me.

"I owe you. Honestly, what do you want?"

Carol's eyebrows form together in confusion. "Nothing."

"Nobody wants nothing." I don't stop the words before they leave my mouth.

"Some people do things just to help others, Medeia." She tilts her heads and looks in my eyes. "You've never met someone like that, have you?"

"Carol, I apologize, I just—" I straighten up. "Only my mother. She's the only one I knew to do that. I'm sorry that I assumed you were after something." She smiles a soft motherly way and slaps my shoulder.

"I liked being Medeia. Maybe we can do it again sometime."

"God, I hope not." I wipe sweat from my brow as I hear the entrance bell signaling Thomas and Anna's departure.

"Cheer up. It's Friday." Carol laughs and heads back to her work.

Friday. First Paycheck.

Fourteen

JOHN LEFT THIS MORNING for a week-long conference in Colorado. My step is lighter knowing I can watch his greedy whore and work without his involvement this week. Not having to hide for a couple of days feels like the sun is shining on me.

I hit the treadmill at the gym hard this morning in anger, spiking the speed up every time I saw Anna giggling at the muscular man next to her. She has my husband and a boyfriend, and she still wants more.

She starts to bounce out of the gym, curls still intact, I shut the machine down and head straight for the door. I throw my hoodie up over my head as the cold air of early morning seeps in on the other side of the gym entrance. Still content to bounce, Anna makes her way to her car. A Mercedes SUV. How did she afford that on her salary? Was this a present from my husband? The make and model matches mine except in color. Hers is white; mine is black.

I make a beeline for my car, one row over and wait to see which direction she goes. Right. I back out and keep a comfortable difference between us. She won't lose me. I need to know about her. Why does she have him eating out of her hand? What can I expose? I can't get a good read from social media, or her behavior at the gym. I need to observe her when no one else is around. When it's just her, no muscular men to impress and no John.

She takes a turn down a residential road, so I do the same. She's heading home, I know because I've passed by her address several times this weekend losing my nerve to look upon the woman my husband leaves me for. She pulls into a spot alongside the narrow road, so I continue my way down the street slowly and turn down the next road and park.

I didn't think this far ahead. I'll get out, that's what I'll do. I can't observe her from here, and she'll notice if I park close by. Shit. What do I do? Do I walk the sidewalk? I'll give her time to get inside then I'll loop the car back around. Yes.

I drop my head against the steering wheel and push down, causing my neck to ache. *What were you thinking, Medeia?* The radio is off. I don't know why. Too scared she may hear me? The only sound is my shallow breathing and scuffing of feet outside. Huh?

I look up to see a most familiar blonde jogging past on the sidewalk. Is she a runner? What the heck was the point in the gym? Status? Couldn't she simply say that she ran?

I take in the surroundings as she turns the corner; it isn't the classiest neighborhood. A bunch of apartment buildings lined up one after another, typically rented out to college students and single mothers. They're cheap. I know because of my search for rentals in the area on the burner phone. Some people wrote reviews on Google that the upkeep here is awful on the landlord's part and stuff is breaking left and right. The outsides of the buildings do look in need of an overhaul. I'm glad I didn't put this on the list of potential apartments, although I'm sad that I won't be Anna's neighbor.

This must be why Anna doesn't post many pictures of her home or morning run. Anna stores her life on the internet, and she maintains a particular appearance so that no one can know her surroundings. Perhaps that's why she drives a Mercedes Benz SUV; she is desperate to be considered successful and prosperous. Her choice in John becomes a little clearer. Who better to screw than the CEO and founder of the company she's working at currently?

Was the SUV hush money? There's a nagging feeling in my stomach about the vehicle. It's time to dig up Anna's past a little. I put the car in drive and pull out of my spot, and I make sure to pass Anna on my way out of the side streets. She's panting, and her curls no longer bounce. I want to stop and take a picture of her to show all her followers the secret behind it all, but it does nothing except make her human. I don't want her to be that.

Medeia's Journal

DEAR ANNA,

You run after the gym, but not at the gym. You don't even work out at the gym; it's all for the show on your Facebook. Why do you go?

I have nothing to do all week with John gone. I'm surprised you didn't head off to the conference with him. Did some old cock block at the office stop it from happening? Poor girl.

Don't worry. We can hang out

Fifteen

I LOVE THE FEELING of yoga pants in public. John would lose his mind if he knew I was out in broad daylight donning them on my body. To him, these only exist for working out. Ridiculous. These are pants. Delicious, movable pants.

Anna has taken me to a health food store today. I like new adventures, and heck, I can't deny that I should eat healthily, so I get out of my car to browse, as well — no harm in that. I pull my baseball cap down lower on my head and zip my hoodie up tighter. No need for a cart, so I swipe a basket at the door. They call the place Simply Fresh, and the prices are simply outrageous. Slap an organic sticker on it, and they're sending their kids off to college with your week's grocery bill. Anna sure does enjoy the rich life, and so do I. Something we have in common, along with John.

I poke around at a few things and keep my distance. Anna has on a cute little crop-top today, hoping to gather some attention from the men in the store. It's working, too. One man's wife already slapped his stomach over the crank of his neck toward Anna's midriff.

I stare from the safety of the tall baked goods rack at the way Anna's head moves when a male is near. She immediately slows down and browses the item closest to her. There's a hip-popping stance she takes that I attempt to imitate and regret almost instantly as searing pain shoots down my leg. How does she do that? And what's the benefit?

I soon find out, as the target of her act takes notice of her rear end and strikes up a conversation. Anna pretends to be uninterested at first, giving him short responses to his questions and not making direct eye contact. I move away from the rack and risk the danger of being seen in the aisle she's in, and I take residence farther down but within hearing distance, pretending to be interested in a box of granola cereal mixed with seeds, sans booty pop stance. I watch them in the reflection of the mirror over top of the produce at the end of the aisle.

"So, uh..." The young man starts to stutter as his confidence fades from Anna's cold shoulder. "Do you like that cereal?" He points to the box in her hand.

"Well." She puts it back on the shelf. "It's not as good as this one." Then I watch Anna turn her back toward the man and fold her body in half so that her ass protrudes in his direction and grab a box of cereal from the bottom shelf. He about faints in the aisle. I'm not sure which one of us has our mouths open wider. When she pops back up, the smirk on her face tells me she knows what she's doing. "Here. Try this one. It's delicious." She flips her hair and walks away. Like a puppy, he trails her.

"Wow. Yeah, definitely, I will. Hey, do you shop here often? Maybe we could meet up sometime?" His voice fades a little as he rounds the corner into the next aisle. I strategically place myself at the end cap, hunting down some protein snacks.

"That sounds wonderful," she purrs. "I'm Anna." She holds out her hand, and he dives at the possibility of touching her.

"Michael." He grins and grips her hand firmly. "How about we shop together today?"

"Perfect." She removes her hand from his and links her arm around his as they walk and talk down the rest of the aisle. "It's always nice to shop with someone." Her voice takes on a seductive purr.

She's a damn professional. Wife duty sex with John on Sunday night puts me at even more of a risk for some second-hand funk. Great. As if those ten minutes weren't painful and disgusting enough, now I need to worry about all the men who have climbed into Anna's bed lately.

I abandon my Anna mission on the search for makeup that won't break my skin out into a rash, and maybe a bar of soap. If I'm here then I might as well buy something, and these options seem like the only ones that get me out of here for a minimal amount of damage. I'm not going to be eating cereal with seeds in it. I may like John's money, but I've never gotten used to the trendy things that are somehow assigned to the rich. Healthy organic food doesn't taste better than the way my mother made Spam a meal for dinner. The luxurious skin care doesn't feel better than Vaseline. But the security, the security, feels fantastic.

As fate designs it, Anna and her new boy-toy are at the register lines the same time as me, although in a different lane. He's still fawning all over her, and she's trying to stay blissfully unaware. I watch as she searches in her small cross-body purse for something.

"Oh, my goodness," she finally mutters.

"What? What's wrong?" He takes the moment of stress to touch her back in a loving way.

"I forgot my card at home today. Damn." She stomps her feet, mad at herself. "No groceries for me this week. I have to get to my job right after this, so I can't make a run home." She slaps her hip with one hand while she bites the forefinger nail of the other, trying to come up with a solution.

"Hey, don't worry about it. I'll pay for you. No problem." Knight in shining armor.

"Oh, my goodness, you would? That's amazing. Thank you. Thank you so much." She hugs him before he can remove his arm from the front of his body, strategically placing her breast on his hand. It's evident in his mind that he's going to score big with this.

I roll my eyes and focus on the line moving in front of me. I'm next.

"Hello." I beam at the cashier behind the belt.

"Hello, ma'am. How are you today?" She doesn't even look up to meet my eyes, just goes through the motions of her job, sliding the barcodes in front of the scanner.

"I'm well, and yourself?"

"Fine. Fine," she rushes. "That will be $28.32." For some fucking soap?

"Here you go." I hand over two twenty-dollar bills.

"Out of $40." She pokes a few buttons on the touchscreen, and the drawer next to her hip pops out. "Your change is going to be $11.68." She puts the bills on top of the receipt and rips it from the machine, placing the mound directly in my hand before topping it with the coins.

"Thank you," I say and scoop my bag up.

"Yup." And just like that, she moves on to the next customer in line. Unaware that customer service isn't the job for her. I don't look like my usual 'let me speak to the manager' self, so she treats me like any other human being. That's why money is so important. It changes the way people see you. Even if Vaseline feels better on the skin, the hundred-dollar eye cream feels more powerful sliding across the barcode scanner. The heels may hurt, but their red bottoms let the world know that you have it all. Reminds me how worthless it is not to appear as if you drip money.

I don't look back as I make my way to the vehicle. I'm glad to be leaving ahead of her; that way I can ready myself in the car for our next stop. She said she was going to work, but I swore John would have had her start by now; it's nearly nine in the morning. And he isn't there, so what would she be doing? He typically gives his secretaries time off or requires them to work a half week when he leaves for a conference.

Anna beams alongside her new meal ticket just seconds after I'm seated in my driver's seat. She is still profusely thanking the kind stranger for his actions. He eats up the attention and like a good boy loads the trunk of her car up with her items.

Maybe she's ready to move on to someone her age. Perhaps she'll leave John alone, but doesn't she have Thomas for that?

Anna recites her number for the man as he punches it into his phone. It's obvious he wants to kiss her goodbye, considering this meeting and purchase of food to be equivalent to a date, but Anna shuts him down with a quick peck on his cheek. Ouch. He doesn't notice the send-off as he watches her pull out of her spot and waves to her taillights.

Now, it's my turn to hang out with Anna, sorry Michael.

I pull out and keep my distance safely undetectable. When Anna gets to the main entrance of the shopping center, she turns right instead of the left that would take her to the office. *Where are you going, Anna?* In a half mile, we take another right into a different shopping plaza and pull into a Starbucks drive-thru.

She doesn't have any money on her, but maybe she has an app on her phone or a gift card. I follow behind her—this hasn't always been my first choice in coffee places, but I won't deny their ability to make a good cup, and I could still use some.

Anna shouts her order into the drive-thru box, making sure to lean out the window and enunciate her words. I cringe, thinking about the person's ears on the other end of the line. *There's no need to shout, Anna. They can hear you just fine.*

I'm right behind and next to order. I ask for a simple black coffee, and the lady is happy to oblige, glad I didn't feel the need to yell my order or make her repeat it twice as Anna did. I grab the change from the grocery store out of my hoodie pocket and ready myself for the first window. I round the circle portion that leads to the next step, and Anna has her credit card hanging out her window for the woman to take.

No money, my ass. She played that man for free groceries, and he fell right into her plan. Wow. I don't know if

I'm impressed or even more irritated with her. Those groceries probably cost that boy close to a hundred dollars, and he handed it over with no doubt in her and didn't know her but for a few minutes.

She speeds off toward the stop sign coming out of the plaza and heads away from the main road. *So, we aren't going home to put your groceries away, or to work. Where are we going now, Anna dear?*

I thank the lady for my coffee and do my best to catch up with Anna. I pray she didn't take any more turns down the road, and I'm in luck. She's stuck behind an eighteen-wheeler crawling ten miles per hour under the speed limit. I'm two cars behind her, and I can see her irritated acrylic nails waving out the window.

We drive for a good twenty minutes out of town to a more rural area. My coffee is gone, and I wonder how much farther Anna is going to take us when she finally flips the turn signal on for a left turn into an old trailer park. I go straight on the main road and find a street that turns upward behind the trailer park so that I can observe from there. Two Mercedes may cause folks there to take notice.

I park off on a lookout point and roll my window down for a clearer view. I watch as Anna grabs two bags of groceries from the trunk of her SUV. She hides out of sight of the home's occupants, trying to catch her breath. I take out my phone and open the camera app to zoom in on the scene.

She looks nervous, picking at her clothes and trying to yank the crop-top downward suddenly. No longer the confident woman conning a man for free groceries in the health food store. She seems like a lost child.

She squares her shoulders and puffs out a deep breath, getting the nerve to walk to the front door, continuously yanking her shirt downward. It takes a minute before someone answers her knocks. A larger woman still wearing her nightgown and curlers swings the door open with great agitation. She pushes the screen door open, advancing out onto the porch toward her in a threatening manner with the butt of a cigarette hanging limply from her mouth. She doesn't want Anna there.

Anna doesn't retaliate, simply holds the groceries up as a peace offering and points to her car to indicate that she has more. This softens the older woman as she takes the bags from Anna and turns to put them inside the house. Anna runs to the car, delighted to finish off the grocery delivery. She returns almost immediately with the last three bags, which the older lady offers to take from her. Anna tells her she has it, but the older lady insists again, so Anna relents.

She follows behind and holds the screen door open, but when the older lady crosses the threshold, she slams the door in Anna's face. Anna's hand on the doorknob jiggling tells me that they locked her out. The cries begin to shake Anna's body, and my grip on the phone goes limp.

Fuck. That was cold.

I look down and notice my camera had landed on something when the phone relaxed in my hand — their mailbox. I zoom in a little more to try to read the name on the side.

Trayor.

That's Anna's mother.

Medeia's Journal

DEAR ANNA,
   Shit.

Sixteen

I LEFT ANNA CRYING on the porch of her parent's house. I wanted to know everything about her, but some stuff is making me feel sorry for her, and that can't happen because I loathe her. I drop my keys on the foyer table with a loud clang. The marble protests the abuse. Anna is sulking, and she won't be much fun to watch today anymore. Her mother did her over, and now she's stewing in those mommy issues.

I text Jane to hang out with me tonight. We still need to celebrate my job finding. Alcohol. I need alcohol today. I head straight to the kitchen. Hannah is gone, I gave her the week off with John away. I deserve the house to myself without someone who is probably paid to spy and tell John I dare to be casual or unclean. Plus, I can cook for myself.

I yank the vodka from the cabinet over the refrigerator — no text from Jane. I guess I will party by myself today. I twist the cap off, no need for a glass; it only makes dirty dishes. Bottoms up.

Why is there ringing? What is that? I lift my head off the area rug of the living room. How did I get here? My tongue feels fuzzy, and I shake my head around. Yuck. Vodka, that's how I got here. There's still ringing. Ugh, my phone.

"Hello?" but there's no answer, just more ringing. Oh, wrong phone.

"Hello?" I answer into the other receiver without looking at the name.

"What the fuck is going on there?" John screams down the line, and I sober up quick.

"Honey, hi." I push myself up to a seated position on the floor, reeling from the room spinning around me.

"Hi? Hi? I've been calling you over and over, what are you doing?" he barks.

"I apologize. I have a migraine today, and I was taking a small nap hoping to help ease the pain. I guess I didn't hear the phone ringing." I instantly rise off the floor, grabbing the arm of the couch to help sturdy my feet. I begin to tidy up the area around me at the sound of my husband's angry voice.

"I thought you were off cheating on me." His voice sounds hurt. I roll my eyes and indeed cause myself a headache. *No, I'm not the cheater, dear husband.*

"Absolutely not. What a horrible thing to do to a person. I would never be so cold." I dig in; I want him to prove me wrong and have emotions.

"Do you think you need to go to the doctor for this headache?" *I don't need any more pills, John.* I shake the phone violently in my hand.

"No. No. I fell asleep in an awkward position last night. Migraine was just a dramatic word on my part. I should have said an intense headache instead," I coo down the line. Ever so polite and meek, meanwhile flashing my smooth, newly painted middle finger toward the phone.

"The cook emailed me that you sent her away for the week." He doesn't sound pleased.

"Oh, honey. I'm fine cooking my own dinners for one week. I like to do it." I put the throw pillows back onto the couch.

"Only you could stomach your cooking." He chuckles like it's a joke. *Fuck off, John.* I don't say anything to the comment, just shuffle the paper plate that holds no remains of the delicious Portobello mushroom sandwich I made for lunch today toward the kitchen.

"I don't mean it like that, Medeia. You're so huffy when you have a headache. I was trying to be funny."

"I know. Just a joke, right?" I dump the plate in the trash can.

"Are you taking a tone with me?" I can see him ducking into a corner somewhere now, out of sight of others to make the conversation private. "Is this about the job?"

"No, I'm sorry. I was trying to focus in on something, and my eyesight is still blurry from the headache."

"You should take some pills."

"I don't need to."

"Well since you're too busy to talk to me, maybe I should let you go." Pouty toddler.

"It may be a good idea. I should lie down. Hope you're having a marvelous time, darling." *I hope you die in a plane crash, darling.*

Nothing but the phone signaling he's hung up. No love lost. It rings again in my hand. Fuck. This is going to be the lecture of a lifetime now.

"Yes, dear." It's singsong, but I can't hide the irritation.

"Dinner, darling?" I hear a feminine giggle.

"Jane?" I hold the phone away and see her name instead of the other J.

"Who were you expecting?" she asks.

"The dickhead who told me my food was inedible," I slip and slam the bottle that once held vodka into the trash. "I didn't think I gave you this number. I thought you were a burner caller."

"Shit. Sorry. Is the dickhead going to be even grumpier? Your husband is the dickhead, right?" She clarifies.

"Yeah." I realize my slip, exposing any part of my non-perfect life to a stranger. "I mean, I'm sorry; I didn't mean to project like that."

"No sweat. If you can't talk about it with your girlfriends, who can you tell?"

"My therapist." Another slip.

Jane laughs. "You're spilling all the beans. I like it. So, dinner?"

"Sounds good. Where at?"

"A little mom-and-pop place called Dangeil's. I'll text you the address." She cheers. "Meet you in twenty?"

I look at the clock. I hadn't realized it was evening already. 6:30 to be exact. "Shit," I mutter.

"Okay, thirty?" She mistakes my curse for lack of time.

"No. Ugh." I run my hand down my face. "I'm drunk. I can't drive."

"Starting the party without me?" She laughs.

"Something like that. Do you think you could pick me up? I'll text you the address."

"I got a better idea. I'll call the pizza shop, you text me the address, and we will stay in tonight. Need me to bring anything?"

"Wine," I spit out.

"Aren't you already drunk?" She bursts into a deep cackle.

"What if it wears off?" I raise my eyebrows, smiling.

"Good point. Wine it is. Text me the address." With that, she clicks off the line, and before I forget, I send her our address from the burner phone and waddle to the bathroom to relieve myself. A little bit of the woozy feeling has worn off after a good emptying of my system. I walk a bit better back to the couch and slump down. I smile to no one and throw my feet up on the coffee table.

John hates feet on the furniture. He would scream if he saw it. I rub my heels back and forth all over the table, bursting into a rage of laughter. I hold my stomach and scream out into the emptiness. He hates any loud noise, as well. I jump from the couch searching for the remote control for the TV. I know there is a music channel on here somewhere. I blare the jazz channel. Something John told me was music for the dumb people. I hold both middle fingers up in the air and move my body to the sound coming through the surround system.

It's not long before the doorbell screeches through the music and I'm dancing my way over to answer it.

"Jane!" I yell when I pull the door back to her smiling face.

"Crazy lady!" She laughs. "May I come in?"

"Come in. Come in. Come in. Join the fun. We're doing everything my husband hates." I pull her into the living room, leaving the front door open behind us.

Jane sets the pizza and wine on the coffee table and immediately joins in on the dance party.

"I'm going to go shut the door," she says as she shakes her body back to the entrance. I open the pizza box on top. Pepperoni. Delicious. I dive in for a slice. John would scold the calories.

"What else does your husband hate?" She strips her coat off and leans back out of the room, looking for a coat rack. I point to the couch with a determined eyebrow shimmy. Without a care, she tosses the coat on the sofa.

"Everything," I shout. "Me." I laugh into her face. I smack her arm because I want her attention for my next words, even if she is already looking at me. "But he doesn't hate his whore." I wave my pizza in her face then bite a considerable chunk and search to switch the music to rap because John hates that, too.

"Shit, Medeia."

"Hmm?" I look at her face, and she's stunned by my omission. "Oh—" I wave her off— "I've known for a few weeks now; don't beat yourself up." I find the rap and start bouncing my body. It feels good to move without a rigid board up my back for once.

"And you're still here?" She's pointing around to the house.

"Well, I'm poor without him." I catch her face screw up in disgust. "Don't give me that." I mute the TV. "I'm working on a plan."

She holds her hands up in surrender. "I apologize. Do you want to talk about it?"

"No. There's no saving my marriage. There's no going to my childhood home."

"You could live with me," she offers.

"I hardly know you. I mean I like you, but we don't know each other yet."

She nods. "I can understand that. I do. If ever you need a place, though."

I grab her hand and squeeze. "You're the first I'll call." I wink at her, and she smiles a sad smile.

"So, pizza?" she tries to rally.

"Pizza." I shake the slice I still have in my hand at her and turn the sound back on the TV. We continue dancing until I can't feel my legs, and I forget why I stopped moving my body this way so many years ago.

Medeia's Journal

DEAR ANNA,

I'll see you in the morning at the gym. I'll be hungover, but I'd never miss a chance to see you.

Seventeen

"SO, I THOUGHT ABOUT it after I went home last night, and I looked it up. It's perfect." Jane is buzzing as she approaches me next to the treadmills. My head is fuzzy and hanging on the front half of the machine.

"Thought of what?" I groan. Hangovers hurt.

"Security cameras. They have ones you can watch what's happening from your phone. Technology is sick. Anyway, you could set some up in the warehouse and nail his ass." She punches the air like she's sinking a fist into John's face.

"Warehouse?" What did I tell her last night? Does she know who Anna is?

"That's the only thing you said last night. I see it on your face. Relax, you're very private. You said that you saw a mattress at the warehouse. I figured this is the way that you can catch the asshole."

"I did that." I groan again. "The divorce lawyer only said that maybe it could help."

Jane's shoulders sag. She wanted to be a helper, but the fact that Jane was on the same wavelength felt like a kinship.

"If it doesn't work, maybe I can find a way to use it as blackmail." I put my hand to my chin.

"Speaking of blackmail." Jane points down over the balcony. I look in the direction of her finger. Anna is late today. I thought she wasn't coming at all. Wait. What?

"Blackmail? What kind of gossip do you hold?" I try not to look personally involved in the matter. "I need someone else's drama for a minute."

"Well, that girl down there, the one with the blonde curls that never mess up."

I nod. I know who.

"Well, it's just that the guys around here talk a lot, and none of them will touch her because she used to date an old boss and blackmailed him into giving her his wife's Mercedes SUV. Everyone around here is scared what they'll lose if they touch her."

"Huh." Well, that explains why Anna drives such an expensive car around. She got it the same way she got groceries yesterday. I'm a little relieved to hear it wasn't John who purchased the vehicle for her.

"That's not the only time, either. She's made a trainer here give her a lifetime membership because he was banging her and didn't want his fiancé to find out. I think she's even gotten a nose job out of her manipulation skills." She points down at Anna posing for a lifting selfie. "She's a snake."

I sink to my butt and look down the glass balcony at Anna. I look at all the people around her rolling their eyes or abandoning their posts to get far away. She is a pariah. Why can't John stay away? Is he aware of her reputation?

"Why are you smiling?" Jane cuts into my thoughts.

"Just thinking about the karma in the world and how it's hitting this girl. How I hope one day it will hit my husband just as well."

She smiles down at me. "It will. It will." She seems confident in her conviction.

"Yeah, I think it just might." I smile down at Anna. I feel like a run before work today after all.

Medeia's Journal

DEAR ANNA,

Do you run this often to keep physically fit or to outrun the problems of your life? I've noticed that your face looks less troubled when you finish. You won't outrun me. I wonder if I can be as good at blackmail as you are.

Eighteen

JOHN LEFT ME A VOICEMAIL to pick up some files for him at the office today so that he can work on them when he comes home tonight, earlier than planned. I can't say the enthusiasm wasn't hard to fake. I almost broke character and told him to stay exactly where he was forever.

Luckily, Anna has the day off and won't be there to recognize the person who has been following her lately. She won't see the silhouette of my body and remember someone at the grocery store looking the same way.

When I step into the office, everyone says hello, but they don't bother to make eye contact with me. I wonder what stories pass around here about me. John may be painting me as a horrible mean wife, wouldn't be the first time he's managed to get people to shun me by inflating characteristic traits of mine into something unimaginably evil. That's what he's managed to do with his family. That's why every gathering is uncomfortable with them.

John's office sits on the top floor of the building. He overlooks not only everything inside the building but everything outside of it. His corner office is obscenely huge and not at all humble. Go big or go home. John has designed for his own office to have a separate waiting area with Anna's desk—you need to walk through two doors before finally entering his space. He keeps Anna just as isolated in her own four walls as he does me in the house.

I glance at her desk as I walk in, it's vacant. Easily accessible and concealed if I wanted to peek inside. I linger with my hand on the door that leads to my husband's office. Just one look won't hurt. I abandon the knob and check the glass doors leading out. There's no one around. I lurk over and duck behind her desk, adrenaline rushing through my body.

I open the top drawer and find a key and a bunch of lip balms. Anna's top side drawer holds a mirror and a spare makeup bag. The vanity of this girl is insane. Her bottom drawer is empty but lockable. This must be where she keeps her purse for the workday.

The left-hand side of the desk holds online business-related documents. Dammit. There's nothing here. I slam the drawer, pissed. I wanted to find something, to hold on to something of hers and steal it for myself like she did my life.

I head into my husband's office and push open the door. Inside on a riser sits my husband's desk with space for two others to sit in front of him. I need to climb the two stairs to reach the precipice. Show off. This looks ridiculous. Another power play of John's to let everyone know that he feels they are beneath him. I walk behind his desk. His drawers hold nothing, as well.

The top of his desk is even more disappointing, not a personal photo to be found. Just six months ago, a picture of him and I sat front and center, smiling at him all day. I'm gone now. He's already removing me from his life. I wonder how much money I'll have saved up before he pulls the plug.

I grab the files he asked for and dart out of his office. I stop by Anna's desk one more time to grab a key. There is one thing of hers that I would love to check out.

Nineteen

I TRY TO TELL MYSELF it's too risky. I might get caught, but I want it so badly it's eating at my soul. I place gloves on my hands to keep from leaving fingerprints and slip shower caps on my shoes to keep from tracking dirt or anything incriminating inside. The dark of the night covers me and borrowing Jane's car helps me blend into the neighborhood around here.

The office desk didn't give enough insight except for the fact that Anna must have parched lips for how much lip balm she keeps on hand. Following her has only proven to me that most of what I see is a façade and she is suffering from severe mommy issues.

I don't need to break the door open because she leaves a spare key to her apartment in the top drawer of her desk at work. She's even the kind of brainiac that needs to label that it's for her apartment. How did she get a job working at John's company when she can't remember what her apartment key looks like or the fact that the only key in the top drawer of her desk belongs to her residence?

No one is around outside, the chill of the weather shoving them indoors. I made sure Anna's apartment building didn't have security cameras before coming here. Isn't that sad? She doesn't value herself or her life enough to have security cameras in place.

I value mine, that's why our entire home has them. Probably why John never brings her to our house for one of their little lovemaking sessions. I check the cameras religiously every single day. Honestly, it's always been an obsession. Security of my family and belongings, of what's mine, is something I take seriously. This act tonight feels merely like an extension of it. I'm checking on what belongs to me—*had* belonged to me.

Anna isn't home this evening. I know because she's off at a club. At least that's what her recent status on Facebook reported. I wonder if she'll play the forgotten card trick on an unsuspecting man tonight and get free drinks. I laugh in the hollow space of the entry to her apartment and close the door gently behind me. I don't dare turn on the lights; instead, I give myself a few minutes for my eyes to adjust to the darkness.

A sweet and citrusy smell surrounds this area. It must be the remnants of a candle or a room spray. Anna is conscious of the way her home smells. Well done. I give her kudos for that. That's a sign of someone who takes pride in the things she's worked hard for. It's evident that Anna and I share similar backgrounds of being brought up poor. We champion and value things a little differently because she also enjoys working hard to take things that aren't hers.

I walk through the living room that's connected off the small entryway. The décor is basic enough. Not a lot of thought in style or design placed inside here. It's functional as if that's all it needs to be. Anna is a no-fuss kind of decorator with only one picture hanging on her wall. It isn't a family portrait or a photo that would mean something to her. It is just a meaningless piece of art bought by the dozens at a warehouse store. She seems to lack a creative spirit when it comes to designing her space—what a shame. I don't see any personal photos lying around. I haven't seen her hang out with many people, either, as I watched her. Anna's even flying solo tonight at the club. I bet she won't come home that way. She must not be close to the members of her family. I know she isn't particularly cozy with her mother, but I wonder if she even has friends.

There's no flow in this room; I bang my knee into an oversized coffee table that doesn't fit in the space, leaving only a tight area to scooch around the couch. I creep down the hallway to the kitchen, rubbing the pain in my knee away. There are three shelves placed in an even row going down the hall, and they all house creepy stuffed animals. A thing some people collect as they have a uniquely large head design, but a woman of Anna's age should be out of this hobby by now, shouldn't she? Or at least hide them where only she can enjoy whatever pleasure she gets out of collecting these obscure little things. I run my finger along the edge of the first shelf. Dust. *Come on, Anna, get your shit together.*

What does John see in her? It's clear she doesn't have any personality that isn't picked straight out of whatever chain home store she shops, and the little bit she does have is somewhat disturbing and thin. I enter the kitchen and open the fridge. *Cheap beer. How tacky, Anna. Perhaps you should try a boxed wine to whet your palate for the finer things in life.* I suppress a giggle. Is this her appeal? She's just a girl, whereas I am a woman. *Even just grab a malt beverage for God's sake,*

Anna. The rest of the fridge is close to bare, having lost her groceries to her mom.

I look in the freezer. It's stocked. For being a svelte girl who shops at the whole foods store, she sure does like to snack on the freezer meals and ice cream. It's probably all for show. Her social media feeds are flooded with photos of her eating healthy meals. What would her following think if they caught a glimpse of the real, unedited, unfiltered Anna? I see a lot of the chicken nugget trays as if she's still a toddler. There is a bag with dinosaur shaped ones. Oh, for the love. *Come on, John. I give you class and sophistication, and you take this toddler nonsense over me?* I shut the door and peer into the cabinets, not many baking dishes to be found.

Anna is the type of girl who has her food to-go or delivered. She doesn't cook or bake. I wonder how she manages those pictures on her feed. There isn't much to be found in this kitchen at all that supports the life she puts out there for the world. The truth behind her mask is that Anna is still poor and lonely.

John comes home to me, but he happily leaves that space for someone whose life is just as fake as the ten pounds of makeup on her face. From the looks of the apartment, there isn't much to Anna. She keeps herself alive to be a toy for the men she wants in her life, waiting for the day when it pays off.

I'm pleased that I decided to come here this evening. I hesitated for so long, believing that what I saw on Anna's social media was enough to catch a glimpse inside her world. It wasn't. It is all a lie; she isn't that person at all. Nor is she the woman at the gym working out on the weight machines, she prefers to run outside. She wasn't the woman with a fancy SUV because she worked hard at her job, she got that nugget from blackmailing her ex. Anna is a woman devoid of any real personality of her own. She keeps throwing things at the wall, hoping something sticks for her.

I make my way farther down the hallway. The bathroom is littered with a ton of makeup that's more expensive than the living room furniture. She spends hours in here dolling herself up only to have that work smeared across her whorish face. I look in the bathtub, her hair from shaving in the bath is scattered all over the white porcelain. Every woman knows to shave in the shower instead. Her mother never taught her the secret. Good God. And who doesn't clean the tub out afterward? Disgusting.

I roll my eyes at the mildew on her shower curtain. *What a winner, John. Good choice. I can see why you like her so much. No wonder she's okay with just the mattress on the cement floor of a warehouse. She makes you take her there instead of inviting you back to this dump because she's ashamed of her neighborhood.* I wonder if she has John fooled into believing she came from money, as well, and that's why they don't use her apartment that doesn't have a roommate as her email said. Another stretch of the truth from Anna. I should keep a tally mark of lies and compare John and Anna to find out who has the most.

I wander down the rest of the hallway. All that's left is Anna's bedroom. This apartment is tiny, but it works for a single girl working twenty minutes away. She doesn't have any animals to keep her company—no one to miss her when she's gone. I push open the bedroom door; it's made of white wood and covered with scarves dangling across the top so that it cannot shut properly.

I gasp.

Here is where she saved her personality. A forgotten bed-side table light illuminates the one bright red wall the head-board butts up against. Making the bed the main feature and first thing your eyes are drawn to. The frame is an extrava-gantly detailed king-size mahogany wood housing. The posts shoot up above the mattress, and she's fashioned a proper canopy across the top. White tulle hangs down in a seductive way instead of looking like a tacky teen's room, and it reach-es down to the foot of the bed. Her sheets are silky red un-derneath a luxurious black comforter. Down. Real down. I'd bet my life on it. It's underneath a duvet cover, but I can tell. She has matching nightstands harboring on either side of the bed. The reason why a single woman would need two is be-yond me until I open them. Sex accessories galore. Toys and lubes and condoms. Sweet God. Jezebel.

In the corner, she has a hammock chair hanging from the ceiling instead of a traditional sitting chair. Scattered along the macramé cord seat are fuzzy pink handcuffs and a whip. There is trunk underneath the only window in the room. The window is fashioned with a double curtain rod that com-pletes the look of the room with both red and black thick light-blocking curtains. There is a white shag area rug against the hardwood floor that aids in pulling the whole place to-gether. So, Anna's personality is sex.

A trunk sits alone at the foot of her bed. Inside is where Anna has her private possessions tucked away. Neatly placed with care are photos and journals. Memories she strives to keep safe, alongside her sins of today. I pick up a picture of her and John that tops one tower of possessions. I hold it to the window to have light from the street lamp illuminate his frozen face—a moment in time that they captured forever. They look happy. It's evident to the naked eye that they just finished having sex. The bed sheet seductively pulled over her breast, her hair disheveled but it's clear she ran a quick hand through it so that the picture would give a look that she was longing to achieve. John is smiling his sleepy sated smile after he's had an orgasm—selfishly, usually without asking if I finished. It's clear he's the one holding up the camera to take the photo. I look for some clue as to what he sees in her. Her makeup is smudged, and she doesn't look like the done-up supermodel I see all the time. She's wrecked, and he loves it. He gets to know this side of her as if it is a gift from the heavens, something she doesn't show anyone but him. He's privileged.

I'm surprised John likes a girl that has two nightstands full of goodies. I could hardly get him to take a shower with me through the years of our marriage. Any time I dared to ever suggest anything outside of the box when we were making love, he ran off and lost his nerve to finish. Now, I barely make it through the ten minutes of missionary style without throwing up all over him. Sleeping with the enemy.

I take the photo and jam it into my pocket. It may be foolish. Anna might look at it every night for all I know, longing to be the wife he so desperately needs. The one he has now is not fulfilling his needs, and she would never let that happen. She is just showing him the love he deserves.

She may look at this picture and see her future alongside him.

I plan on studying this picture until it talks to me, tells me all the reasons I lost my husband's love and why she has earned it. If it would just tell me what makes the two smiling into the camera so deliriously fucking happy, maybe there could be peace in my heart. What makes another so fascinating that they're worth ripping your spouse's heart out?

Why is it worth dying for?

A slam against the outside door makes me jump. Fuck. I dart off into the bathroom and climb into the tub, drawing the shower curtain half closed. When the door opens all that fills the apartment is sounds of Anna's moaning and the feeling of déjà vu.

"Hold on. Hold on." She demands.

"Come on, baby."

"No, my bedroom. Not here." She breaths between kisses and attempting to shut the door behind her.

Their shadows pass by the doorway as Anna leads a new man to her sex treasure chest. Not John. Not Thomas. Not Michael. I exit out of the tub and grab the lipstick off Anna's shelf.

"Holy shit. Your room is sick." The guy has more of surfer dude tone in his voice than John's professional one or Thomas's easy going one.

I roll my eyes at the continued moaning as he kicks the door shut. This is my chance. I slink out, careful not to put myself in the sliver of the light from the door that won't close because of those damn scarves.

"Let me freshen up."

Fuck. This girl. I dart to the kitchen as I hear Anna's heels on the floor again. She flicks on the bathroom light, and I hear the faucet running. It feels like forever before the water kicks off and she's heading back to entertain her guest.

"Where were we?" She puts on her best seductive voice for the man.

"Bring that sweet ass over here." She giggles and I hear her jump on the bed.

I duck around the half wall of the kitchen into the living room space and stare down the hallway. A part of me wants to watch and see what Anna does to drive these men insane. Why can't I even hold on to my husband and she has four guys eating out of the palm of her hand? I don't go. Instead I make my way to the front door. I take a deep breath before I turn the knob and allow only enough room to squeeze myself outside.

Anna is a greedy whore.

Medeia's Journal

DEAR ANNA,

Your red lipstick looks better on me. I swiped it from your bathroom. It seems fabulous with my skin tone. I've seen you wearing it lately. It must have been your new favorite. You looked like a drowned heroin addict when you wore it. You should thank me for stealing it. I'm saving you. You could lose John with that look.

Speaking of John, he hates the lipstick on me. I loathe you and the oxygen that finds its way into your lungs and sustains your pathetic life.

As for me, I look like a 50's movie star. Unfortunately, I'm playing the most tragic role.

Twenty

"MRS. MOORE."

"Medeia, please." The irritation hums through my veins at the lawyer's exasperation for me daring to retake a moment of his time today.

"Well, frankly, it's going to be Mrs. Moore because I feel like you need a reality check about what you're trying to accomplish here. There's no way in my professional opinion that you'll be able to come out of this divorce with anything." He taps his pen off his desk. He looks younger than me and too fresh in the world yet, but I have a terrible feeling when a lawyer looking for experience won't take a case. He should be the greediest looking for work, shouldn't he?

"But he's cheating on me!" I hold my phone up in protest, showing the screenshot of their night together in the warehouse.

"Might I suggest that you consider that an indiscretion and go on with your marriage. Better than being a poor, single woman." He looks at my clothes up and down. "Are you ready to give up what luxuries his money affords you?" He shuffles the papers I've brought him back into the folder and holds them out for me to take home.

"That's it?" I'm baffled. "You told me to get proof; now you say just to ignore his infidelity?"

"Afraid so." He shakes the folder impatiently, waiting for me to grab it. I rip it from his hands and flip the strap of my purse around my shoulder.

"Thanks for nothing." I bite out.

"No offense, Mrs. Moore —" he says the name with such irritation — "but what did you expect when you signed that prenup?"

"Fidelity. Like an asshole, that's what I expected. Good day, Mr. No Good Useless Lawyer." He salutes me, and I slam his door behind me.

I throw the papers in the garbage outside of his office. "What good are they anyway?" I shout at the can.

"Ma'am?"

"What?" I shout at the receptionist. She's an older lady cowering behind her ancient computer monitor.

"Are you alright? Would you like some tea?"

"I want some fucking vodka. A whole bottle as big as that man's ego in there." I point at the door that I just exited containing the biggest asshole I've ever met.

"I, um."

"Oh, shut up," I shout at her and take off for the exit. I'd slam that door, too, if it let me.

I make it home in record time and pour whiskey into a mug and take it to the sunroom. I don't even shed my purse or shoes at the door. Fuck it, what's the point? All I want is to get drunk. I chug the mug down in a few seconds. The alcohol burns my throat and brings tears to my eyes. I want more. I throw my purse on the floor and spin in my seat to head back to the kitchen for the bottle.

"Do you think I'm stupid?" John encompasses the doorway before I can get out.

"What?" I notice my work lanyard dangling from his left hand. "No, I just—"

"Oh, I want to hear how you explain your way out of this Medeia. I specifically told you no job." He advances toward me and chucks the lanyard at my face. It bounces off my shoulder and lands on the table behind me. I fall back into my seat.

I look for the words as I stare down at my nametag—another thing of mine for him to take. I wipe my forehead, praying the lie comes to me, but John has had more time to prepare than I.

"Let me tell you this, Medeia." My name sounds like a curse. "No job. I told you no job. You make me look weak. The world will peer in here and think that something is wrong, that I can't provide all of a sudden. You don't care what kind of risk that puts on us, do you?" He moves his hand, and I flinch, but he grabs the lanyard and chucks it across the room. *Something* is wrong here, but it's not our finances. "Quit."

"John, it's just a job." He lunges forward so that his nose is touching mine, and it's the most violent feeling I ever felt by another human's face.

"You're so stupid. You don't get it, do you? No man in my position has a wife that works. You're just meant to sit here and look pretty, and you can't even manage that." He flicks his wrist into my hair indicating the style not being suitable.

"I look just fine." I clench my teeth.

"You smell of alcohol. Bad day at your *job*?"

"No. Just a bad day."

"Why don't you take some pills? Does Dr. Janson know that you like to drink in the middle of the afternoon?" The devil inside John smirks at me.

"Why are you home?"

"I had to deal with this." He points at me.

"John," I start.

"Quit." He finishes.

He storms off, and I'm left alone, lonelier than before. I hold my face in my hands and cry. I'm fucked.

Medeia's Journal

DEAR ANNA,

Thanks for telling John about my job. I know it was you. You heard my name spoken and you lead him on to it. Thanks, bitch. You'll get yours. Trust me. I'll find a way.

Twenty-One

"MEDEIA. I'M WORRIED. You haven't said a word in twenty minutes." I scooch down into Dr. Janson's couch further and bring about my large sweatshirt around me. My hair is unwashed, and I have no makeup on. I've chosen the most massive sweatshirt in my closet.

"Please, Medeia."

"He made me quit." I sniff.

"Who made you quit? Quit what?" Les is concerned. His voice is not a distant professional; he's invested. It makes me feel a small light in the dark.

"John." I sigh and wipe the tear rolling on my cheek. "I got a job. Secretly. He won't let me work. He said it makes him weak."

"You were working? I'm sorry, Medeia. Why did John make you quit?"

"I didn't know that wanting to feel independent was such a dirty thing." I ignore his questioning, lost in my own mind.

"It's not." Les drops his pad into the side of his chair. He's not taking notes right now. "Tell me about it, Medeia. Get it off your chest. I can see in your eyes that you're living in a past moment, and I can't help you if you don't let me come there, too." I shift in my seat taking in his face. He wants to know.

"Did I ever tell you about my siblings?" I push the brim of my baseball cap up so that Les can see me.

"Not nearly enough."

"I have a younger sister and brother, Ophelia and Hank." I smile mentioning their names.

"What do they do?"

"I don't know." My smile fades. "John made me agree that they were worthless to our lives. Our *rich* lives."

"Tell me about the past. I don't want to hear about John."

My eyes fill with tears. "Me either." A sad smile lifts Les's lips.

"When I was eighteen, I moved out. God, I couldn't stand being in that shack any longer. I told my mother that I was taking Ophelia and Hank with me. She tried to protest, but I packed their bags and told her they were going. She didn't fight because at that second my father came in drunk and throwing his bottles. I think she was relieved that someone was getting her children out of there. She never believed that she could do it."

"How did Ophelia and Hank feel about moving?" Les leans back in his chair.

"Mad at first, until we got there. They each had their own rooms. I rented a two-bedroom apartment and gave them the bedrooms. I slept on the little futon in the living room. I felt blessed to have a new home; I didn't care about having my own room. The place was small, not much bigger than the house we left, but it didn't have the threat of my dad in it. The carpet was stained, but we loved it because it wasn't giving us splinters like the damaged hardwood floor of the shack. I bought Ophelia a birthday cake, and she cried the whole time that we sang. We never got such a luxury before. We thought we were rich."

"You became a mother to them."

"I could never replace my mother," I argue. "I couldn't see working three jobs and not doing it for a purpose. They were my purpose."

"What happened?"

"Hank graduated and soon so did Ophelia. I met John and—" I wave to the air "—that was that."

Les doesn't respond. He lets me fill in our silence when I'm ready to answer his unspoken questions.

"I dropped them for John and his lifestyle."

"You had to make a choice."

"Don't do that. Don't try and put salve on the wounds I've created. I did wrong."

"I—" but he stops himself. "I won't."

"Our session is up," I announce. Les sadly nods as I gather my purse. "Les?"

"Yeah?"

I walk over to him, lean my body down and hug him. "Thank you." Les's arm reaches up to embrace me back.

"Any time."

It's a windy day on the top of the bridge, even more with the cars rushing behind me as I stand on the pathway. The wind does nothing to chill me. I feel dead inside already. I lean my head against the metal beam and look out on the river's dark water.

"Me-Me"

"Phil." I laugh as Ophelia scrunches up her nose. "What's up, sugar cube?"

"There are clothes on my bed." She's confused.

"Yes." I smile.

"Why?" She scratches her leg and hitches up her too tight short sleeve dress.

"Because you need school clothes."

"They're for me?" As the realization dawns on her, I watch pure joy seep into my sister's young fifteen-year-old face. "Seriously?"

"Well, they won't fit Hank." I laugh. I have been dying for her to notice the clothes on her bed.

"Very funny," Hank grumbles from the couch as he's watching a movie.

"You got me school clothes?" Ophelia asks for confirmation. She's terrified that's it's just a dream she'll be forced to wake up from and go back to reality.

"I got you both clothes." I sip my coffee and puff out the newspaper in front of me, trying to act casual as if new clothing isn't a monumental thing. But it is. To my siblings and I, it's a rare thing.

"You got me clothes?" Hank jumps up from the couch, no longer acting like a cool sixteen-year-old as he darts for his room. "Oh my god! Phil! Come look!"

Ophelia takes off after my brother and with them out of the room I let the ear-splitting smile take over my face.

"Fashion show!" Ophelia yells.

I remember that day like it was only five minutes ago. I can still smell the vanilla air freshener trying to mask the mildew smell when I think about it — the rundown green carpet stained from the previous owners. The walls needed a few coats of paint, but it was home. No one was going to hurt us anymore.

Except, I hurt them.

I climb the railing and sit on top of it. I should jump and end it all. What good am I to this world? John has made sure that I'll be left with the karma I deserve for leaving my siblings behind. I look down at the river. I wonder if it will be the fall, the water, or the cold that kills me.

I could haunt John.

All his belittling comments he's stained my soul with would be buried with me. Anna would be welcomed in as a natural moving on process. No one would ever know what they did.

I put my leg back over toward the pathway and make the other one follow. I jump back down on the path and start walking to my car.

The idea of John winning doesn't sit right with me.

Twenty-Two

INSTEAD OF JUMPING off the bridge, I drive to one of my favorite gift shop style stores with little figurines and trinkets in it. They annoy the hell out of John every time I purchase a new one. If I can't divorce him, the least I can do is irk him. A small bit of power I can hold on to for the time being.

I pop in and wave at the lady behind the counter. She's not the old lady I'm used to, and I'm not in the mood for conversation, so I'm more than delighted to know that she as well wants to be left to her devices with the simple headbob she offers me. I don't look like myself today. I look at least ten pounds heavier than I am. I wish to be swallowed whole in comfort today. I probably give off a hot mess vibe that screams trouble.

I head to the back of the store because I like to work my way from the back to the front. It feels more efficient that way, giving everything a once-over and freeing myself from the possibility of impulse buys when I see an item twice.

I hear a familiar voice talking with the cashier over the low volume of Motown hits playing on the stereo. I try to place it before showing my undone face, just in case it's one of the snobby wives that I'm supposed to play nice with. I peek my head around the etagere to see.

It's Anna. My heart skips a beat, and I duck behind the ceramic dolls. Their voices are soft murmurs, so I slink away from the speaker to hear them better than the blues. I want to rush up there and punch her. I can't believe she made John think she went to a bookstore on her own accord. She's the "wait for the movie" type. She doesn't read — too busy screwing every guy in sight to open a book.

"Samantha, I have news. It's about John." She's leaning against the small sliver of the wall in front of the register. She's cautiously examining her manicure, a tick of fret, while her friend rolls her eyes and continues her organizing behind the mahogany countertop.

I crouch down in the nearest aisle so that to the cashier, it only looks like I am browsing the items on the lower shelf. I don't want to risk being called out for eavesdropping, so I pretend I don't hear them gossiping.

"Did his wife finally take an ax to him for cheating on her?" She slams down a roll of tape in frustration at another employee's displacement. "Here it is," she mumbles toward the tape.

"Samantha!" Anna scolds her, but Samantha shrugs. It's obvious she's familiar with the situation and no fan of John's behavior. "We are in love. How can you say that? He's coming up with a plan so that we can be together soon." Anna reeks of desperation—a high-pitched voice, and she's shuffling from left to right. She's in love and craving the world to bend to her because of it.

"Fat chance." The stuffy cashier with her frizzy hair and pimply face scoffs at her. I wonder how these two ladies know each other. They are complete contrasts. Anna has long, smooth, blonde hair that looks like she takes time to maintain it and make it healthy. She has a long, slender body that shows she works out, and her nails are acrylic, but at least she pays attention to their aesthetics. Samantha has a muffin top, shoveling her face full of chocolate cake from the vending machine, and you can see the remnants of what used to be nail polish only on the middle finger of her right hand.

"Sounds like the usual married man chatter." Samantha raises her eyebrows as if it were as simple as that.

"He is. He promised me." It's more of a question, longing for her friend to jump on board at the slight hope of possibility, than a statement with real conviction.

"Why? Because he loves you?" Samantha mocks her with a smoochy face. "Come on, Anna. It's the same thing that happened with Blake, and that's how you became this guy's secretary. Remember? You needed a new job to get away from the last married boss you were screwing. Now you got this position, and you're screwing this boss." *Tough love, Samantha.* She doesn't pull any punches. I like her. I don't know her, and from this standpoint, she's supposed to be Anna's friend, but I feel like she is more on my team than allowing her loyalties to lie with Anna.

"No, he told me his plan. That's why I know he's going to leave her." The plan excites Anna, but Samantha doesn't take the bait and continues cleaning her workspace. "Samantha!"

"What?" Samantha looks up from the note on the desk she was taping down.

"Ask me about the plan." Anna's tone is the definition of annoyance.

"No."

"I'm going to tell you anyway."

Samantha rolls her eyes.

"It's brilliant. Her mother passed away a few months ago I think, or it may have been a year." She touches her finger to her chin but waves it off. "Doesn't matter. The point is she's mentally unstable. I'm talking a mental breakdown that led her to be in the hospital and weekly therapy sessions."

Samantha glares at Anna.

"So, he's been able to get her to ask for higher dosages of medicine. He's hellbent on sending her to a facility once he's convinced her she's crazy enough. Then, after a few months of that, he can divorce her for irreconcilable differences because he can't handle the stress of losing his wife to mental illness. She won't be able to fight him and gain any money that way because she'll already be clinically insane." She drums out a beat on the countertop. I slap my hand on my mouth to keep from throwing up on the thin carpeting.

Samantha slams down on Anna's happy hands. "That's sick."

Anna rips her hands out from underneath her friend's firm grip. "What?" She looks down from where she was envisioning her future life and shrugs at her friend. "He's generous enough to offer to pay for her to stay there. Something about her being the reason he was able to keep out of jail when he was younger over being falsely accused."

"This could put you both in jail. You should stop that thinking right now. You're the other woman, Anna. The only thing the two of you deserve is poverty and shame." I am Team Samantha. She may not be able to uphold her appearance, but her morals are genuinely intact, and I smile at the lost art she is in this world. She sees through the lies that John is feeding Anna.

"She doesn't deserve him, Samantha."

"I agree with you. She doesn't deserve a two-timing lying scumbag. And neither do you; you need to rise above this and drop his ass." Samantha begins to restock the candy at the front of the store.

"It's love, Sammy. Love. You don't just walk away from that."

"You do if it's a ribbon wrapped around a pile of dog shit." She slams candy bars into their spaces. "Why can't anyone else bother to fill these? They look at them all day long from behind the counter. They know when they're empty."

"Sam, I want you to be happy for me."

"I'm not." She puts the candy box down and grips both of her friend's shoulders in her sausage-fingered hands. "You are not living to your potential. You are just someone else's whore."

"Jesus, Sam."

"It's true." Samantha lets go of Anna and fills the candy etagere some more.

Anna insists that John is hers. But he isn't. I look down at my left hand; he made a solemn promise to me to only be my man. Forsake all others. He isn't hers in law. I have his name; I gave that identifying mark up to embrace his. He lives with me. He gets mail at my house. All the invitations say Mr. & Mrs. John Moore, and that doesn't mean Anna. It means me, Medeia Moore. His wife. I didn't go through the hell of it to have someone rip the title and not only leave me broke but deranged.

I slump down on the floor beside the turtles, no longer strong enough to squat. How could John do this to me? I gave him everything. He still wants to take more from me.

"And what about Thomas?" Samantha's words haul me up on my knees.

"What about him? We still see each other." Anna vigorously fluffs her hair up. How dare Samantha not understand.

"This isn't normal, Anna. Most people don't seriously date two guys at once."

"Well, John has *her*, so why can't I have Thomas?"

Samantha throws her hands up in defeat; she's talking to a wall. "You have Thomas, the guy from the club, the married John, and the guy from Simply Fresh."

"I got to go. Meeting Thomas for dinner. Don't tell him anything?" She points her coffin-styled manicure at Samantha's face.

"I wouldn't dream of doing your job for you." She pushes Anna's finger out of the way and shakes her head as her friend storms off. When the door shuts, Samantha goes back to her work, like her friend didn't just plot to have someone committed to a mental facility. As if all of that is normal in her world. It must be for Anna. How many times has she done this before?

Once Anna leaves, I gather myself off the floor, grab one of the antique turtles from the bottom to avoid suspicion and pay for it. Samantha switches into the best-cashier-ever mode as she hands me polite talk along with my receipt as if I didn't just hear what kind of nasty human-being she associates with in her down time.

I walk out to my car and throw the turtle on the seat next to me. *Samantha has given me an intriguing idea to take an ax to you, John. Well, I think a double murder sounds better.*

Medeia's Journal

DEAR ANNA

I've decided what I'm going to do. I'm making my own plans, too.

Twenty-Three

"HEADING OUT FOR DRINKS with some business associates. I'll be back late." John fiddles with the watch on his wrist.

"Okay, dear." I look up from my book and flash him my best smile.

"Glad to see you're no longer mad, Medeia."

"How could I be, dear? You made your point crystal clear." *Sharp as a knife.*

"I won't be long." John kisses the top of my head.

"Take your time, dear." I look back to my book and pretend to read as John saunters to the door. Off to his whore.

I wait until I hear the motor of the garage door opener shut off, indicating that the door has closed, before I get up and make my move toward my car. I know where John's going, so I'm not afraid of losing him. I press the button to lift the garage door for myself. Instead of focusing on gaining my security, I need to switch directions to taking John's away.

I pull into a parking lot near the warehouse, close enough for the camera app to work, and I turn up the volume after I put the car in park. Thanks to John for making me quit, I now have free time to replace their batteries and make sure they're always working. The show must go on.

"I'm sorry, I missed you too much today. I had to see you." Anna is already waiting on their mattress when I hear

John's footsteps hit the top stair. I don't see him yet. Dinner with Thomas must not have been enough for her.

"Never apologize for that." He rushes and holds her, lifting her into his arms. *Asshole.*

"Tell me again, John."

John pulls his head away so he can better look her in the eye.

"Tell me again how we are going to be together. The plan. I need to hear it again." She's desperate, doubting her love's abilities to leave his wife.

He motions for her to sit on the mattress, preparing her for a story, a fairytale. One that they don't know I will stop and turn into an absolute tragedy.

"Don't worry, Anna. Medeia does what I tell her. She won't be hard to convince that she needs to go to the facility. I just got her to up her dosage again. I think at least two more times of raising it should be enough. She's weak. Not like you, sweet Anna." He brushes her hair back from her face. "I can't wait to wake up next to you every single day."

It's all true. John just confirmed it. Heat rises in my chest as my body attempts to battle the adrenaline of the truth.

"Couldn't you just commit her now?" She's begging him, grabbing onto his chest. I punch the top of my steering wheel imagining it as her face.

"Anna, trust me. This is delicate. It's going to happen, but we only have one shot at it. It has to be perfect so that it sticks. She's not there yet." He kisses her forehead.

"I wish she'd overdose and die, then we wouldn't have to wait anymore," she whines into his shoulder. I hold my middle finger up toward the phone.

"I thought she would early on, right after her mother died. She was so messed up." I see a flicker of care on his face, and my heart jumps. I'm not the only one to notice it, though.

"Why don't you remind her of what her mother looked like lying on the floor in her own blood? Maybe that can push it along." I turn the phone over toward my lap. The image of my mother's death is conjuring up effortlessly in my mind at Anna's words. How does she know? John told my secret to his dirty little secret.

"Anna. Don't talk like that. We are together now; let's not talk about her. I want to make love to you." They begin kissing, and I turn the phone off.

My hand is around my throat; suddenly it's hard to breathe in the car. I roll down my window and the night air rushes in and chills my bones. The cruelty that's plotted against me, the way they disregard my mother and make love on their concrete nest of lies, chokes the oxygen out of my body. They aren't good people. I agree with Samantha, they deserve nothing but poverty and shame, but I can't think of a way to bring about that.

I can't get a divorce. John will be searching for clues that I didn't quit my job now. And he'll be trying to up my medication. I get nothing from the prenup; I have nowhere to go. I feel helpless in the fight for my own life.

I want to take Anna from him. He's taken everything from me. I won't get her to pull away and go to Thomas; she's in love with John's money. Thomas is backup—just something to keep John's attention, to make him fight for her. Even if she did leave him, how long would I have until another Anna came along? Where would it leave me? I'd still be stuck in this marriage with John.

I look over the parking lot and find a couple kissing on a nearby bench. I drive off to give them privacy, praying they aren't another lousy pair of cheaters.

Anna wants me to overdose, and John seems disappointed that I haven't done it. I mean nothing — nothing to no one. They couldn't even spare humanity for my mother's demise, so I won't spare any for theirs. It clicks in my head what I need to do. It's the only thing that's left.

I will kill them

I will kill Anna and John.

Twenty-Four

"I'M SO SORRY, MAGGIE, I wish that I could stay," I start.

"Wish you could stay? Wait, why are you quitting?" Now is the time to spill the beans; the more people that know the character traits of my husband the better character witnesses I will have to account for the evil man he is.

"I'm sorry." I start to cry. "My husband won't let me have a job. I was coming here in secret, and he found out, now I need to quit."

Maggie grabs ahold of me in a tight embrace. "Oh, darling." She doesn't know what to say.

"I don't know what to do." I know what I need to do. It's the only way out of the wall they've cornered me in — take John and Anna away from the world.

"You always have a safe space here." I like Maggie, I honestly do, but I can tell this is out of her depth. She's not Jane. Jane feels more like a ride-or-die kind of girl. When I said that I needed to quit, she asked me what my plan was to get back at John.

"Thank you, Maggie. Sincerely. I'll be alright." I squeeze her back and make to leave. "I do need to get going. Perhaps John is right; this isn't a good idea right now when I'm still recovering mentally from my mother's passing."

"Oh." She's stunned. "I hadn't realized, dear. I'm so sorry for your loss. You were easily becoming the best employee I ever had. You changed my mind about you."

"Thank you. Goodbye, Maggie."

Without John, I proved myself to be capable of holding my own. I am not the weak woman he has dedicated years to impose upon me. I was beginning to show it to myself when he once again grabbed it from my reach. I won't stop now and go back to being oppressed under his thumb.

Maggie waves. Her new favorite employee has a bully husband, and she's mentally unstable; it's too much to handle. I head from Maggie's store to Dr. Janson's office. Much to John's dismay, I was about to get a whole lot better and go down in dosage instead of up.

When I come into the office, I smile at the receptionist, and it takes her by surprise. I'm not usually this cheery. Changing your direction in a plan can have that effect on you, plotting to rid yourself of your worst demons makes your steps lighter. I wanted to skip, but I fear to be too obvious.

"Hello, Helen." My smile never fades.

"Well, hello, Medeia. How are you?"

"I'm wonderful. I'm a little early, just going to sit and read a magazine." I point toward the chair in the corner.

"Oh, he's ready for you whenever you are." She beams.

"Oh, perfect. Thank you." I tap on her desk and make my way through the door leading to the hallway taking me to my new future.

Today is going to be the start of a new Medeia, one that John will lose control of, but I plan to do it the same way he took it from me—deliberate and without his knowledge. By the time he realizes that the power has slipped through his fingers, it'll be too late for him to gain it back.

I rap three times on the door to alert Dr. Janson that I'm here before walking in and shutting it behind me.

"Hello, Les." I smile, and it has the same effect on him as the receptionist.

"Hello, Medeia. You look well." He scrunches his eyebrows up in surprise.

"I feel well, Les." I pop down on the couch and bounce a bit. "I tried something new."

"That is?" He grabs a pencil from his desk and moves to sit next to me in his usual lounge chair.

"I went to the gym." I smile. "And guess what else?" I lean in and look left and right with mock conspiracy. He leans in and plays along, happy to see a good mood returning.

"What?" he whispers.

"I made a friend." I smile again. "An actual friend, Les. Do you know how long it has been since I have hung out with anyone but my husband? Since my mother died. I either hung out with my mother or my husband. And now I have a friend!"

Les's laughter is contagious, and I join in. "Why has it been so long since you had a friend?"

"Oh, John doesn't let me have friends that he doesn't approve of first." I wave my hand as if it's no big deal, but I know how sharp Les is and he didn't miss my confession. "I'm keeping Jane a secret. He's already made me quit the job; I don't want him to make me quit a friend, as well."

Les's laughter stops dead, and his face falls into a deep sadness.

"He's always worried about someone trying to infiltrate his company through me, so if he doesn't know the people, I'm not allowed to hang out with them." I shrug. It's my life, and I act as calmly as I have let myself be about it for the last ten years of my life.

"That doesn't sound right." He grabs his notepad from the table and jots a few things down.

"I quit today." I change the subject. I need for those notes to hold a lot of things— I have no time to waste.

"How does that make you feel?" I see Les scribbling notes on his pad between the scrunched eyebrows that cause worry lines of age to appear on his forehead.

"Well..." I scrunch my eyebrows in comparison and wonder how deep the lines in my forehead area. "I'm not happy about it."

"Where were you working?"

"Mugs and Books."

"Was that a career for you?" The question feels stupid leaving his lips, and I can tell it tasted terrible.

"No, but it was a lot of fun, and I was feeling stronger. I didn't know that was wrong."

"It's not." It's the first time I watch contention take place between Les and me. He will make a great character witness, as will his notes.

I fluff the throw pillow next to me. "Can we talk about lowering my medication, please? I don't like the increase."

"Uh, certainly. Do you feel these extra things you've been doing have helped improve your mood?" I can tell there are more questions that Dr. Janson wants to ask.

"Well, I was understandably sad about having to quit my job, but I realize now that getting out of the house was the main boost in my mood. So long as I continue to branch out and meet people, I think I can maintain a good mood. Then I want to get off the medication eventually."

"It's a fabulous idea, Medeia. But you just came in upset the other day."

"Les, can I be honest with you?" I perk up on the couch.

"I had hoped that's what you always were." I nod.

"Blunt. Blunt is a better word." I decide.

"Okay. Be blunt."

"I felt an emotion fiercely the other day, and I didn't sulk. I didn't hide it, swallow it up until I took a shower where I could cry. I let myself feel it. I never did that before, and I feel like that's an improvement. Don't you?"

"It is Medeia." He agrees.

"I knew to come to you that day."

"Yes, you did." He places his pen to his lips.

"Everyone has sad days like that. The emotion isn't saved only for the medically diagnosed people. Sadness doesn't discriminate."

"Yes. That's also true." Les bites his lip and flips through some notes of mine.

"So?" I tilt my head.

"Let's lower your dosage." He smiles.

"Wonderful. I can't wait to tell John."

Medeia's Journal

DEAR ANNA,

Allow me to introduce myself.

I'm a smart bitch from the streets, not a doll in a Versace dress. That's the role that I've been playing. I have done a lot of horrible things to obtain money in my life. Killing you and John won't even come close to the worst.

I have covered up my father's crimes just so my family could have groceries for a week. A week. That's all the money it took to motivate my father to mug someone. He even hurt a man so severely that he died three days later. Just for enough cash to buy one bottle of gin. That's it.

Don't be fooled by what you see. I'm not a dumb trophy wife.

Twenty-Five

"ISN'T IT GREAT, HONEY? Dr. Janson is going to start decreasing my medication. I don't know if it's the gym or the other things he's suggested I try, but I am feeling so much better these days." My shoulders can't help but do a happy shimmy.

John drops his spoon with a sudden clang. "He said what? Are you sure?" John pushes his bowl away; he's lost his appetite.

"Right? I was as shocked as you at first." I dive into my soup. Delicious. "But, it's wonderful news, babe. I'm on the mend."

"Don't talk with your mouth full like that," he scolds.

"Oh, honey." I wave him off. *You can't break my mood, John.*

"I think you should get a second opinion about that." He's grasping for control, trying to clasp his greedy hands around it. This is the first time he's felt me have the upper hand. He doesn't know that I realize what position I'm in. He still thinks there's time to convince me to crawl back under his thumb.

"You said Dr. Janson was the most qualified therapist there is when I needed to start going to one. I don't understand." I tilt my head like a dog begging for answers.

"He is. I mean, yes, yes, he's qualified. This is a huge step, though; that's all." A nervous giggle passes my husband's lips, and I record the sound to memory.

"Well, John, with situational depression you're not meant to stay on medication forever."

He nods along. He doesn't have time to plot his next move.

"Do you think I'm crazy, John?"

"No." It's his immediate response, but the second it leaves his lips, I can tell he regrets it. Telling me, I'm not crazy doesn't help to convince me later that I am. "I think you are in a delicate state, though. I want to know that you won't crash like that again. I hated seeing you so out of it in the hospital, babe. It was scary." With clear eyes, I see John's calculating ways to play on my emotions. There's even a quick, instinctive urge in my chest to cave to him, but I resist because my heart won't drive my life anymore, and neither will John.

"I feel stronger now than I ever have, babe." I clear my bowl and his from the table, walking back to the kitchen for the evening dishes, smiling at the dumbfounded look on my husband's face. "Don't worry about me." *Worry about your girlfriend.*

JOHN DOESN'T TAKE THE news of my decrease in medication well. The next three days he brews on it, his agitation growing because he can't find a way to make me spin around the drain. With less medication in my system, the fog begins to lift. As my mind grows stronger, so does my will to see John pay for those wasted years.

I'm sitting in a lounge chair in the sunroom reflecting on the years under John's rule. It's a new meditation form for me; it brings me focus every morning while I watch the day come to life before me. There's no chance for positivity in our relationship, so I let the lousy parts fuel my will to push forward in the plan. I've stayed longer this morning, chancing to entertain myself with visions of John and Anna's murder and how I'll accomplish it.

I hear a slam of the front door.

"John?" I call out. "Is that you, honey?" Every time I use an endearment toward him, I think about washing my mouth out with a bathroom cleaner.

There's no reply, so I unfold my legs and set my now-cold coffee down to investigate. It's only ten in the morning; he's back awful early from work. I find John in his office, briefcase dropped on the floor and the drawer containing the gin open. My husband throws his legs on top of the desk and goes to pour himself a glass of gin before deciding to hell with the glass, letting it shatter on the floor with a simple flick of his wrist. He chugs straight from the bottle.

"John," I scold.

"What?" he seethes.

"I bought you those glasses." I point to the shattered pieces of thick etched glass on the floor. John's answer is an evil laugh as he tosses back another gulp of gin.

"*You* bought them for me? You don't buy anything. It's my money." He leans over his desk toward me. It's clear he already downed his reservoir of gin in his office at work before coming home. Why couldn't he have just wrecked his car and died? I match him. I am tired of his shit.

"Yes. *I* bought them for you when *I* was allowed a job during our engagement." I lean forward on the desk and get into his face. I have the power now. *I will kill you and your girlfriend.*

"So..." He leans back. "This is the warm reception I get coming home today?" His left arm swirls the air, while his right clasps the bottle.

"Why are you home so early, *dear*?" I stand straight up. I want John to feel small under my glare.

"I finally smacked the smug look off that asshole, Kalen." He lies back in the chair and closes his eyes in meditation.

"You did what?" I shout.

"He had it coming." He flings his eyes open. "The police, however..."

"The police?" I screech and start pacing the floor in front of his desk.

"God, Medeia, you're so annoying." He slams the rest of the gin down.

"What did the police say?" I'm anxious, no need to pretend.

"Asked him if he wanted to press charges. Is there any more gin in this house?"

I look into his glazed eyes. John won't remember anything tomorrow. "Does he?" I ask.

"Does who?" John's mouth is nothing but lax and slurring.

"Does Kalen want to press charges against you?" Drunk John is exasperating.

"I don't know." He shrugs. "Where's the gin?"

"You drank it all. Do you want vodka?" I grab the vodka bottle from his cabinet and set it on the desk.

"Mmm. Vodka." He twists the cap off with ease and chugs at least a third of the full bottle down in one take.

"This is bad, John. What happens if he presses charges?" I worry my bottom lip.

"Jail?" He laughs. "I honestly don't know right now. I think I'm drunk." He leans back in his chair, and the whole thing tumbles over, and he falls straight on his ass.

"Dammit!" I scream and leave John to his office and his drink. There's no sense in trying to get anything from him, not when he's this obnoxious with alcohol. He's going to mess up my plans again.

I stew all day around the house, trying to come up with a counter attack in my head, so John's possible dance with the law doesn't ruin my plans. He can't be dead and in jail at the same time. The idea of John going to jail is attractive.

Then it hits me.

The best way to succeed would be to make John the accused. Yes, I've been focusing on getting my revenge in the wrong direction this whole time. John doesn't need to die alongside his beloved Anna; he needs to be the one to kill her. It's much more satisfying to have John's name besmirched.

Every little detail comes flying into my mind like I've unlocked something I always could do— just like my father, I can plan a heinous crime. I have so much foundation to lay to make the case solid. I need to cut down enough on my medication and intercept texts from Anna to create a quarrel between them. I can make it look like she was leaving him.

I'm so caught up in the planning that I forget all about John in his office until curiosity gets the better of me and I go to check on him. Sure enough, he has at least gained enough consciousness to set his chair back upright, although he can't manage to put his body in that same position. He's slumped over his desk, clinging to the next empty bottle of alcohol. The vodka and gin have been tossed to the floor and remain in shards alongside the glass.

I dart to the front entrance and grab my shoes so that I don't wind up with a bloody foot. I make a note to tell the housekeeper to do a thorough vacuum in here when she comes this weekend. I'll do the best I can once I throw John in bed. I'd rather let him stew in here, but the part I need to play to convince a jury and everyone in the world reading the newspaper after Anna's death. That I was a caring wife, involves acting like I don't know.

I remove the bottle from his hand, and this causes John to wake up.

"No. No, I need that," he whines and grabs the thin air.

"It's empty, John." I walk over to his side of the desk, careful where I step, and offer my hand to help him up. "Come on; let's get you to bed."

"I need a shower." It's all I can do not to throw up. I don't want to care for John. I don't want to be his crutch up the stairs. And I surely don't want to be the one washing him, sponging off his skin soaked from alcohol spills and pores clogged with cigar smoke.

"John, it can wait until the morning."

"Medeia," he pleads.

"Let's see how you do going up the stairs first." He nods and allows me to pull him up on his unsteady feet. I duck my body underneath his arm, the stench of his body odor clinging to my shirt.

I want to watch the blood flow out of his throat, but that's not the prize anymore. They'll suspect the wife. How could I have ever loved this man? Even when he is cleaned up and put together, he will barely exist as a thin shell of what he's supposed to be. It's all a front. Behind his charming smile and well-groomed demeanor at a dinner party is just a serpent covered in scales and slimy skin of sin. He's no prize to win, I see it now. I used to believe with my whole heart that he was my knight in shining armor, the only man that I needed, the only one worthy. He'd catch me if I fell, care for me, love me, forsake all others. It was a lie. A damn good one that I believed for sixteen years.

I hobble under the weight of my husband as we trek to the master bathroom on the second floor, the one that connects to our bedroom. I strain with every step under his full weight because he's decided not to help me at all. Carrying the burden that is John feels like an ironic metaphor to our life together. I laugh.

He scowls. "What's so funny?"

"Just thinking how I'm glad I skipped leg day at the gym this morning." The lie comes quickly from my mouth, and I'm proud to have the skill of my youth returning with ease.

"Oh."

I lean him against the sink once we reach the bathroom and start to walk away when he reaches for my hand like a tree's roots jutting from the dirt and trying to trip you on your escape.

"Medeia, you still look so sad." He's staring through me and not at me.

You look like a piece of shit.

I grimace. "I'm fine, John."

"I think you need the medication." He almost plants his mouth on the edge of the marble counter but catches himself in time. Damn.

"I think you need to sober up." I turn the bathtub faucet over.

"This is only one time. I'm upset by the day I've had," he defends.

"And I'm upset by my mother's death."

He glares at me. I've matched him in wit. Most of my body, the repetition burned into me, tells me to hold my tongue, but I let the new part win — the old Medeia.

"Fine." He tries to shove me out of the way, but I dodge him with ease, and he stumbles into the wall. He uses the towel bar to steady his steps to the tub. He gets in with his clothes still on.

Where is Anna now, John? She isn't here to strip the wet clothes clinging to your body so that you can get clean. It doesn't matter how hard you scrub in here, or how hard I do when I end up helping you because you're too intoxicated to complete the task yourself, you'll never be able to wash off the stain of your soul, John. For that, you will pay the ultimate repentance, for which I have scheduled the meeting.

"Can you..." He pauses and rubs his pathetic hand down his equally worthless face. "Can you help me?" He seems embarrassed, the weight of his uselessness coming to light in the tub.

I swallow back the bile at the thought of being this man's crutch any longer. I nod and move from my perch on the toilet lid to the edge of the tub. I take the washcloth from him. *Sure, darling, I'll help you. Your whore isn't here to see you in your crippled state, no. You save that version for your wife.*

It takes effort, but I get John dried and into bed. I rub the pain in my back and move to the closet to change my soggy clothes. When I come back into our bedroom, John's loud snoring signals he's finally asleep. I sigh. I turn out the light and make to close the door when I notice a light shining from John's phone. I walk back and check the screen.

Anna.

I don't condone the violence you showed today, John. I talked Kalen into not pressing charges, but this better be the last time.

So, Anna's the reason the bottles ran dry so fast today. *Your girlfriend was mad at you, John.* I back up the text messages in his cloud to make sure they stay there for when I need them. *No one will be shocked by your violent ways.*

"Idiot." I toss the phone down and hit him square in his unconscious face.

Medeia's Journal

DEAR ANNA,

You required a Mercedes SUV to date your old boss. Free expensive groceries for Michael at the store to talk to you. Free gym membership for the trainer's fiance's ignorant bliss. Yet, you are satisfied with a mattress on the ground when it comes to John.

You love him.

I hate you.

Not because you fell in love with my husband, that I believe you couldn't control. The legs you held open for him you could, but that's a different story. What I hate most about you is that you are less than me; there is nothing I could have done better to hold onto the attention of my husband. I gave him everything, took his every comment to heart and molded myself to become the perfect bride for John.

But he still chooses you.

That's why I hate you.

Twenty-Six

INTERCEPTING TEXT MESSAGES from Anna has been easier than I thought it would be. I can't do a thing about them when he is at work when she's right in front of him, but at home, I do my best. It works out perfectly to spark self-esteem issues in Anna. She notes to John several times that she realizes he's home with *me* and wondering if he's changing his mind.

I know your wife may be at home, but that never stopped you from texting me before.

John, naturally, is taken aback by this, considering she was the one not texting him. Only, he didn't see the messages she was sending him because I deleted them before he could read them. The misunderstanding leaves enough room for doubt in Anna's mind, and she starts a quarrel to make John prove he loves her. John doesn't like to be told what to do.

Maybe you need to relax. You already know my feelings for you, why do I need to prove it over and over?

That's what people do in a relationship.

I'm married, Anna. What do you propose I do?

Dead silence on her part. Or at least—that's how I make it look. I delete the paragraph rant about how she wants to be needed considering all that she is giving up in her life to be with a married man. It was compelling stuff. She made some persuasive points. Too bad John won't see them. He believes he's getting the silent treatment, so he serves her the same platter.

They play into the game like easy pawns. Anna doesn't even try to use a code for the fact that she wants her lover to lock up his wife in a crazy house. Maybe I am insane, but at least I won't be dead in a month.

I watch as my husband obsessively checks his phone all night while we are watching a movie in the living room. He wants to remain silent and not be the one to break first, but the wait is killing him. The fact that Anna has no permanent attachment to him leaves him nervous.

"Expecting a call, hon?" I ask as I throw some more popcorn into my mouth.

"Mind your business."

I lift my right shoulder at him; I don't care enough to give him a full shrug.

"I was just wondering if everything at work is okay after the fight with Kalen."

"Huh? Oh. It's fine," he mutters, slamming his phone down on the cushion.

"Good. Good." I turn my attention back to the television, thankful for a funny part in the movie so I can laugh out loud at the pouty toddler of a grown man on the couch beside me. "Isn't this nice, John?"

"What?" he grumbles. He is not finding the movie funny at all because he's missed all the jokes.

"You and me, sitting on the couch watching a movie. Just like old times." I want to jam a fistful of popcorn in his mouth and hold it there until he chokes on it and gasps his last breath.

"You mean listening to you chomp down on popcorn and miss every line of the movie?" He growls. "Your nails are chipped, too. It is like old times."

"Huh." I stare down at my nails, and sure enough, three of them are sporting chips in them, and I hadn't noticed. Working and going to the gym have taken a toll on my appearance. I smile down at my nails. They're fucking beautiful. Perfection.

I place the popcorn bowl on the table in surrender. "I think I'm going to go take a walk around the neighborhood. Do you want to come with me?" I stand up from the couch, tugging down my shirt.

He looks at his phone again. Nothing.

"Fine." He stands up and flicks the television off.

"Perfect. Then I can pick your brain to get ideas for your birthday coming up."

John turns to me and genuinely smiles. "Birthday? Planning something?" He winks. Anna is forgotten just like that. This is him. I knew I didn't marry an evil creature; it's what he became. I see my John staring back at me now, and I lose my breath. It is like old times.

"Um. Maybe," I stutter.

He laughs. "You never were good at keeping a secret." He ruffles the top of my hair. "Come on; let's go." He holds his arm out for me to take and we walk, linked together, to get our jackets and shoes.

"So," I start to stumble in my speech under the careful watch of John. He sees me. He's looking at me again. "I was thinking of planning something, but I want your input if you'd prefer for it to be small and intimate, or large and extravagant."

"Intimate," he whispers in my ear, and the hairs on the back of my neck stand up. I zip my jacket up farther to protect myself from any more of that nonsense. So much of my body betrays me, telling me I want to lean into him, but the logic side needs to win.

"It can be done," I chirp.

"Do it at the house. Make it easier on yourself to plan." He drops his arm and links his hand in with mine as we turn to the right out of our driveway and head instinctively through our old routine of walks. This was something we used to do all the time when we were first married.

"Good idea." His hand feels foreign yet good in mine. I want to melt in, but his hand has held another's, and I need to keep telling myself that over and over.

"Don't you just love this plan, John?" I smile clinging to my husband's arm. It's been a month in our new home, and I'm still floating on cloud nine.

"Mmm."

"This could be our thing, John— walking at night." He smiles down at me. Everything feels simple and easy.

To the neighbors peeking out while we retell old stories from our dating past, we look like a happy couple spending time together, and that's what I want them to see. A part of me aches in grief that it isn't what we are. John was the love of my life, my best friend. Life and money changed us. Power took over John, and he needed to implement it in every aspect of his life, until one day he woke up and I didn't hold his attention anymore, his secretary did.

Was it my fault for being able to be manipulated? I thought I was merely making my husband happy. Was it all John's fault for seizing the opportunity to make me weak? Or could the whole thing be blamed on Anna for recognizing the qualities in John that made it easy for her to get what she wanted?

"Remember the crazy neighbor that used to live there?" He points at a house on the corner that has sat with a for sale sign in the yard for two years now.

"Yeah, they're never going to sell that house after the newspaper article they printed." I wince.

"Shit on the walls. Painting an entire room with human feces." He screws his face up in disgust as I imagine mine looks, as well.

"That's the kind of people who belong on medication. Not me," I whisper.

John drops his head and the conversation.

We make it back around to the house, the fresh air feeling excellent and dizzying. I feel like a young girl again. This was the first night in a long time that I didn't hate everything about John. Maybe he could change.

"I'm sorry I didn't come to your mom's funeral." He whispers it into the night sky—not at my face.

"It's okay." He would never be able to repair the damage that leaving me alone at a time like that caused, but his remorse felt soothing. We stand in the front yard and look at the night around us.

"I'm going to stay out here for a little bit." He looks worried. I know when John has that face that it's best to leave him alone with it.

"Okay. Good night, John. I had a nice time walking with you again." I don't even have to lie.

"Me too, Medeia." He looks confused by it. "Me, too."

Medeia's Journal

DEAR ANNA,

You didn't know John before, that John will always be mine. The new John you can have.

Twenty-Seven

JOHN SENT A TEXT TO Anna before he came to bed, telling her that he didn't know if he wanted to go through with the plan anymore. It was the first line of communication between them since the silence fell, and I can't believe John was the one to break it.

She responded at two o'clock in the morning, waking John from his sleep. She called him a coward. It was odd to read the words of someone playing John's usual role of twisting words to him. I hated her with each curse word she threw at him. I read them while he showered in the morning, washing away the things she called him.

End it then, John. Be a big man about it and end it with me. Since suddenly you have a conscience for what you've been planning on doing. I didn't start this. You're the one who did. And look how far you are in. If you end this, I'm telling.

I don't want to do that, Anna. I'm just saying she doesn't deserve this.

If you leave me now, I'll make sure the whole world knows about us and your plan.

Don't do that.

Are you going to go through with it or not, John?

I don't know.

There's no other way. You're a coward. I love you more than she does. I deserve the life with you.

He stopped texting her after that. I was nervous for his response, but two things were for sure either way — I'm not going to a damn mental facility, and Anna will die. I throw the covers off me and jump out of bed for coffee — a victory for me. Anna threatened him. I have motives all around.

It doesn't matter if John has grown a conscience toward me or not, Anna sure hasn't, and I damn sure wasn't about to give up my freedom for either of them. I am not going to be the stepping stone they push into the dirt to build the foundation for their new life together.

As I wait for the machine to brew, the knife slab on the countertop lures me away. I raise one of the knives to my neck and press down just a little. I debate if this will do the trick. Nah, too small of a handle for control of the blade. I put it back into the slot of the knife slab. The butcher knife is the only one I can think of, but it's more noticeable when it's missing. I'm looking for a strong second that could pass the inspection of my husband, but not an officer who is looking for the murder weapon in our home.

I pick up one of the steak knives. No. I mean, it works for the fact that there's always a slot missing a knife, so I could easily rearrange the knives from day to day to throw off the scent, but it's not going to work to cut through a neck. It needs to be sharper. Besides, they can hardly cut through John's well-done steak, how can it push through the layers of human flesh? Who eats a steak well-done, anyway?

I look at the bread knife. No. Paring knife? No. What the hell? Butcher's knife is the only one I want. The only one. How would I easily hide that it is missing? John would notice. Then when it all comes out, he'll be suspicious of me and sell me out for Anna and for that night.

Wait. I open the utensil drawer and find just what I want — the butcher knife from my grandmother. It's a special knife that came only by itself in its own sheath. *Thanks, Grandma.* It lies now alongside the watermelon knife, cantaloupe knife, and another knife. So, I have options. Around every corner, there is a rainbow. Using her knife would be fitting, considering my grandma was a feisty old woman who threatened to cut the balls of any man that dare cross her. I guess she'll get her wish after all, in a way. I'm going to metaphorically cut John's balls off when I slit the throat of his mistress.

I hear John's loud footsteps enter the room. He drags his toes off the ground before lifting them to make a new footprint. The tops of his shoes are always a little more worn down than a normal man's, and it looks atrocious and sloppy.

"What are you doing?" He's displeased, the moment we found last night is long forgotten. I nod at the drawer in solidification. This ends soon.

"Trying to find the apple slicer. I wanted to munch on an apple and some peanut butter." I smile while I think about what kitchen utensil that I would love to see jutting out of his neck.

"It's right there in front of you, don't you look?" he snaps.

"Oh." I grab the apple slicer and hold it up proudly. He rolls his eyes. I want to take the device down his penis and cut it into five even pieces with the middle sorted out. Give

Anna more things to suck on this evening when I thoughtfully send the parts to her in a large envelope mailer.

"Great, now do you think you could make something edible for breakfast today? That would be a real triumph," he giggles, but the cruel words aren't covered up by the laughter this morning.

I think about putting some laxative in his food, something that would cause him some pain tonight. I settle for spitting in his food the next time I fix his plate.

"So, I'm not the best cook, but there are worse things." I plan on putting the positive, smiling face on because I know how much it gets under John's skin when he can't get my goat. He hates when he's trying to draw a fight to make me the bad guy and it backfires on him.

He scoffs. "Like what?"

"Well, at least I'm good in bed," I venture.

"Yeah, that doesn't feed my stomach and sustain life, though." At least I have the compliment of pleasing a selfish man in the bedroom.

"Well, if my cooking is so bad, John, you can make breakfast," I quip.

"If I cook, I'm making breakfast for myself, and that's it. I'm not serving you," he warns.

That used to get him what he wanted — threatening what would happen if I didn't do something for him. It doesn't now. The veil is off; these words bring anger to me instead of a morbid fear. Standing before him in the kitchen, I only see him for the little bully he is and think about grabbing the skillet and beating his head like it was a tennis ball. I would be the Wimbledon champion here in my kitchen. I'd stand over his lifeless body and accept my gold medal.

Instead of giving in to the fantasy or his nasty words, I flash my pearly white teeth his way.

"Okay, dear. I'm not that hungry, anyway." I slice the apple, grab the jar of peanut butter, and leave the idiot standing in the kitchen with his threat backfiring. *Make your breakfast, you cowardly bitch. I'm not here to serve you. You got away with that shit for far too long now. No more. If Anna can persuade you in a short text conversation to turn against me, then I hope God has mercy on both of your souls, because I won't.*

Medeia's Journal

DEAR ANNA,

Everything you do is right. And everything I do is wrong.

I watch you feed John pizza, and he doesn't snap on you for being too lazy to fix him something better. I watch you gorge on three slices, and he smiles, impressed, instead of rolling his eyes in disgust. Whenever you act like me, I feel a kinship with you. Perhaps we are John's type, but you were the better option. The traits that turn him off from me turn him on to you.

That isn't fair.

I wanted my husband. I wanted our marriage. I wanted a life.

You took it.

Maybe it's because you didn't have a stable life growing up. Your father ran off, and your mother was a whore sleeping around with men and leaving you home alone. I've come across all the times the cops were called on her for leaving too young of a child at home without supervision. She lost you to her mother, and she didn't bother to fight.

He won't fight for you, either.

He'll be the death of you.

Twenty-Eight

I'M IMPRESSED THAT Anna can keep up with all the men without any of them realizing the other ones exist. I think about finding a way to blow her cover, but I hate to take something so precious away from a dying woman, so I watch.

I watch as she and Thomas play the same twisted love games in her apartment that she plays with John at the warehouse. I snuck into her apartment again recently and added a camera just for her own TV show. She likes to be the center of attention, so I made her the star. She makes sure to use the same things on each of them, either it's her only bag of tricks or she doesn't want to expose herself by slipping up in dirty talk about previous lovemaking sessions. All the one-night stands have begun to fade as Thomas pushes himself into her life, and John pushes for their plan.

Thomas isn't a remarkable person. I've followed him twice now, and he's squeaky clean. He has a good relationship with his mother and works hard at his job that doesn't pay nearly as much as John's, but he doesn't seem to mind because he gets to run his own business and follow his passion. That's what his Facebook is all about, following his passion. Thomas will be another victim of this tragic love affair. He's too good for her, but he loves Anna all the same. He is buying her flowers every Friday on his way home from work.

I watch them sit and wilt on her dining room table every week before he replenishes them for her. She doesn't appreciate the gesture; instead, she expects it to be done.

I haven't seen her mouth a thank you yet. I barely need to turn on the camera app when I want to watch Anna's place because the visual of it all is readily available since she hates to draw her curtains closed — always longing to be the main focus in all aspects of her life, even the ones that are meant to be private.

She likes to undress with her blinds open, and there's a neighbor boy across the street that appreciates this. She knows. I watch as she looks for his attention before she gets down to her task. What's the point in shedding her clothing if it isn't a show, as well? Anna has a small tattoo on her upper right shoulder. It looks a little bit like a bird or possibly a butterfly—either way, an animal with wings. Maybe something she's always longed to be able to do: fly. I could make her fly. I'll grab her by the hair and toss her out the window so she can test those imaginary wings.

The gym is still my favorite place to watch Anna. Jane doesn't particularly care for my favorite blonde for her own reasons, but she doesn't know mine. She makes the game a lot more fun with her intentionally cruel narrative.

"I think her tits are fake."

"They are," I blurt. Running and talking has become a lot easier for me. I feel everything about me growing stronger.

"How do you know?" Jane is a little out of breath today. She said she downed a bottle of wine last night in celebration of an anniversary. The way her eyes looked off into the distance when she said it, left me curious about what kind of anniversary it was.

"What's the anniversary you celebrated last night?"

"Anniversary of my ex-husband's death." I think that's why I'm so drawn to Jane. She's blunt where I've needed to be censored the past ten years. I notice she never gives this attention to anyone else in the gym. Not even a simple hello to another person working out. She's only ever talked to me from what I've gathered. Can she read my thoughts? Why are we drawn to one another?

"How?" Spending time with Jane has stripped me of a level of censorship, as well.

"Heart attack." She winks at me in a smooth serious movement. At that moment, I stumble on the treadmill but gain my footing before falling and causing everyone in the gym to look at me. Could Jane be just like me? "What?" She shrugs.

"Why did you guys divorce?" My interest in Jane has peaked.

"Cheated on me," she pants. "Hey, this is the first time you've asked questions about me. I've answered, now be fair and do the same." She nods toward Anna.

"Her high school photo on Facebook shows her flat chested. There's no way those are real, especially the rippling on the sides. She got ones put in that are too big for her body type. Did you fare in the divorce?"

"No, fucker took everything, but his life insurance still had my name on it. Do you know her? Are you stalking the gym trollop?" I note Jane's comment about life insurance.

"That's the bitch fucking my husband." It's Jane's turn to stumble on the treadmill.

"Would you like to come to my husband's birthday party this weekend? I'm not allowed friends he doesn't approve of, and he'll hate you."

"Is wavy tits coming, as well?" She points to Anna taking another selfie.

"Of course, it wouldn't be a party without her." I laugh, but it has no humor.

Jane shuts down her treadmill. We still have ten minutes left to go, but she dismounts and leans in over the handle of mine. "What's in your head?"

"What's in yours?" I mimic the seriousness.

"I'll tell you my dirty secret if you share too." I've followed Jane without her knowing. I wanted to understand her character when no one was around because she kept pushing herself into my life. She is what everyone hopes to be, a great person. She feeds other people's meters, holds doors open for the next person behind her, cries when she sees mistreatment, and I listened in from the bathroom stall of a restaurant as she helped a young girl get herself out of date that she felt unsafe in. There was also something darker about Jane that drew me in, her ex-husband's money. How did she end up in a decent house when the old newspaper gossips about him taking everything? Jane is the only one I can tell my secret to, and I'm dying to let it out.

I slam the stop button on the treadmill. "Breakfast?"

"Drive-thru. My car," she directs, grabbing her water bottle and towel off the treadmill.

"Done." We walk out with a purpose, each of us dying to know what the other one is dying to tell.

The second we get in the car Jane demands to be informed. "Spill."

"Are you wearing a wire?" I say it to break the seriousness in the air and make it lighter., but Jane lifts her shirt and shows me nothing but skin.

"Jesus, Jane, I was only joking."

"Now, you." She's serious.

"Are you off your rocker?" I lift my shirt anyway, and Jane searches my back, as well. She nods when she's satisfied, and I put my shirt back down as she pulls out of the parking lot.

"I switched my ex-husband's heart medication with a placebo before I moved out." She spits it all over the dashboard, and the air in the car is thick but not uncomfortable. I nod along. "It took several months, but it caught up to him. No one knows. His family didn't want an autopsy because of his heart history."

"You got away with it." It's not a question, but a statement.

"Yeah." She bows her head at the red light.

"Did he hit you?"

"Every single day."

I knew this already by the way Jane flinches when people yell, and she always tries to be louder than them to put a brave face on. "John and Anna plan on making me think I'm crazy so he can put me in a mental facility."

"How can they do that?" She stares over at me, thirsting for more.

"Well," I say as she turns into the drive-thru lane. "When my mother passed away last year, I had a mental breakdown and was put on medication. However, it was diagnosed as situational depression, not long-term. John has been manipulating me to have me tell the doctor to raise my doses. That is, until now." I pause so Jane can give the speaker our breakfast order. Once she receives the total and moves up one in line, she shuts the window again and turns to me. It's too juicy to let a whisper hit the outside air.

"Ever since I saw them in a restaurant window, I've opened my eyes to his manipulation techniques. Now, I know everything they're planning. I'm one step ahead. I know that they want me to be committed. I plan on stopping them."

"How? Do you need help?" Jane, my ride-or-die, has been found.

"Thank you!" she shouts out to the worker in the window, and we park in a spot on the corner lot to talk and eat.

"Jane—" I gather her attention to my face— "I want to kill her."

"Naturally." She bites into her burrito.

"No. No." I interrupt and place my hand on her forearm. "I want to kill her." I pronounce each word slowly.

Jane doesn't flinch. The color in her skin remains; she isn't frightened. I watch as the wheels in her mind spin. "Why not him?"

"I thought about it. That was the original plan, but it's stupid. They'll suspect me. The wife is the first to be suspected. I'm not in the situation you were, John has no heart history, and I am sure I'm on no life insurance policy. I need him to be the one in jail." I pick at my sandwich. "I want to take her from him the way he has taken my ability to be an independent human being."

"Fair enough." She slurps at her coffee. "Tell me more. There's more on your face that you're proud of figuring out. You seem confident about pulling this off. Spill."

"John has a criminal record." I smile at her.

"For?" She scooches up in her seat.

"Beating a man into a coma when he was in college. I thought it was a bar fight and the guy dropped the charges. That's what John told me. When my then-boyfriend was on what I thought was a three-month trip for his graduation present, he was actually serving jail time."

"So, he's prone to violence. Has he hit you?" The burrito pauses in the air.

"No. He'll shove me out of his way from time to time, but it's more fun for John when he verbally belittles me."

"Bastard."

I nod and bite into my breakfast burrito.

"How can we prove that he verbally abuses you?" Jane is seeking out the flaws in my plan. She wants me to succeed. I can feel it.

"Oh, well, my therapist has taken outstanding notes on what we discuss there. I've made it a point to not only tell him about everything John calls me but also the fact that he doesn't let me have a job or friends. And I've let him know that it's John who doesn't think my medicine is working and needs to be increased."

"Brilliant." She stabs the burrito in the air, and lettuce falls on my arm. "More. I'll be your fresh eyes to the plan.

Tell me more." She grabs the piece of lettuce and shoves it in her mouth.

"Jane, he just got into a physical altercation at work, as well."

"It's the fucking universe smiling on you." She cackles.

"They fuck in the warehouse that was supposed to be my real estate office. The one thing I worked so hard to complete classes for, he took away from me and told me I couldn't work. That it was insulting to him."

"And you can't have friends?"

"No, and I've told my therapist as much. Not unless John approves of them. He claims that people will try to use me to infiltrate his company, but I realize it's because if I told anyone else about him, they would point out the obvious abuse to me."

"What is he? A spy?"

"CPA."

"Loaded. I can tell from your house."

I nod.

"Prenup?"

"Unfortunately." I sigh.

"You get nothing, huh?"

I nod again.

"I've been there. Legal representation?"

"I tried, but the divorce lawyer I spoke to just laughed at me, even after I gathered proof."

"No, I mean, did you have a lawyer look over the prenup before you signed?" Her coffee lingers in the air.

"No." I'm confused.

"It may be null then." She sips and nods.

"Huh?"

"My divorce lawyer told me that I would have had a bet-ter chance of getting our prenup thrown out had I not had a lawyer look over it before I signed. But, unfortunately, I did, and I told him I didn't care because I loved Stewart." Her face turns up in disgust at the words.

"Huh?" I kiss her on the forehead. "That's wonderful news."

"But you should still kill the bitch." She finishes her first burrito and unwraps her second.

"You're not a normal person, are you?" My coffee warms my hand as I wait for Jane to confirm what I already know.

She shakes her head.

There's silence in the car while we finish our respective meals.

"Jane?" I venture.

"Yeah."

"My father killed my mother when he was in a drunken rage. I was supposed to meet her that morning." I stare out my window, even though I'm not looking at Jane I know she is giving me her undivided attention. "When she didn't show up, I drove there. The medics were already there. She was on the floor in a pool of blood, and he just sat there on the porch."

"I'm sorry, Medeia."

"I don't want to be like him."

"You're not; this is justified." Jane starts.

"Is it?" I turn my head to her. "I always felt if I followed John's rules for the wealthy lifestyle that I would never be tempted to commit all the crimes that my father did because he was poor. Now here I am, contemplating the worst one."

"I can tell you aren't your father. You're in a survival situation in my eyes."

"I could just blackmail John with his crimes that I have covered up." I laugh toward my lap in reverie.

"What?"

"John beat this guy senseless one night when we were dating. I mean, I watched his eyes glow red as he kept punching him. When I was finally able to pull him off the guy, it was awful. I covered it up. John was so terrified, I know now that it is because he didn't want to go back to jail, but I told him not to worry because I knew what to do. I cleaned up the scene. I got rid of anything that would prove that John was there. Then, I drove the guy to the emergency room and told the nurse that I watched him get jumped by two guys. I gave them descriptions far from John's own that they wouldn't look for him. John told me he was grateful and knew that I was the girl to marry, but I had to promise to leave my poor criminal ways."

"Jesus."

"I can't use it against him, though. I thought I could."

"Because you assisted him." Jane finishes my thought.

"And the expertise my father gave me in covering up crimes could make me a suspect if Anna disappears."

"Yeah."

"After all of that, John wants to take the rest of my life away." I look at her, tears filling my eyes. "I can't let him."

She grabs my face with a hand on either side of it and shakes me gently. "Then don't."

Medeia's Journal

DEAR ANNA,

I have tried on five different dresses for you. I'm nervous to see you tonight.

Twenty-Nine

I CHOOSE A NIGHT THAT John is working late — really working. I know he is because Anna is one of the first to arrive. Decked out in her best dress, hair done perfectly, and nails freshly painted. I gush over her as any good hostess would do. She brought a small gift for John. I take it from her for the gift table, knowing full well I will toss it in the trash.

"You look amazing, Medeia." She mispronounces my name on purpose, and I think about spilling her blood here all over her sunshiny yellow dress.

"Thank you so much, Anna." I do a small turn in my dress for her. "Only the best for a night as grand as this." I watch as she tries to hide her growing repugnance at my trim body.

I have a black lace dress that hits just above the knees, showing off my fabulous legs. And, since John didn't give me children in our long and torturous marriage, I show off my perky breasts in the deep v-cut neckline. The cap sleeves scream elegant, while everything else screams sex.

I am dark. Anna is light.

My nails are painted blood red to her nude color; my heels are spiked and black while her sandals are nude, as well. I make sure to show her my Louboutin shoes and gush at their price. Anna speaks my language when it comes to money.

"Just follow me, and I'll introduce you to some people." I hand the present to Jane with a wink. She wanted to fill in as a waitress. I told her it was nonsense, that I wanted her as my friend, but she insisted it was for the best in the long run of the plan. She could be my ears to the behind-the-scenes of the party.

"Anna, this is John's aunt, Mary," I say as I scooch Anna closer to Mary.

"You realize that's a summer color, sweetie, and this is the damn winter?" She scoffs at Anna's outstretched hand. "I'm not shaking hands, sorry, not my thing." Mary is the meanest old lady you'll ever meet. She hates everyone but me for some reason. Anna is no exception, and I'm glad she doesn't disappoint me.

"Mary, have they come by with your old-fashioned yet?" I don't make to correct her comment to Anna. My tone is sweet, and she changes hers to match.

"No, dear, but I'm getting antsy." She grabs my arm in a kind way, something Anna takes notice of immediately. I watch in my peripheral vision as she mashes her lips together in embarrassment at not having impressed one of John's relatives. She wants them to choose her over me, and all of them would, except for Mary that's why I've let them meet.

"I'll grab you one in a minute, and if they do come before then, you'll simply have two." I wink.

"Angel. An absolute angel." She blows me a kiss, and I smile — *Angel of Death.*

"Come on, Anna, let's go see what's taking them so long on the drink order at the bar." I guide her with a hand on her back. Her long blonde hair grazes my thumb, and it takes everything in me not to reach up and yank on it, forcing her head to fling backward. With her neck exposed like that, I would stab her with a shrimp fork. Instead, I squeeze her close like old friends.

"It's so wonderful to have someone here who isn't John's family." I giggle like we are conspiring together. She melts a little at my effort. I know how to play her. She doesn't receive female love, only competition, and stripped bare of the prized bull she longs to own, John, she can't help but give in to me.

When we reach the large hall in the house, it's buzzing with people. Anna stands back in awe at the glamour of it all. She loves the grandeur of the house, and I note her taking it in while I shuffle her alongside me, room to room. She's thinking about how it can all be hers soon. It's that thought that keeps my smile toward her genuine because I find her funny.

"I do hope you'll forgive me, Anna," I say after we drop off Aunt Mary's drink. "I have to leave you to fend for yourself out here while I make sure everything is running smoothly. Hostess job never ends."

"Oh, um," Anna stumbles. She hadn't realized she got accustomed to my presence. "Yeah, we'll catch up later."

"Of course, my dear. I wouldn't miss it." I touch her arm with a wink and turn toward the kitchen leaving her with a disgruntled Aunt Mary who quickly walks off. Anna stands in the party, the gigantic house she wants, all alone, like I have for ten years.

I step off the kitchen into the sunroom and stare out the window.

"Like a ninja," Jane says behind me.

"I want to throw up."

"Better not. These weird fancy mini toast things the caterer made are delicious, and you'll be missing out."

I laugh at her. "They're ridiculous, aren't they?"

"I remember them at every damn function my ex-husband had. I still don't know the name."

"Neither do I." I shrug. "Do I look all right?"

"For the hundredth time?"

I nod.

"Fucking fabulous. Now, go out there and make her feel like shit because she can't be you." She smacks my backside as I walk past her.

"Hey, Jane?"

"You're so needy," she jokes. "What?" She's exaggerating; I see the twinkle in her eye at our bond.

"Thanks for being my friend. I never had one before," I admit.

"Ever?"

"Kids don't like the poor girl who smells because there's no running water at her house." I choke on the words and the pain of my childhood. I never felt good enough in my entire life.

"Kids are dickholes. We would have been friends even then." She stares out the sunroom window, the same way I do every morning.

"Yeah, right." I roll my eyes.

"We stinky poor kids have to stick together." At that moment, when she looks me in the eye, I see myself. We were meant to find each other, Jane and me. Our souls have been pushing us to meet.

I smile.

"Now get the hell out there," she demands.

I salute.

The party roars on as the rest of the guestlist pours into the house. Intimate to John meant fifty people. That was larger than any birthday party I ever had. Even in the beginning years of our marriage, I only invited my mother, but she stopped coming, and John stopped putting anything together. Birthdays just went by like any other day of the week for me.

As the time approaches for John to come home, I dim the lights. I had everyone park at a specific location, hiring a valet of sorts to shuttle them in. Money really could buy anything, even dumb stuff like that. He wouldn't notice a car in the driveway, though, and I pray he'll watch his underhanded comments when interacting with me as he first walks in. They didn't need to see it, especially Anna. I want her to feel betrayed by him before she commits betrayal herself.

His car pulls into the driveway, and no one else is around the front entrance but me. Anna has pushed her way through the crowd so that she may be front and center for the event. She wants to have this moment every day of her life, the man of her dreams coming home to her.

If she could convince a man to put his wife away in a mental facility, what makes her think he wouldn't turn on her someday? I've watched her confidence fade as I ooze grace out of every pore tonight, guiding her around for the first half hour. How can she be so sure of herself that a man wouldn't leave her?

As the key turns in the knob, I steady myself. Showtime.

"Welcome home, honey," I drip.

John takes one look at me, and his reaction is exactly what I want. "Holy shit."

I giggle. "Come have dinner with me."

"Are you sure dinner is what you want?" *Pig.*

"Yes. Come on." I grab ahold of his arm and straighten his tie up. He looks at me funny, but I just grin. When we turn the corner of the entryway that leads into the formal dining room, the people there and throughout the attached den area shout—"Surprise!"

It rings out in a well-rehearsed chorus.

"Wow." John is stunned and smiling from ear to ear. "Honey, this is wonderful." He leans down to kiss my cheek. I take notice of Anna's pissy face and laugh.

I grab a glass of wine from the tray by the doorway. "Happy Birthday, John. I hope this year of life brings you what you deserve." I toast my glass to him and watch as everyone in the room does the same. *I just made fifty of your closest friends and family toast to your demise, John. I understand why you get high on power.*

Overcome with gratefulness, he bows his head, notices Anna's presence in the front row, and stalls with his body awkwardly bent forward for a few seconds before he remembers to finish the motion.

The party has just begun.

Medeia's Journal

DEAR ANNA,

Don't pick at your nails when you're nervous. It's annoying and tacky.

Thirty

I WALK THE PARTY FLOATING from one person to the next, being the gracious hostess on the outside while keeping a watch on my husband and his mistress. Jane is my other pair of eyes. She's under strict orders to not let Anna and John sneak off anywhere in my house.

It was the only rule I gave her, the rest she comes up with instinctively herself. She passes by at times to whisper in my ear that she gave Anna a piece of shrimp that fell on the floor. Even tells me she spit in the glass of wine for John. Little things that I imagine only a great girlfriend would know to do to keep your spirits up.

I'm looking fabulous on the outside, but inside is a different story. I feel like a fraud. I am continually sucking my stomach in to look thinner in my killer outfit, passing on food to stay that way, leaning against a wall in a sexy manner but really to ease the pain in my feet. I long to make Anna believe she's less than. I want her to know me as a person, to truly see John's lies, and to give her one last chance to realize what she's doing.

That's what I keep telling myself as I stare at her from across the room. When in fact, I hunger for her pain to come no matter what. I spend every morning waking up pissed off that I let someone trap me inside this life. I go to bed pissed

193

off that I'm not free of the chains. I don't want her to walk away. I don't want John to walk away. I want them to crawl.

"About a quarter of the alcohol is left to serve, and your feet are killing you. I think it's cake time." Jane winks as she hands me another glass of wine.

"Thanks."

"You all right?" She looks concerned.

"No. But, is anyone?" I take a sip of the wine. Jane bites her lip. There's no comeback for that in her arsenal. She walks away toward the kitchen. I watch John come and graze his hand up Anna's back, and I turn to grab his cake before I see too much and smash his face into it.

The catering staff is waiting for me in the kitchen. It feels odd to be the one in charge, but that's how life is going to be from now on.

"I would like to thank you all for tonight, for your hard work, for putting up with, at the very least, one asshole out there—" they giggle— "and for making such damn good food. Now, let's light this cake on fire and get these people out of my house so I can soak my feet." I have won them over; no one has spit in my food this evening but reports throughout the night from Jane tell me that other guests didn't fare as well.

They graciously load my arms up with the cake and light the candles for me. I look up at all their faces and imagine they're here for a birthday party to celebrate me. This is what it would feel like to be gathered around by smiling faces who genuinely like you and don't feel obligated because you're their boss's wife. I tell my tears to haul back inside as I turn toward the living room where the party has decided to assemble. One of the waitstaff kills the lights for me before I walk inside.

Everyone joins in the old song, wishing John the happiest of birthdays. I glare toward Anna as he reluctantly leaves her side to be the center of attention by me. I steel myself away from jealousy, for she will be forever associated with John's green-eyed monster soon.

I know something she doesn't, and once this asshole blows out these candles, I'll be more than happy to reveal it.

Make a wish, John.

Everyone claps at my husband's ability to blow out a few candles on a cake, but they didn't feel the shower of spit that I did. I won't be eating a single piece of that now, not that this dress would allow me anyway.

"If I can have your attention, everyone," I shout, and the room quiets down. "Thank you so much. I don't think I could work at that volume all night." I'm greeted with smiles. "I'm going to put down this fabulous cake and say a few words if you'll indulge me." Jane appears like a right-hand man to take the cake from me. I smile in passing.

"I want to thank everyone for coming out tonight and for helping me keep this party a secret. As most of you know, I am horrible at keeping secrets." I'm met with giggles at the flaw in my character. I chance a look in Anna's direction. *I have managed to keep a few of yours, Anna.* "Ok, on a more serious note, thank you for coming out and filling our home with love and laughter this evening, it is truly appreciated. I can't believe I have spent a decade as this man's wife, and I get to celebrate his birthday alongside him still." John reaches for my hands, not one to be outdone. "But, enough about him." The crowd laughs. "I want to say a special thank you for the waitstaff and catering team. The food was phenomenal, and I know a lot of you have been asking to meet the chef, and I've kept you away because I had a party to pull off, but I've asked him to come out and join us now for some cake. His name is Thomas Pole, and I'm sure he'll be embarrassed, but let's clap anyway, huh?" I watch the blood drain from Anna's face, and I wish it could leave her body altogether tonight, but good things come to those who wait.

Thomas's face, however, is a bashful shade of red as the crowd hollers his praise as he steps into the room. *I was trying to help your boyfriend's side business, Anna. Don't you like rich men?* He is welcomed in the crowd, and the guests sing his praises as he makes his way through, attempting to swallow all the compliments.

"The party was amazing, baby." John is in my ear, and I smell the alcohol seeping from his pores. He's drunk again and clapping the loudest for Thomas.

"Thanks. Only the best for you, babe." I curl under his arm and take my place at his side, more so for the gain of directing his body to face toward the crowd, toward Anna and Thomas, whose face just lit up at the sight of his girlfriend. Underneath my hand, John's body stiffens.

Anna openly welcomes the kiss that Thomas plants on her face, and while still under the scrutiny of the crowd, he gets a big cheer for his act.

"Oh. I didn't know Anna knew the chef." I turn toward John. "You know sometimes you are right, this town is so small."

"Yes," he grits out. "Very small, indeed."

Medeia's Journal

DEAR ANNA,

John hasn't left the house in a couple of days to meet you. Was there a fight?

Thirty-One

I MAKE SURE TO SEND Anna a muffin basket and an apology note explaining how sorry I am that we didn't get to spend more time together at the party as I had hoped. She's such an asset to the company and my husband that I am eternally grateful for her. At least that's what is now on file at the basket company. I whistle all day throughout the house.

John is in an irritable mood again. According to his phone, it is all because his girlfriend has a boyfriend. How strange, my husband wanted fidelity from her but never bothered to think she might like the same.

"What are you doing?"

I leap out of my skin at the sound of my husband's voice behind me in the sunroom. "Jesus, John. I spilled coffee on this note." I sop it up with my napkin, but it remains unsalvageable.

"What note?" He's bored. *Go away, John. Make up with your mistress so that I may kill her with a good motive.*

"Thank-you notes for your party. I didn't think you would write them, but if you want to shock the pants off some of your family members, there're still a few to go." I smile at him.

"No. You've got that handled."

I roll my eyes when I turn back around so he can't see me. That's the only kind of job he allows me to have — boring perfect housewife jobs.

"Do you need something, darling?" I rewrite my note to John's cousin Grace while talking over my shoulder.

"I'm bored," he whines.

"I noticed."

"Well." He decides upon entering the room and taking up residence next to me at the little table in here.

"Well?" I repeat, not looking up from the correspondence.

"I'm bored." The draw of the last word makes me want to punch him.

"Aunt Mary needs a thank-you card," I sing as I lick the envelope of another thank-you card done and cross Grace's name off the list.

"Nah, she likes you better anyway." *That's because you're a dick, John.*

"You could go watch some television," I offer.

"I already tried that." He gets up and paces in front of the floor-to-ceiling picture window, observing the view I dearly love of the backyard. Stripped of his secret mistress, John finds it difficult to settle into tame married life.

"John, is something bothering you?" I need him to go away so that I might have a moment's peace. I don't want a repeat of the walk we took around the neighborhood. I want to feel dead inside toward him. His ability to act human complicates that at times.

"I fought with a friend." He tells the window and not me.

"Then go make up." *Go away.*

"Is that what you're supposed to do? Just make up. What if I was right?" He glares at me.

"Well, seeing as I have no experience in having friends because I was a disgusting kid with greasy hair and poor fitting clothes, only to become a teenager with three jobs and a mortgage to pay off, and no time for a single friend because I had two siblings to support during that time, then I became an adult still supporting those children through school and taking classes at night, I would say my friend advice is extremely limited."

"Hmm. What about when you became a married woman without all those problems?" he quips.

"Well, my husband doesn't like me having friends he hasn't pre-approved, and they all turn out to be boring duds of human brain cells and shopping bags when he does pair me up with someone." I seal up another thank-you card.

"You hate the rich. Do you realize you are rich?" He laughs, but it's an epiphany. I'm not rich. Not because I don't have my own money, but because no matter what lessons John has crammed into my skull, I'll never act like those we are surrounded by. I'll always be the poor girl from the shack, and I'm okay with it. I'm finally okay with it.

"*You* are rich, John. I'm not allowed a job." I begin the next letter, but I can still see his head bobbing up and down in the corner.

"You speak a little bit more frankly now with your medication decreasing." His tone hints toward an edge in his temper.

"I apologize, the party was quite stressful, and I'm just trying to do it right so that I do the name of being your wife justice." I smile at him. He softens. I've learned an extra thing or two about being manipulative since I opened my eyes up to John's trait. It's not a hard thing to pick up on, although one that leaves you feeling rather slimy even if it just saved me a nasty fight with my husband.

"So, I just make up with this friend?" He sits down at the table across from me. *Are you really asking your wife relationship advice for your girlfriend, John? Tacky.*

"Yes. I imagine no friend that leaves you pacing the house is one that is easily tossed aside." I raise my eyebrows toward him.

He nods and bounces a beat out on the table before slapping the right hand down and pointing at me. He sets to exit the room.

"I'll be out tonight," he claims.

"Okay," I shout back.

"Hey, Medeia."

I look over as he hovers backward in the doorway and I exhale an annoyed sigh. "I think you should make a friend. You'd be good at it." *What?*

"I'll try."

He taps the doorframe and heads out the door with a sad look in his eyes. I throw my head into my hands. Why is he trying to resemble a human again? Is this the universe's way of telling me that I need to cancel the idea of killing Anna? I don't want John back. I don't want Anna living in my house with her smug face. I want her dead. I want him to pay.

Thirty-Two

CURIOSITY KILLED THE cat. My mother said that to me every time I opened the oven to see what she was making. I couldn't help but follow John out tonight. Maybe boredom is contagious, but suddenly, after he left, thank-you notes didn't hold my attention anymore. I had a bigger job to perfect as his wife.

Sure enough, John is sitting outside the warehouse waiting for Anna. She must be late because he keeps opening the car door and walking around it before deciding to get back in. I pop some cashews into my mouth as I sit in my car facing the opposite direction on the road. He's not looking for my car, so I'm not at all worried about being seen. Still, I park a safe distance away and use my side mirrors to watch what's going on before I can turn on the app for the cameras inside.

Anna's car finally pulls up. John jumps out of the vehicle with relief. I cross my fingers that she'll keep driving and run him over, but she proves herself to be too chicken shit to stop his evil ways. He goes to hold her when she climbs out, and she shoves his arms away. I wait for him to get mad at her for the violent action, but it doesn't come.

She isn't you, Medeia. He doesn't get mad at her like that.

She points to the door inside — she wants privacy for the fight, not in the middle of the parking lot. I laugh and flick on the camera app. I've installed a few extra inside the

202

building this week when I came to change the batteries so that I won't miss anything.

She stops just short of the inside door, refusing to go up to the mattress with him.

"What do you want, John?" she groans.

"I'm sorry, I overreacted. I was an asshole." His voice is soft and pleading. I imagine that's what it would sound like if he were begging for his life.

"You called me a whore," she spits.

Ouch, John. Maybe he does get mad at her as he does me.

"I know, and I feel sick about it." *No, he doesn't, Anna. He's a dickhead.* He tries to reach out and embrace her again, but she backs away from his advances. I laugh.

"That hurt me, John. You have Medeia at night. I have no one. Thomas was just a friend, and I felt something for him. You weren't leaving your wife and kept telling me that the plan needed time because it was delicate. What was I supposed to do?" *Stop believing married men when they say that they'll leave their wives when you've already spread your legs to them?*

"I was wrong. I got angry when I saw you with Thomas. I guess I liked the idea of knowing it was just you and me. I hadn't thought of Medeia the way you think of Thomas in a long time. It hurt." I flip the burner phone over, so I don't see his lying face anymore. *Really! Because you got off pretty good the night of the party.*

"I'd like it to be just you and me, John."

I grab the phone and see Anna step forward to his open arms. She's buying the glittered turd he's selling.

"I love you, Anna." John holds her tight.

"What?"

"WHAT?" I scream in the car.

"I do. I love you." He kisses her forehead. I throw my cashews on the dashboard.

"I love you, John." They kiss and embrace before heading upstairs to the mattress.

Anna must die. Tomorrow. They're fucking up the planned motive — I can't wait.

Medeia's Journal

DEAR ANNA,

I hate you. He walked you home tonight, and you two stared at each other like lovesick puppies.

He loves you.

I hate you.

Know that there is a balance in our world, because as strong as his love is for you, my hate will always be the equivalent. I don't want John. He feels more like your sloppy seconds than my husband, and I'm the one who had him first.

I want revenge. I want freedom. I want what I'm owed for ten years of marriage to that prick.

I need to be ready.

Tomorrow night, you die, dear Anna.

Thirty-Three

I HAVE BEEN AWAKE SINCE three in the morning. The beast inside of me has been stirring for a lot longer. Anna finally took John to her apartment last night, and he didn't look at her in disgust. He must have a thing for the poor girls. Instead, he told her he wanted to walk her home like a real date. I watched as he kissed her at the entryway to her building.

They're in love.

If the sight wasn't enough, the foul mood that John displayed when he got home signaled the shift in seriousness between their relationship and the growing need to rid himself of me.

Like a good wife, I am going to solve that for him tonight.

I stare as he sleeps next to me, unaware of the hate he created, the evil he orchestrated with Anna. His eyelashes flutter as the dream in his mind shifts plot. What kind of man will John be when he wakes up to find his beloved dead underneath him? Are his thoughts preparing him for the task?

I throw my side of the covers off and make my way into the bathroom by way of the closet, touching his line of suits as I go. Which will he wear to court? I close the bathroom door behind me and take note of my appearance in the mirror.

There's beauty and disgust. I can look at the parts that are becoming my own with joy, the strength in my posture, and the lift in my chin. The hollow look in my eyes comes from John, where he has emptied my soul for his benefit. I tear my burner phone from the pocket of my robe.

On the third ring, Jane answers.

"It's early," she whines.

"Want to go shopping tonight?" I whisper and poke at the dull skin around my eyes.

"Okay. You could have asked me at the gym this morning, you know?" She rolls over in her bed, and I hear the shuffling of her pillows.

"It's not Thursday."

"I switched shifts this week so that I can go to the gym in the morning now." I hear her yawn after.

"I'll see you there." I hang up. I head back to the closet and take down a pair of workout clothes and put them on. I throw my pajamas on the floor. I'm tired of hiding them in the chest.

"Aren't you going to pick those up?" John grumbles as he bumps into the doorway coming in.

"Later," I say. "I'm late for the gym."

"You wouldn't need to go if you didn't shove pastries in your mouth when you're bored." He shuts the door, and I advance toward it before stopping cold and flipping the door off. He has become more blatantly rude, no longer hiding the meaning of his words with tact and a smile.

I grab my shoes and run down the steps, and quickly scratch a note out to John that I'll be shopping this evening and missing dinner. Christmas is only a month and a half away now. He won't be shocked to find me heading out for sales — he expects it. Another job that's left for me to do.

I look around the house one more time. This will be the last morning I wake up to go to the gym and see Anna. This will be the last day that John wakes up to see Anna. Who said Mondays were horrible?

I slam the door behind me. It feels good. No wonder John does it. I smile into the dark morning and head off to meet Jane at the treadmills. I'm early, but I can't stay in this house any longer with that man — the devil I married.

"How long have you been here?" Jane stretches her arms above her head and leans forward to touch her toes.

"About a half hour already." I pop out my earbuds to talk with Jane.

"Why?" She hops on to her treadmill and begins to work the buttons.

"I needed the extra run." I'm not even panting anymore. I wonder if Anna could outrun me now.

"So, what are we going shopping for tonight?" Jane starts at a slow trot, getting her legs warmed up.

"Christmas."

"I don't shop for that until the week before," she groans.

"Well, you have to come with me. I need to pick out something fabulous for myself from John." I stare down over the wall at a familiar blonde taking her morning spot at the weights. Jane follows my gaze.

She bursts into a full run, our eyes never leaving Anna. "What time?"

Medeia's Journal

DEAR ANNA,

He isn't worth it. You don't know him as I do, so listen carefully and with an open mind when I tell you to run. Run away from him as fast as you can. He doesn't love anyone but himself. He will use you only for as long as you are benefiting him, and even then, he finds a way to be bored with you. In that regard, I guess you are perfect for each other.

He'll be the death of you. I've already died.

There, now I feel like I did my part in giving you a fair chance to survive.

Thirty-Four

WHEN I ARRIVE HOME, un-showered from the gym and running over the plan with Jane for a couple of hours while doing errands, the last thing I expect to see is my husband's car. This is far past the time that he should have been at work and too soon for him to be home. I hide the fast food I grabbed for lunch after grocery shopping in my purse before I get out of the car.

I find him in the kitchen bent over his computer, typing.

"Hi, honey. I thought you'd be at work." I set a small amount of grocery bags down on the countertop and go about putting them away.

"Sorry to disappoint you, Medeia. I took a short day today at the office." He doesn't look up but remains hunched into the screen in front of him.

That's not what disappoints me about you, John.

"I'm just surprised is all." I put the rest of the produce away in the fridge and fold up my reusable bags and stick them in their designated drawer.

"Oh, your father passed away last week. I guess his drinking finally caught up to him."

The ice of his voice rolls up my body until my breathing seizes. I don't turn around, but I imagine he's smiling at my reaction.

"He what?" I stutter.

"Yeah. Sorry, we missed the funeral. I can give you the details of where he's buried if you'd like." He says it as if we missed a movie coming out in theaters, not the death of someone who is partly responsible for my being. Nothing stops his incessant tapping on the keys. I finally turn to face him. Lucifer is looking straight into my soul.

"How long did you know?" My voice is a growl.

"A few days." He looks back down to his screen and continues as if he told me that the price of pork was higher at the grocery store this week and I missed a sale. "Are you all right?" The reaction to this question piques his curiosity, however.

"Am I all right?" I grip the countertop of the bar opposite of where he's sitting. "Why did you keep it from me?" I grind my teeth.

"I was only thinking of your mental health, dear. Besides, he killed your mother. I didn't think it was that important." He shrugs. I think about all the knives in the slab — my hand aches to grip one.

I grab my heart. The tormenter of my youth is gone, yet I feel no relief because it was my current one who informed me of it.

"Do I need to fetch some of your pills or call an ambulance?" I catch his grin before I nearly black out from the misery, and it pulls me to the light. His cold and calculated words mean to drive me to the edge so that he can use my breakdown to advance the relationship with his girlfriend further. He doesn't care about the death of anyone unless he can use it to his advantage.

"No. I'm fine." I place the bread inside the bread box and the cereal into the pantry.

"What?" The typing stops.

"Did you get my note, dear? I'm heading out to do some Christmas shopping soon, and I don't imagine I'll be back until late. Don't wait on me for dinner." I'm staring at the macaroni box, trying not to let the tears fall. I won't play into his game.

"As long as you think you're all right. Remember what he did to your mother, and how you found her in a pool of her blood on the same floor that you learned how to walk on? Geez, I don't know how I'd be holding up if I were you. Maybe you should lie down; I'll get you your medicine. Maybe call Dr. Janson?"

"I recall what he did, John. Thank you for reminding me." I turn and face him. "I'm going to get a shower now, and then I'll be going out." I don't let him respond, and I push the image of my mother's body aside, replacing it with happy memories instead as I take the stairs two at a time longing for the comfort of the cascading water. I lock the door.

When I get the water hot enough to remind me of hell, I slump onto the tile and place my washcloth in my mouth and clasp around it with both hands so that there is no noise when I scream for my mother. Her body was lying awkwardly on the floor of that damn house. The blood spilled from her head because he couldn't control his anger. Now, he's dead, and I feel no redemption for my mother in that fact.

I keep my shower to the minimum time, even though my tears have yet to finish, and I do my makeup in record speed. My eyes don't look swollen at all as I exit into the closet. There is not a trace of pain for John to poke at.

"I just wanted to make sure you're all right, Medeia." John is sitting on the ottoman in the middle of the enormous closet space.

"I'm fine. Do you think your Aunt Mary will like a new shawl? I noticed the one she was wearing at the party was a little frayed at the edges. Possibly I can find something in a similar color and fabric for her." I grab my black turtleneck and black jeans and slip them on.

"Are you going to go visit his grave?" He keeps pushing.

"No. Are candles too cheap for Grace? I never know what to get her." I pull a blue cardigan on and search for my new favorite pair of black boots.

"I wonder if your sister or brother came to the funeral? They must be furious at you not to call." He twirls in the ottoman to face me no matter where I am at in the room. I need to leave so I can breathe. He's stifling me.

"They don't know my number. You changed it." I slip the boots on over my pants and grab a black jacket that allows me to move, going in and out of stores and not getting too hot.

"Still. They know where we live. They could have at least rang the doorbell."

Before I walk out of the doorway, I jolt back and glare at him. "You told them they were worthless and never to come around, and now you're surprised that they listened? Really?" I advance toward him, and he dares to look surprised. "You made me agree in front of them that they weren't to come around anymore because you felt Hank was a thief and

Ophelia was no better. You gave me no choice but to shut them out because of your money."

He tries to refute, but I yank my coat on and dart downstairs, rushing to the kitchen for my purse. I open the garage door and shimmy the bag I have prepared for tonight out of its hiding spot and into the car before John can even make it down the steps.

"Medeia!" I hear him screaming when I shut the driver's door of my car. I crank the music on the radio. I see him step out of the house and into the garage. I wave as I quickly reverse down the driveway and bolt off down the road.

I want to cut his throat. I want to make him bleed all over the expensive rugs in our house. *This is the wrong day to remind me of what you stole, John.*

Thirty-Five

THE HOUSE IS THE SAME as I remember, just more rot with age. The grass around the front has grown up to the base of the windows in some spots because my father always loathed doing yard work. The haphazard stairs remain, leading to the wooden front porch, dried with the sun's strength and neglect of proper maintenance.

This is the house that determined my outcome. In school, it was the thorn that kept me beaten down when I would walk the halls. When I got older, it decided who I thought I deserved in life. Now, it holds power over me of what I'll soon become. A murderer, just like my father. He killed my mother by shoving her; she lost her footing and hit her head off the edge of the table.

He killed himself with the bottle when they let him off easy — no conviction — condemning him to live out his life sentence here, where it all happened. Waking up and walking the floor stained from her last breaths. She wasn't significant enough to the world to lock him away. No amount of screams that tore from my body changed the mind of the judge who threw the case out for lack of evidence that it wasn't just an accident. No matter the cry of his history of violence.

She didn't matter enough.

I am going to make sure that Anna matters enough to the world that they lock John away for it. I will make her name go down in history so that they don't forget the pain he caused in this life. My father got his for my mother. A life for a —

My father stumbles in a drunken stupor out onto the porch and tosses some lunch scraps out to the stray cats circling his feet and hollers at them to be patient.

He's not dead.

I watch like I'm a kid again, as my father puts the drink to his lips and downs an entire beer bottle in a matter of seconds. Still a drunk, but still very much alive. He turns and fails to enter the doorway twice before success is his, and he's back inside. Back to his second six pack that I imagine is almost gone for the day. He moved on to liquor at nightfall in the later years.

The front door shuts just as I open my driver's door. There's no one coming on the street — an empty spot in the country with no neighbors around, just farmland. I run across the road and duck down in the weeds until I make it to the side of the house. I edge closer to the open window I know belongs to the living room.

My father groans as he takes residence in his favorite lounge chair that's near the window but facing the television on the opposite side of the room. I exhale and steady my nerves before raising myself on my tiptoes to peer inside.

The smell of body odor and garbage assaults my nasal passages as I struggle to keep quiet. How can anyone be used to that stench? I look at the back of my father's head, his bald spot taking up much more space than I recall. He's alive.

I turn my head slightly to see the spot on the floor where my mother laid now covered with a torn area rug that used to be in my bedroom. He's covered her up.

"Maria!" He calls out, and for a small second, I convince myself that I'll see my mother come around the corner from the kitchen at any moment. My father just rose from the dead, why can't she?

"Maria, I miss you." He begins to sob as the soap operas do little to drown him out. I let my heels touch the earth, and I melt to the ground in a squatted position.

I miss her, too, Dad.

I walk back to the road, and I put the car into drive — he doesn't even notice me sitting on the side of the road. The liquor stole the best of his eyesight long ago.

It was all a lie, cleverly orchestrated by my husband so that he may send me off to a mental facility to please his money-hungry girlfriend. My father didn't die, nor did my siblings come to town and not reach out to me. He wanted to push me over the edge. I would have sounded crazy had I ranted to the doctor that my father was dead when he wasn't.

He won't get away with it. I stab the accelerator to the floor. I'll take what's his with the same dedication he puts forth into stealing the stability of my mind.

Medeia's Journal

DEAR ANNA,

I hope you wear your best dress tonight to meet John. This will be the last time that you can impress the world with the veneer you put on over your average frame. No one ever told you that you are merely average with an innate ability to play up your better features.

You are still special to me, though. I see the side of you that the world isn't allowed, so I know you find me special, too.

Thirty-Six

"HOW CAN I SHOP, JANE? This feels awkward."

"Just gives you something to steady your mind." She holds up a red sweater for my approval. I nod. It looks great with her skin tone.

"I thought you were helping *me* Christmas shop?"

"I am. I'm giving *you* ideas on what to buy me." She smiles.

"You really aren't normal, Jane." I jab the words with a little bit of irritation, but Jane doesn't mind.

"You think you are?" she jokes. "Look, if you think about it too much, you won't go through with it. And trust me, right now they are sending texts back and forth like mad about him lying to you over your dad being dead."

"Yeah. Probably getting a good laugh at me." I bounce my head off the wall behind me. "Jane?"

"Hmm?"

"Do you think I'm crazy?" I ask.

"Oh, yes, darling, but all the good ones are." She doesn't look up from the sweaters she's perusing.

"I'm serious."

"No, I don't think you're crazy." She sighs and draws her attention to me. "You're a fighter, just trying to survive. If you don't look out for yourself, who will? Huh? He's taken everyone from you. He's even attempted to fucking take you from you. And you're still here. Now, you need to do this last step for your freedom. I don't see it any other way." She turns back to the sweaters. "Not any other way that's satisfying and filled with perfect justice." She holds up a purple sweater, and I nod my approval again.

We finish up most of my Christmas shopping. Just in case the need for me being on some cameras is necessary, besides two birds and one stone. If I do get caught, at least people will still receive their presents. I grab Aunt Mary a new shawl and a pendant to close it with. I buy John's cousin Grace candles and a cashmere scarf. I even purchase John a gift. It will be something useful for his repentance in prison, a new toothbrush. Maybe he can whittle it into a shank to protect himself.

"Do you have everything? Are you ready?" Jane asks when we are about to part.

"Yes," I say as I pack the bags into the trunk of my SUV. "I am now more than ever."

"I wish you luck," she says as her feet dance back and forth. "I can't believe he told you that your father was dead."

"He's a sick man." I shut the trunk. "I'll drive you back to your car if you'd like."

"No, I'll walk." She embraces me. "This might make me a horrible person to anyone else, but I hope you get away with it. You deserve your freedom. You deserve a life," she whispers in my ear.

"I'll see you in the morning?" I try to keep it as casual as possible in case a camera catches our interaction.

"Always." She smiles and walks away toward her car, and I make my move to the driver's door.

"Hey, Medeia," Jane shouts, and I turn my head in response.

"You're the only friend I've ever had, too."

I flash her a small smile, and she turns back to her walk. We are kindred spirits walking in the day carrying demons from the nights of our past. No one saw them, but the trained eyes of others who wore the same disguise of normalcy, and even most of them turned away, not willing to bring to the surface their own or make room for someone else's. Jane saw mine and lunged to hold my head above the water they wanted to drown me in because they had done the same to her.

I take myself to some mom-and-pop places that aren't too far from the warehouse, but distant enough so as not to raise skepticism. There won't be any sign of me near the crime, because I will be somewhere else during the time. I tuck my cell phones by a tree outside of the mom-and-pop stores where no one's naked eye can spot it, and no cell phone location tower could place me anywhere but here—planting my alibi where it needs to be. I can't chance someone texting or calling me when I'm at the warehouse tonight and have my location pinned. I've seen that be the demise of so many people in a situation like this. They're too attached to the things that will harm them. I plan to retrieve my phone after the deed is complete and even purchase myself a little victory trinket from one of the shops. But now is not the time for shopping, it's time for my revenge.

The last time that Anna's lungs will fill with life-giving oxygen.

I leave and head toward the warehouse. The sky is growing dark now; it is the perfect disguise. No one will see me coming around the back of the building, and this part of the lot is unseen from the road. I walk from the street over, where I park the car. The only streetlight here is conveniently busted. I have a couple of punk kids to thank for that. From the warehouse looking toward the street, there is nothing but the back of the buildings to see — not a soul in sight. Behind the warehouse, where I creep up and duck down, there is only a river after a scattering of trees.

They aren't here yet when I arrive, but they come almost simultaneously, their practiced dance of deceit in this place down pat. They exit their respective cars in silence and reach for each other's hands and head for the door of the warehouse. They look longingly at each other. The severity of the moment is not lost on them. It wasn't just a simple tryst to either one. They are in love. I can see it on their faces as he opens the door for her one last time.

I let my footsteps mark the anthem of tonight. I allow a piano to play in my mind of retribution and sin. I open the back door and turn to look toward the street where my car sits. I could run. I could forget this whole thing. A sliver of logic tells me that I'm taking it too far once I close this door behind me. There's no coming back from where I'm heading.

The fantasy of murdering someone isn't completely abnormal. I've read it somewhere. The act of doing it is. Putting the idea in motion is beyond typical spectrums. I am crazy, no matter how Jane or I justify it. *But they made me.*

I close the door slowly, staring out into the night and pushing down that last part of me that wants to go home. I swallow it whole with the jaws of the monster they made me become.

The back door closes beneath my fingertips with finality, and no part of me wishes to leave now. I don't even hear the flick of the lock, but I feel it beneath my hand. I feel the knife in my jacket again for the eighth time since I came to the warehouse. I already have my gloves on, and I slipped shower caps on my feet before entering the building. I'm jealous that John has Anna. Jealousy is a very powerful motive.

And so is revenge.

Thirty-Seven

"DO YOU THINK SHE'S run off?" I hear Anna's nasally voice above me in the loft.

"I don't know. She had some crazy eyes when I told her, so I bet she's going to break." John sounds out of breath already.

"Oh John, that turns me on. We're closer and closer to being together."

I wish I still had the cameras up in the warehouse so that I could see exactly where they are positioned in their makeshift room. I don't want to chance mistakes when I need the scene to be set correctly. I couldn't risk leaving the cameras up and having footage leading to me being caught. Plus, there won't be a lot of time afterward to clean up and hide them. They'll be looking for fresh marks, not ones made with Anna's shoes weeks ago. I want to laugh when I look down at how stylish her boots appear on my feet even with the shower caps on the bottom. A bonus for me that we wear the same size.

I wait until her obnoxious moans of foreplay reach a volume that would drown out my light footsteps before making my way up the stairs. I crouch to the floor in a deep squat and begin my practiced walk over to the outer portion of the cardboard box hallway that lines their love nest. The shower caps on my shoes make the task slippery and hard, but it's the only way to walk. I must keep myself low enough not to be spotted by the windows. We are facing the river from here, and the romantic candlelight won't illuminate me to any boats passing by, but I still take no chances.

There is a slight opening where they always place food and stuff as a makeshift table. I've watched with bile threatening my throat as she would feed him grapes and shit. It was sickening. I chance a peek through the small hole.

His face is buried between her thighs, and her eyes are closed. She's rocking her hips back and forth against his face, begging him not to stop. It's my chance. I grab the bottle of wine on their table. They already popped the cork, so I don't need to worry myself with the noise.

I am a perfectionist, and I won't get sloppy now. This moment has run through my mind more than a million times. I need to execute it flawlessly and not allow their carelessness to rub off or have my emotions cloud the vision of what needs to be done. I take a deep breath and let my ears go deaf to my surroundings.

I dump the crushed-up pills into the bottle through a paper funnel I made, watching as no powder dares to caress the neck. Perfect. I swirl the bottle slowly until all visible trace is gone. I recheck my small peephole. John has come up for air and is now dominating over top of Anna, getting his victory kiss for making her cum. I push the cork in and set the bottle exactly where it was and wait for what I know will come next.

"Let's have a drink," he commands. It's what they always do — foreplay, drinking, more foreplay, and sex. Then they lie cuddled up on the floor mattress for a half hour just touching each other and appreciating the closeness—not tonight. Their boring routine will be the end of them. I hold my breath as the shadow of my husband's hand retrieves the bottle and evenly distributes the contents between two glasses.

Bottoms up, John and Anna.

I wait, holding my body up on aching legs, as they share their romantic ten-dollar bottle of wine. I push myself past the pain. *Soon, legs, soon we can walk but not on this side of the boxes.* After one glass they're ready to go at it again, and Anna assumes her position on her knees. The slurping threatens to break my exterior so carefully constructed for tonight. I sing any song I can think of in my head to avoid letting her penetrate the calm this all requires.

"Be on top, John. You know, missionary. Let's go old school. I feel like it's our first time together," Anna purrs. She's a twig, so I know the medicine will work its way into her system faster than his.

"Anything you want, Anna. I love you. I can't wait to hold you in my arms every night and fall asleep next to you." The words fall from his lips so easily. I've never heard the sound his lips make this close before when he tells his whore the same things that he swore only to say to me.

It burns me up inside like a wildfire that cannot be contained. John loves Anna. I sink forward, pressing my face into my knees, and close my eyes. A tear drips down my cheek, and I do my best to shove the feeling down deep. He's not the man I married, not the one that I fell in love with so many years ago. He doesn't even closely resemble the one who loved me back. He's a horrible human being now. This is Anna's John, not mine.

I focus on the shower caps covering the boots. Not a single mark left behind. I pat the knife inside my pocket. The only mark will be that of a scorned lover, but not this one. I won't be in this warehouse, except for a faint memory of me and a time I thought I would become an independent woman alongside my husband. A time when I had dreams to make security for not only myself but my future family. He tore it all away. There's none of that Medeia left. Not even in the certificate buried behind the boxes.

"John, I don't feel right." I hear the force behind Anna's words as she tries to push them past her lips and fight the sleep taking over. I pick my head up.

Their groans start to slow in repetition, and I can tell it's taking strenuous force for John to keep going.

"John, I feel funny." She's breathy.

"Anna, are you still awake?" he grunts into her. "I'm gonna cum."

Before she can respond, and I know she can't, he falls on top of her. Ironically, instead of finishing together, they pass out together. How fitting. I almost want to tell my husband when he wakes up that at least he conked out at the same time as his lover. *You two must be truly synced.*

I begin to make my way down to the end of the box-made hallway, and I give it another five minutes to make sure they won't be fighting the pills. I hear John's distinct snoring, and I don't hear Anna protesting having his dick inside her since he fell asleep on top of her. They're out.

My moment has arrived. I turn the corner of the boxes, and finally, stand up in the cover and sanctuary they provide from the outside world. I head toward the sleeping lovers. Slow and deliberate, every step is a victory, a memory. *Remember when you told me that I was crazy?* Step. *Remember making me quit my job?* Step. *How about every time you suggested that I up my medication?* Step. *How about when Anna smiled and held my hand at the party as if she wasn't a snake trying to ruin my life?* Step. *What about every I love you?* Step. *What about today, when you told me my father was dead? Do you remember it all, John?* Step. *Because I do.*

I make it to them. They're lightly snoring and still connected. She did tell him she always wanted to play house with him, sleep next to him, and wake up next to him. I made the bitch's dream come true. Well, everything except waking up. I cannot fulfill that dream, and I won't give in to their happily ever after. I'm not that big of a person.

I waste no time because the longer I stand here, the more the scene threatens to bust down my walls. I straddle over my husband's back and lift the top portion of him. He's heavy, but the adrenaline gives me strength. Revenge gives me strength and the fact that I'm ridding the world of two destructive, calculating people makes him lighter than a toothpick. I'm holding my naked husband above his lover after drugging them with the same pills John wanted me to increase for myself. I push it down. It's just mechanics. I need to think of the moves and not the reason.

I place the knife inside his right hand, and cup mine over the top of his. Now comes the part that I have dreamed of every night since committing to the idea. The scene that I have played over again in my mind with great pleasure. The reality is so much better than anything I could have daydreamed before. Watching my husband's hand come up to Anna's soft white throat and press the blade in is everything I have longed for and more. It only fits that he be the one to end what he started, to take out the stain on our marriage. To punish himself for what he has done. To take away his happiness, just like he stole mine. That's what he does. He ruins everything.

He glides the blade over with quick, angry ease. The blood squirts his face, narrowly missing mine. And there's a gurgle to be heard, and Anna's eyes try to fling open, but she bleeds out before the strength returns. I stand up and ease my husband back down, his face near the wound. How remorseful he is for what he has done, he's holding her without care of the blood. *What did you do, John? You had to kill the one thing you loved and couldn't let go.*

My husband killed Anna.

Medeia's Journal

DEAR ANNA,

I think about your last breaths. The last thing you said. The last moment your eyes were open. I feel privileged to have known that they were your final moments because I took care of honoring them.

You knew something was wrong. You would never fall asleep on your lover. It wasn't the wine; you knew it because you're an avid drinker and can handle a bottle a night all on your own. So why now? Why would you be too drunk that the room spun around now? Why?

I liked the last look in your eyes when he slit your throat, the way you fought to look around, how you felt betrayed by him. I hope you know that your lover didn't stop screwing you when you fell asleep. He just assumed you had your eyes closed in ecstasy. You were a hole for him.

And that's the man you risked your life to be with in the evenings.

He's the man who killed you.

Was it worth it, Anna?

Thirty-Eight

I SWITCH THE BOTTLE of wine with another empty bottle from one of their previous meetings here. I pour the remaining wine from their glasses into a sandwich bag and then put the cups into another plastic bag. I saved two cups from a time that they forgot to clean up after and put those on the makeshift table area. No trace of the pills here. I finish cleaning up, and I look down on the scene one last time. Nothing left but them.

The ending of a part of our story. At least to one of the chapters, Anna's chapter. I try not to think about the family who will miss her or the horrible life they will live knowing what happened to her. I put my mind at ease about the even score we had to settle. Here's the thing, your parents will try to raise you so that you do right and not wrong. They'll give you all the tools you need to change a red situation to green, but you're on your own when you start fucking people's husbands.

I hope her family finds peace. Even her mother, whose guilt will consume her when she remembers the door that she recently slammed in her daughter's face. They can find closure in the fact that John will be behind bars and out of society, that someone will pay for what happened to this girl. They'll paint her as an innocent girl who got tangled in the wrong situation by love. That's how they'll portray her.

Her friend Samantha and I will know the truth. Jane will know the truth. Anna hunted for the married men, to mess with their lives and tempt her fate. She loved luring them away from things. It gave her a thrill because she had done it so many times before to leave the man dry of something in blackmail. It was different with John. Different with me. She loved him and attached herself most precariously. It led to her destruction.

Anna's blood glimmers in the flickering of the candle-light. I wonder what the scene looks like with the bright overhead lights blaring down. But, for now, it's just poetic. A little bit romantic. If I slit John's throat as well, they could be like Romeo and Juliet. Except, I want my ending where he pays for all that he's done to me. I don't want to romanticize their blatant abuse of my mental state. I want the world to flick on the bright lights and call attention to what happened here, to the horrible things these two were plotting to do.

I walk out of the building with intent. So many people rush this part on those tv shows because they are frightened and need to get away. But this is where I need to be the most cautious. If my father taught me anything useful, it's this. What could scare you? You're the scariest thing there is now. When I get closer to the car, I take the gloves and shower caps off and deposit them into the plastic bag along with the wine bottle, wine, and cups. I was never here.

I'm tempted to stay and see what happens when John wakes up, but that's too risky and indulgent. I need to remain focused. I can't be here. I can't run the chance of being seen. I also can't mess with my alibi not being stable. I'm off to dispose of this evidence and finish my shopping. I let go of the fact that this is one of the pieces of the puzzle I can't see or have control over. I hand this over to my husband and rely on him to do his part. A difficult task in my mind because John has proven himself to be unreliable. That's how we got in this entire situation. I take a deep breath and concentrate.

I dump the wine into the river and save the rest of the things to burn at Jane's place. I head off to get my phone and victory reward. I still haven't gotten Jane anything for Christmas yet. And what about Anna? She'll need something acceptable as John's secretary. I always buy the secretaries he has a little chocolate gift pack. I should stop and get her one. Just the same as all the others, so she doesn't realize how special she is to me.

I buy my purchases and linger a little bit at a coffee shop. It's lovely to watch people hustle and bustle on the street and amongst the stores. They're in their cars thinking about how awful the traffic is, and how much they want to go home. They wonder what to buy and try not to feel guilty when they opt for a cheaper present because the other one wasn't exactly in their budget.

They come into the coffee shop and order their pick-me-up to aid them in their energy level to continue shopping or to begin. They don't know how close they are to me. They have no idea the things I've seen and done. They smile at me when we happen to make eye contact. I smile back and even offer up a hello if they are in a close enough range. I exchange pleasantries with several of the customers in the shop and wish them a blessed holiday season as they leave.

Not a single one of them thinks they're talking to a person who just committed a murder.

They have no idea.

And no one ever will.

I give John another hour before I return to the house. When I come in, arms filled with shopping bags, I find him at the dining room table. He's freshly showered, and his neck looks raw from scrubbing. *What was there, John? Blood from your whore?* He's sipping on gin and staring out into space with wild eyes. He looks like my father did that morning. He tries his best to hide it when I enter the room. Will he finally confess to me?

"Hi, honey," I sing. My stomach aches with excitement. I run to him and kiss his cheek. He jumps at the feeling of my touch.

"Hi." He whispers. I watch the ghosts of his past dance across his face. The time that he beat a man into a coma, the time he hit a man so badly that I needed to cover it up for him, the time that he got into an altercation at work, and now the time that he murdered his mistress. Unfortunately, that moment is fuzzy for him I imagine.

"What's the matter?" I ask, ready to take in his confession.

"Something bad happened." He stutters. I bite my lip to keep from smiling.

"What?" He doesn't answer me. Instead he pours himself more drink. "John, you have that same look in your eyes like the night that you beat that man half to death."

"Don't talk about that night." He growls, and I jump back for show. I want John to be terrified of his demons.

"I'm sorry, Medeia. I'm sorry." He scratches his nails deep into his scalp in frustration.

"John?"

"How are you feeling?" he ventures. "You left upset." I watch him swallow down his confession and start up a new lie.

"I'm all right. I mean, it's sad when someone you know that well passes away, but I can't change it." I look him in the eye and long to stare and stain his soul.

"I feel awful," he whispers, near tears.

"Hmm?"

"I did some investigating today when you left," he starts. The lie is on the spot; I can tell by the way his eyes jolt around instead of focusing. "Your father didn't die. He was merely in the hospital is all." He nods excited — he's proud of his lie.

"Oh?" I pull a chair out to sit down. "Huh."

"Are you okay, Medeia?" Now he is nervous. If he doesn't have me now that Anna is gone, who will get him through this? I'm not covering this one up for him. If John confesses right now, I'll turn him over to the police.

"I don't know." I bite my lip. "I mean, I spent all day making peace with his death and the horrible things he did." He grabs for my hand, and it's cold on mine. I think about the last thing our hands did conjoined together. "I guess that work doesn't have to go to waste, does it?"

He shakes his head.

"I still gained some peace from it all. From the torture and hell that others have brought into my life."

"That's a good point." The color is slowly returning to his face as he forces Anna from his mind. He won't be confessing to me.

"Did you do a little shopping?" He laughs at his joke. His ability to change the subject to trivial things is terrifying. *Doesn't Anna matter at all to you?* She's all I could think of for months now.

"Christmas is done," I raise my arms in a victory stance.

"I haven't even started." He stares at the bags with a small smirk playing at how I accomplished the feat in one day. "What can I get you for Christmas, babe?" He seems a little sad when he asks it. He sees his future flash with the riddles of lawyers and plea deals, not Christmas and shopping.

"Oh, I even took care of that for you today, my love. I know how busy and focused you've been at work lately, so I wanted to take the burden from you. I ended up getting myself a little something; I'll just put your name on it," I say. I laugh at my joke, but he is none the wiser to its origin.

I remove my hand from under his and pat his shoulder. "It has been a long day, though." I stand and point to the bags. "Is it all right if I leave these here until the morning? I think with everything that happened today that I should take a shower and get into bed."

"Yeah. Yeah. Sure." He nods to the bags and waves off their existence. "Leave them here."

I head out of the dining room.

"I love you." His shout is desperate and second best.

"Thanks, John." I turn around wondering if this will be the moment that he spills everything, but he's staring out the window into the night again. A shiver runs through me, and I see Anna's lifeless body when I look at him. I killed her, but she's all around.

Thirty-Nine

"SO?" FOR ONCE, JANE has beaten me to the gym this morning, and I'm even twenty minutes early. I've been too anxious to tell her about last night, that I couldn't sleep.

I nod.

"Wow." She hits the buttons on her treadmill and starts at a slow pace. I do the same.

There is silence between us. The words that we long to share with each other are not appropriate for this public space.

"How did the shopping go, once I left you last night?" I pick up on Jane's code.

"It went well. I got something for everyone on my list. I'm done shopping for Christmas." I pick up the pace on my jog. I notice Jane's eyes are looking around the weight area to see if a certain blonde makes her way in today. She needs something to solidify that it's real, that what I say is the truth.

It was her story that convinced me it was possible to pull off, and I checked it out, too. The abuse records were real, as well. I knew Jane was telling the truth when she admitted to killing her husband. I look over toward her. I wonder if the pressure of knowing my secret will only bring her closer or push her to crack.

"Jane?" I startle her.

"Hmm?" She whips her head toward me as she picks up her running pace.

"I hate it when people tell me what gifts they got me, so I won't tell you what I got you as long as you don't tell." I raise my eyebrow.

She is offended immediately. "I would never tell you what I got you. I hate when people ruin a good gift that way." We both nod— we understand.

I face forward, and Jane lingers on my face only a second longer before following my line of sight. It's the first time at the gym that we don't see Anna taking selfies. None of the gym rats downstairs or on the walkway upstairs miss her or ask about her.

Jane takes the bag from me that contains my gloves, shower caps, and John and Anna's plastic cups. We exchange it inside her knit hat she purposely left in my car the night before.

"I'll take care of it." She puts the hat in her purse.

"Thank you, Jane. Seriously, for everything. For your friendship, your trust, your secrets. For you." A tear rolls down my cheek. "I love you like you were a sister to me." I pull her into me.

"I'm so happy that we could save you from your abuser," Jane whispers into my ear as we squeeze each other harder.

I watch as she climbs into her car and drives away. I still have one last person to follow today, and it won't be my paranoid husband who spent the night crying in bed next to me when he thought I was asleep. It will be Samantha. I wonder what my favorite girl is up to today.

I find her waiting for Anna at their weekly lunch spot. Anna is fifteen minutes late, and she's getting impatient that her friend isn't picking up her calls. I sit three tables down from her, reading a book and enjoying some music in my earbuds. They have a delicious fish sandwich here. I can see why this restaurant has become a repeat place for Anna and Samantha.

She dials the number for Anna again only to groan at the beginning of another voicemail message. She raises her hand for the waiter's attention and asks for her meal to be made to go. She is not one to wait long, and she's confident that Anna is mad at her for something, at least that's what I gather from the multiple rantings she's placed into Anna's voicemail.

Anna, I know you're still mad at me but pick up. We need to talk.

I only told you the truth. That's what I always do. I don't understand why you're ghosting me now. Are you too good for friends?

I'm leaving the restaurant, Anna. I can't believe you stood me up. You've changed since John and not in a good way.

She slams the end button on her cell phone and stands up. The waiter comes over with her fish sandwich meal and change. She tells him to keep it and smiles at him, hoping to gain a little approval for her looks, but he's more excited by the ten-dollar tip to notice she did her hair. I notice though. It looks good on her.

I beckon him over, as Samantha makes her way out the door.

"Hi, can I have the check please?" I wink.

"Certainly, miss." He digs into his apron pocket and proceeds to pull my check out. I have the cash already waiting for him.

"Here you go, keep the change. I'm in a bit of a hurry today." I smile and stand up.

"Thank you so much, miss." Two large tips in two minutes. He's one happy guy.

When I walk out of the restaurant, Samantha is hovering over her phone, facing away from me. I linger and pretend to be searching for my keys in my purse.

"Listen, Anna. I'm done. You and John are sick for what you're trying to do to his wife. If you don't like the fact that I told you the truth, then I'm done with it. You deserve John if you're going to be that nasty of a human being. His wife deserves nothing but all of his money in the divorce, and I hope she gets it. You're proving yourself to be no better than your mother." She smashes her finger into the end button and stomps off in the opposite direction as I do.

I head into the store next to the restaurant, a little party place but more so a good cover to watch my favorite human being, Samantha, walks away pissed off and done being friends with Anna. I hadn't realized the bonus that I could take something away from Anna, as well.

Medeia's Journal

DEAR ANNA,

It's been three whole days, and they have yet to report you missing. No one at the office has bothered. Your mother. Your aunt. Your grandmother. No one. Not even Samantha. Are you essential in anyone's life but John's and mine?

Forty

IT HAS TAKEN A LOT of strength and willpower to resist the urge of going to the warehouse and checking on Anna. I feel like I'm neglecting her, leaving her lying there without so much as a visit. I don't even know if she's still there. What did John do to her? Did he take proper care of her? I didn't know she was so unloved until the moments that followed after I watched her bleed out.

It takes a whole week before Samantha reports her missing. I was hoping it would be her no-good mother. If I ever had a kid, I'd be in constant daily contact, and I would know immediately. How terrible, especially since I know how often Anna tried to visit her mother. She still longed to be loved. Maybe that's why Anna felt the need to have men constantly around her. We blame it on daddy issues, which she had, but maybe there's a little bit to do with the neglect of a mother's love in there, too. If her mother had had the proper amount of self-esteem, perhaps she could have passed that healthy self-love image down to her daughter. However, she failed, and Anna turned out to be a whore just like her. I wish I could have done something more for the girl, now. Maybe a bigger basket of muffins.

"John, come here. Come here. Come here." I demand from the living room.

"What?" He shuffles in, unamused.

"Look." I point at the television illuminating the room with the morning news story. "Isn't that Anna?" I turn to see the terror in John's eyes contrast against the pale white of his face as he grips the back of the couch.

"Oh, god," he mumbles.

"It is. Oh, my goodness. That poor girl." I grip my hand around my mouth if only to keep from laughing in John's face about how he's stumbling backward holding the couch for support. He grips the wall as he stumbles out of the room toward the kitchen.

He knows what he did. He can't fathom how he could be so cruel. I am revived by the fact that John doesn't even question that it was his doing; he knows how horrible of a person he is. He doesn't walk around unaware of his temper. Poor Anna.

Her lover betrays her.

I know exactly how that feels. Maybe John is still trying to piece together that night. The only thing he'll remember is drinking and blacking out. That's when his rage must have kicked in, and considering he never reported the incident, that must be what he felt on some level. He didn't want to be bullied by her into throwing me in a mental facility, and he didn't want to lose her if he didn't go through with the plan. If he couldn't have her, no one could. He must think that's what he did. On some level, my husband wanted his mistress to die. He's as guilty as I am.

I am like a kid counting down the days until Christmas while having no real concept of time. I don't know when they will find her body or where he has stashed her. I'm waiting desperately for the moment when it will begin, but then a part of me wants it to take a little longer. What if it wasn't flawless? What if I messed something up? I went over everything at length in my mind every day, all day long. I keep thinking about every step taken. I always stop and ask, *what if they found this?* But then I debunk the question by going over my careful planning.

I envision him slicing her throat open at least a thousand times a day. I remember how he took the blade across her delicate pale throat, and I can't imagine how he could have felt to do such a thing to her. I can't believe how callous he is; it's almost as if he's forgotten about Anna and pushed her from his mind. He dodges the conversation every time I ask him if he's heard anything about the case since she worked so closely with him. How cold.

She's on my mind. Did Anna know she could be so dispensable to another human being? That her life and future wouldn't matter to someone that she had shared such an intimate relationship with and planned her days around? She probably couldn't picture John being this bitter about her. Then again, she never saw his offensive side. She didn't know he could kill her and go on with his daily life as if nothing happened. She probably thought he was an honorable man who would turn himself in and confess. He turned out to be nothing more than an ordinary coward.

"Poor girl," I utter at the TV as I power it down with the remote. "I hope they find her."

Medeia's Journal

DEAR ANNA,

It's almost Christmas time. Your family has been coming out of the woodwork now to make a plea for you to be let go for the holiday season. They believe you have been kidnapped in some conspiracy theory. Wow.

You come from strange folks, with very little intelligence or teeth. Is that why makeup became your shield? Was the reflection of your mother's face looking back at you daily too much to handle? Were the freckles that lined your nose just like your father's—better to digest when you blended concealer over them?

It's a shame that they couldn't act this way when you were alive.

Medeia's Journal

DEAR ANNA,

Ten days have passed, and they finally found a body. I held my breath, thinking about you. We get a lot of bodies in the rivers around here, but not often just thrown in the woods. How could he be so careless with you? I took the time to show you attention, and he threw you out like yesterday's garbage.

Tossed you in the sprinkling of woods along the river as if you were just a piece of litter thrown from a car window. You were more. He left you in the cold for animals to poke at you, for the bitter cold to do it's worse against your naked skin. He didn't care.

Forty-One

I OPEN THE FRONT DOOR after the incessant knocking expecting to find the little girl who has been trolling the neighborhood selling delicious boxes of cookies, but I see an older female flashing a badge in my face.

"Mrs. Moore?"

"Yes? Can I help you?" My stomach drops.

"I'm Detective Mason, ma'am, and I was hoping to ask you a few questions about Anna Trayor." She's pleasant enough. I scrunch my eyes at her.

"Anna Trayor?" I gasp as the last name hits me, but the truth is it's all an act for the officer—the name is burned into every part of my being. "Oh, my god. You mean John's secretary?"

"Yes, ma'am."

"Come in. Come in." I wave for her to come inside. She nods to her partner, another female of similar age but with a bored look on her face. "Oh, I heard about her on the news, how awful. Missing around the holidays."

"Thank you, Mrs. Moore. This here is my partner, Detective Tompson." We exchange nods and handshakes.

"Please come in, sit down." I motion toward the living room. "Can I get you anything to drink?"

They both decline.

"Oh, my goodness. I hope you guys find her." I point to the chairs in the living room for them to occupy.

"Mrs. Moore, I realize that this is an uncomfortable conversation, so please bear with me, but I need to ask you some personal questions about your relationship with your husband."

"John?" They nod. "I apologize; I don't understand what you're saying."

"We spoke to him earlier today, and he's assured us you'd be available to chat." I know that it's a lie because there's no way John would want them speaking to me about the verbal abuse that he has been dishing out the past ten years, or anything relating to him. He wouldn't want the secrets of the past coming into the present.

"Wow. Okay." I sit rigidly on the edge of the couch with my hands clasped between my knees. "I'm sorry, I *really* don't understand. You spoke to John about his secretary, and that makes sense because she worked for him, but what does this have to do with me?" They exchange glances. I slip out of reality for a second and float above the scene, and I replace myself with the empty mind of an unknowing wife.

"Ma'am, are you aware of an affair between your husband and Miss Trayor?" Detective Mason asks.

"A what?" I shout and lean forward. "No. No. No. John isn't having an affair." I shake my head.

The other detective jumps in. "Can you place your husband's whereabouts on the night of November twelfthof this year?"

"Wait. Wait. Go back." I throw my hands up. "An affair? Why do you think John was having an affair with Anna?" I search their faces, one after another. I'll give them one thing; they're excellent at their job because they know to look upon me in empathy.

Detective Tompson moves to sit next to me and grab my hand. "Mrs. Moore, I apologize, but it has come to our attention that your husband has been linked to Anna romantically up until recently."

"How?" I squeeze her hand and rub my forehead with my other hand.

"Well..." She looks to her partner for permission, and she nods. "After talking with several people at your husband's office where Anna worked as well, it has come to our attention that the two were closer than just coworkers. We are trying to confirm the suspicions. Right now, it's gossip. Strong gossip."

"He couldn't be," I stutter.

"Do you know where your husband was the night of November twelfth?" she repeats.

"I don't know. It's hard when you spit out a specific date." I take deep breaths. "Sorry, I'll grab my calendar. I usually write my activities down in there, and it might jolt a memory."

"Thank you, ma'am. That would be helpful." She follows behind me while I retrieve my purse from the hall closet. I unhouse my planner, and she waves for me to follow her back to my own living room.

"Okay..." I settle back down on the couch, Detective Tompson taking up residence next to me again. "November twelfth, I was shopping for Christmas gifts. I met my girlfriend, Jane, up at the stores, and then I shopped longer after she left. John was working from home that day." I look up at their faces. "I remember it now." I gulp. "I came home from the gym and some grocery shopping, and he was bent over his computer in the kitchen when I got home. He told me he took a half day at work. And then..."

"And then what, Mrs. Moore?" Detective Tompson presses.

"He told me that my father passed away. He said he had died and that we missed the funeral." I stare at the floor.

"I'm sorry for your loss," Detective Mason says.

"He didn't die." I correct her. I glance up to watch the shock settle on their faces.

"What?" Detective Tompson echoes the shock on her partner's face in my ear.

"John told me later that night when I got home from shopping that he was misinformed," I state.

"Seems like a pretty big thing to be misinformed about," Detective Mason quips.

"Yeah." I nod. "After he told me that he had died, I remember I went up and took a shower, and left to go shopping." I squeeze the knee of Detective Tompson. "I'm not callous. It hurt. I drove around and parked for a while, making peace with it. I haven't seen my father since the day my mother passed. I don't want to go into details, but I don't exactly have the closest or best relationship with my father."

"I'm sorry to hear that," Detective Tompson says.

"It's..." I shake my hand at them. "I don't know where John was. I think he was home. He was home when I got back, and he was showered so he must have been here awhile."

"Around what time did you get home, ma'am?"

"Oh, I don't know. Maybe nine in the evening."

"How did he seem when you got home?" Detective Mason asks.

"Well, um." I pretend to be dragging the memory up from the depths of my mind. Meanwhile, the face of John that night is a screensaver up there. "A little odd, I guess. He told me he loved me."

"And that's odd?" Detective Mason leans in.

"Lately, yes." I sit back against the couch. "Huh." I pretend to connect the dots. "What's the gossip at his work?"

"Uh, just a few things suggesting Anna and your husband were intimate," Detective Tompson stutters.

"Like what?"

"I don't think I'm at liberty to say those to you and cause you any distress when it may simply be just gossip and lies." She smiles.

"Well, that's shit," I blurt. "Oh, I'm sorry. Just, that's frustrating. See, I'm sitting here with two officers wondering if my husband is cheating on me. I answered your question for the date, and you're going to leave me scratching my head when you go."

"One of the coworkers has pictures of them holding hands, and your husband kissing Miss Trayor." Detective Mason doesn't share the same secrecy policy that her partner does.

"Thank you."

"Thank you, Mrs. Moore." They stand to leave, their use for me over. "If you think of anything else, please don't hesitate to call us."

"You should talk to our chef, Hannah." I slam my planner shut. "You gave me the gossip, so I can at least point you in a direction for John's alibi. That's what you're looking for, isn't it? Why else would you be asking me about a specific date?"

"Chef?" Detective Tompson's prejudice against the rich shines through.

Detective Mason steps in front of her. "Your husband failed to mention this."

I glare at Detective Tompson. "She comes in every night for dinner. It's her job to keep a menu written down. She can confirm his time at home that night. I didn't stay for dinner." I watch a spark shine between them. The dumb rich housewife proved to be useful after all.

"She's dead, isn't she?" I rub my upper arms to ward off the chill.

The detectives don't do well to hide their faces.

"Thank you, Mrs. Moore." Detective Mason shakes my hand.

"Please, call me Medeia. I'm not sure I like that last name right now after hearing my husband cheated."

"Medeia."

Medeia's Journal

DEAR ANNA,

I miss you. My days are empty now that I can't follow you around. I tried to take a selfie today in remembrance of you, and it made me sick. The whole office knew you were a whore. They even took pictures. Funny that none of them ever reached my inbox. I wonder if others were taking your course in blackmail and planning to get raises from John.

Forty-Two

"MEDEIA, I CAN EXPLAIN." John's talking to my back because I refuse to turn around and look at him.

"Hannah, a pleasure to see you." I grab the coat off the rack that our chef just put there. "I'm afraid I need to give you the night off, though. I do apologize for you driving all this way."

"I understand, Mrs. Moore." She puts her coat back on, and I can tell by her face that she has heard John's screams for longer than a minute.

"Mr. Moore. I wanted to speak to you, um, before I go." She nods to me for permission. I grant it.

"What, Hannah? We're a little busy," John barks.

"John," I scold. "Knock it off." He jumps back at the tone of my voice, as does our young chef. Never have I raised my voice to him, I've always been a pushover when it comes to John and arguments, but now that his affair is out in the open for me to react to, it feels wonderful to let go.

"Go on," I coax.

"Well, Mr. Moore..." She looks at me before adding, "Mrs. Moore. I need to resign."

"Okay," I say.

"Why?" John advances toward her, and I intercept by putting myself the middle.

She stares down at the floor and wrings her hands, and I take them in mine to reassure her. "Why, Hannah?" I ask softly.

"The police, Mrs. Moore, came to my house today and asked me a lot of questions." She looks at my husband. "I don't want to work for you anymore, Mr. Moore." Translation: She doesn't want to work for a philandering murder suspect.

"That's fucking ridiculous," John screams. I watch the spittle from his bottom lip fly off toward Hannah's face. "You aren't allowed to quit. It's all hearsay."

"Sir, with all due respect, I don't want to associate myself with you and your case this soon in my career." I watch as she tries to keep a professional head while wiping the spit off her cheek.

"Career?" John laughs like a maniac. "I took you in from culinary school. You are nothing without me. Nothing."

"Enough, John," I scream.

"I understand, Hannah. I'll mail you your last pay." I show her out the door, the whole time protecting her with my arm away from the steam of John's angry breath.

"That's great. That's just fucking wonderful." He points at the door after I close it on our ex-chef's retreating back.

"Can you blame her?" I yell.

"I lost six employees today over this shit. The whole office is going on about an affair with Anna. Now, our cook is gone. What am I supposed to do, Medeia?" He slaps his thighs, out of breath.

"Cook for yourself." I push past him and up the stairs toward our bedroom.

"Where are you going?" I hear him take the stairs two at a time while I calmly stride up them.

"I'm going to my bedroom, John, where I will pack your things." My tone doesn't raise again.

"This is my house!" he shouts.

"Then you can move *your* shit into *your* guest room. I'm not fucking leaving because *your* dick couldn't stay out of *your* secretary's mouth." He slaps me across the face. I slap him back.

"Hit me again, John. I'm sure that's what the police want to hear, how you are so weak in anger that you can strike a woman. Do it. Hit me again, you coward," I seethe in his face, watching my saliva now be the one to fly onto his open lips of shock.

"I'm sorry, Medeia. I didn't..."

"You didn't what? Mean it?"

He nods.

"Which part?"

"All of it." It sounds like a question rather than a statement.

"Forget it, John. I'll pack my things. You can have your big old mansion." I swing my arm around to the empty house. "I won't be sleeping anywhere near a murderer tonight." I will, in fact, forever sleep with a murderer every night for the rest of my life.

"I didn't kill her." He lurches forward and enunciates every word so that they hit the base of my spine one by one.

"Prove it." I pack my stuff to stay at Jane's for the night.

"You don't have anywhere to go. I'm not paying for you to stay in a hotel tonight."

I laugh. "Don't worry about me, John." I had Jane now, and some money saved from my job and taking cash back at stores. I had everything I needed to stand on my feet alone, and it feels good. I don't want to be rich anymore. I want to be free.

"Medeia, wait. I need you." He grabs at my arm, but I dodge his touch. He's begging now. He can't find an angle to work, so he's flailing.

"I'll be back tomorrow morning for the rest of my things, John. Until this is sorted out, or I decide what I need, I won't be in this house with you."

I throw clothes into a suitcase I have inside of the closet, careful not to spill out any of the food or money I have hidden in certain items of clothing. John paces around the room while I pack in a fury. I toss makeup into a bag and zip it up and head out.

"I would never hurt you, Medeia." He yanks on my suitcase as I'm walking down the stairs.

"You just did."

"I apologized for that," he sputters.

"Yeah?"

He nods.

I grab my coat and car keys, then pause. "Then go tell Anna you're sorry, see if it works for her." I shut the door as tears run down John's face.

Medeia's Journal

DEAR ANNA,

I never had a sleepover when I was younger. Hell, I didn't even have friends let alone someone who wanted to have me come over to their house. I like being in Jane's home. It's smaller than mine; it's perfect. Thank you for fucking John and for weirdly giving me my freedom. I hope I gave you yours. I hope now your sins are repented because of the price you paid for them.

By the way, why did you never invite Samantha to sleep over? She's working so hard for you, but I have an awful feeling you weren't the kind of friend she is trying to be for you now.

Forty-Three

THE MORNING BRINGS sunshine to warm my face through the glass doors leading to the balcony of Jane's guest bedroom. Jane's ex-husband was rich. When he passed away, the life insurance money afforded her to buy this charming place with luxurious features.

It was extravagant in the best ways: a balcony off the guest bedroom, a vaulted ceiling in the living room, marble countertops in the kitchen. Aside from those features, it was down to earth everywhere else, and I blame that on Jane. She didn't come from riches, she wasn't ever as poor as I was, but she didn't have a silver spoon anywhere near her mouth for the longest time. Even when she did, she paid dearly for it.

"Coffee?"

I shift in the bed off my stomach where I was watching the sunrise and turn over to Jane's smiling face as she sits on the comforter holding two mugs.

"Yes, please." I take the cup from her and mirror her position in bed.

"Do you want me to come with you today?" I could tell she was nervous, the bruising on my cheek came almost immediately after the slap. I reach to touch the tender spot that she's fixated on.

"No," I decide. "I can't drag you anywhere near this. It needs to be clean."

She reluctantly agrees. "So, I was thinking." She turns her mug in her hand and bites her lip.

"What?" I sip at my coffee, already doing its job at waking me up this morning.

"I hate living alone." She is having a tough time because independence is now the anthem of her core and admitting that she is lonely out loud feels like a betrayal.

"Can I have this room?" I interrupt her. "I love watching sunrises, and it looks gorgeous from this balcony view."

She sighs with relief and leans her head on my shoulder while I look out at the view some more.

"I never had a sister. I was an only child," she whispers.

"I had a brother and a sister," I admit.

"Had?"

"John ran them off." I sip the coffee, hoping to warm the ice of the past.

"Perhaps we need to make it our mission to find them." It wasn't a question, or a statement really; just Jane's way of telling me what the future held.

"I'd like that." I smile into my coffee. "I really would."

After I get dressed, I bid Jane farewell and head back toward the house to pack up the rest of my things. I don't have much, or at least I don't want much. Now that I can be out of that house, I only wish to have what is dear to me. I didn't have time last night to do a final sweep and make sure I had it all. Plus, Jane deserves her Christmas present.

I turn right at the stop sign onto our street, and as I round the last bend to our house, lights catch my eyes. Police lights. Red and blue blaring in the driveway of my marital home. I slow the car to a stop nearby and get out. I don't remember running, but I make it to the door in a hurry only to be caught by a police officer.

"You can't go in there, ma'am," he says as he effortlessly lifts and sets me down in a new spot.

"That's my house. What's going on?" Could John be dead? Did he kill himself? Why are there three cars here? Is that the number they bring to arrest someone or to a suicide?

The officer signals to one of his buddies to come over and escort me off to the side of the yard so that I can no longer get in the way of their job.

"Deputy Byers will fill you in, ma'am, but right now I need to ask that you step away from the entrance." Sure enough, Deputy Byers is gripping my elbow and leading me away from the front porch while the officer at the door returns to standing guard.

"What's going on?" I repeat.

"Hold on, ma'am. I'll answer your question in just a moment, but first I need you to answer some of mine. What's your name?" He is a younger officer, tall and built like he spends his mornings at the gym. The brown locks of his hair flow into his face, and I can tell he takes pride in not only his job but his appearance, as well.

"My name is Medeia Moore, this—" I point to the front door— "is my house."

"Where are you coming from, Medeia?" He raises his eyebrow in question.

"I slept at a friend's house last night. I fought with my husband, and I left," I state. I don't give more away than he's asking, but I know sometimes it's not about the words you say, but more the ones that you don't.

"Is that how you got that bruise?"

"The what?"

"That bruise." He points to my face. "On your cheek there."

"Yes, I slapped him back, though." I want clear transparency when it comes to the cop's impression of me. I don't want him believing I can lie to the authorities.

"That's okay, ma'am." He touches my face for a closer inspection. "You're saying your husband struck you, though?"

"Yes." His hand is pinching my chin, moving my head from side to side looking for other marks.

"Why?" He's bent down oddly so that he can square up with me eye-to-eye. It's a little unnerving and comforting all at once, and I'm not sure what the effect is supposed to be out of the two options.

"I confronted him about the affair he was having at work." I look toward the sky. "Look, tell me honestly, is he dead?"

"No, ma'am. He's alive."

I breathe a sigh of relief and bend my body in half. I don't want John to get out of this that easily. "The detectives told me he was cheating on me with his secretary, so when they left the house, I called down to his office and asked for Regina. She's the nosiest bitch there, so I knew she'd have the scoop. Sure enough, she sent pictures. Pictures. Can you imagine?"

He shakes his head at me. I plop down in the grass on my butt, and he follows in a squat.

"What happened next?"

"Well, I forwarded the photos to the detectives because they mentioned proving their suspicions, and I gave them Regina's number. I was just so mad, I wasn't trying to be an asshole, but I was. And they didn't question everyone down there thoroughly as they claimed, or they'd already have had the photos." He understands and gives up the squat and sits down next to me. "So, he came home pissed off and in a mood. We argued a little, and I saw Hannah's car outside of the window, so I came downstairs to greet her and send her home. I never shout, but, well, this time I did. I shouted and scared her, too."

"Hannah?" he interrupts.

"Our chef."

"Oh." He lifts his eyebrows.

"Look, don't fucking judge me. Yes, we had a chef. I can cook, John will tell you otherwise, but I know how to do it. He's the one who hired her."

He holds his hands up in defense. "I apologize. I meant nothing by it."

I roll my eyes. "Anyway, she quit. Said she couldn't work for him. I understood that. I mean, shit, he screwed his secretary. Who would want to work with a man who did that? And then—" I point around— "obviously something bad happened to his secretary. I asked the detectives if she was dead, and they just looked at each other in this weird way. Clearly, they told John that she died because in our fight when I accused him of being a murderer, all he said was that he didn't kill her. She's dead, right? And why would I stay the night here after that?"

"The secretary or the chef?"

"The secretary." I slam my head into my knee. "This is a horrible game of Clue."

"You didn't hear it from me, but she's dead."

"Oh." I look up into his eyes. "Jesus. I figured that by the look on the detective's faces, but to hear the words. Wow."

He bobs his head. "Is that when he slapped you?" He doesn't suspect me. They all believe it's John. I got away.

"No, he slapped me when I told him he couldn't keep his dick out of his secretary's mouth." I listen to the officer try not to laugh and fail, covering it up with a cough.

"That's not funny."

"I know. I have a horrible sense of humor."

"Now answer my question."

He looks confused.

"What's going on here?"

"Your husband is resisting arrest for the murder of Anna Trayor." He stares at the doorway the whole time, expecting John to be walking out at any moment lead in handcuffs.

"Oh, Jesus." I put my head between my knees again. "How long?"

"We got here around six."

I look at my watch. "Three hours?" I peek at him from the top of my knee.

He only nods.

"You're horrible at this. John doesn't even own a gun. Just go in there and tell him that you'll start breaking the door down if he doesn't get out."

"He does own a gun," he interrupts.

"He what?" I shout. I slam my head down on the ground. *What were you planning on doing with that, John?*

"Are you willing to give a signed statement of everything you just told me."

"Yes."

"Coming out!" I hear the man at the door shouting. My companion jumps off the ground and offers his hand to me. I take it, and once my feet are back on the ground, he places himself in front of me for protection.

It happens in slow motion, the way John's feet hit the sidewalk one by one and the way his head hangs lower at the brightness of the outside light. He's ashamed. He's flanked on each side by an officer, both larger than he is. I see another appear behind him with a gun that he places in a bag for evidence, no less. John's gun. *Why did you own a gun, John?*

They push his head into the backseat of one of the three cruisers parked haphazardly in our driveway, and he flinches from the pain. The other officer shuts the door on him with great finality. Suddenly the sounds come rushing back into my ears, and I hear the shouting and the officer next to me leaving my side.

"I'm fine," I mutter to no one in particular, not sure if anyone even asked.

Then John looks up and spots me. He holds my stare. I find peace in his hollow eyes.

Medeia's Journal

DEAR ANNA,

John will pay for what he did to you. I promise you that.

Forty-Four

I ARRIVE AT THE PRISON right on time on Saturday. I receive a standard search and pat down. Items are asked to be removed from my person because they violate the code. My phone is taken, along with my purse. I no longer have the burner phone on me. Jane and I destroyed it last night since it is no longer valuable. I stand, stripped of everything but the divorce papers, waiting for my husband.

It gives me a slight clue as to what John must be dealing with in here. He could never last without certain luxury items. It was a joke we ran in the house all the time. John isn't the type who can live without a therapeutic mattress or memory foam pillow. Shit, he can't sleep a night without his sound machine.

Here he is in prison, and I'm a hundred percent positive that they do not provide those things. Not even if you fuck a guard for it. I hope the prisoners are lulling him to sleep, making fake wind sounds and teaching him how to fluff his paper-thin pillow to make something more suitable for the herniated disc in his neck. I'm sure they're kind like that in here.

I wait at one of the small tables in the visiting room with a name tag clipped to my shirt that lets everyone know I am just a visitor. I would hate to be confused as anything else in this place. The walls of the large room are cold and con-

267

crete, they let zero amount of heat into the room. I keep my cardigan sweater swirled about me for need rather than want or fashion. The smell of damp despair clings to the air and drowns everyone in misery. The walls are a faded chipped gray that I'm pretty sure was originally white. Behind a bulletin board that has shifted from the nail on the left side, I see a sliver of the room's original color, which was more eggshell than dingy gray.

It is easy to spot the first-timers, we are all nervously fidgeting as if we are in detention for the first time and don't want to get caught even looking in the wrong direction. Especially me, because I know I'm about to see an innocent man. I'm too close to the place that should house me for the crime, and the fear causes my stomach to ache. If they find out they won't let me walk back and get my purse and leave this hole.

The ones who are veterans are relaxed in their chairs and staring at the door they know their loved ones will pop out from any minute. They've accepted that this place has become part of their life's routine. The lawyers in the room shuffle their papers and put them in the area where their client will soon reside.

We are all waiting for someone—someone that we love, someone who is our blood, someone who has wronged us, or someone who is paying us. I wait for closure, as I'm sure some of the anxious others are looking for, as well. There's a young girl, obviously meeting with her father today, practicing her speech at the table near mine. She's planning on getting the words out that have been suppressed by her teeth and tongue for too long. Today is her day for regaining a bit of the strength that her father stole from her. He still holds power over her because she stumbles through the words without confidence. I send out a silent prayer that she will find her voice before her father walks in.

John finally enters the room behind five other prisoners all wearing the same tacky tan scrub uniforms. It screams that they are no better than the other—no matter their crime they'll all be punished and treated the same in here. Murderers. Embezzlers. Thieves. Rapists. Molesters. They all follow the same conduct and rules inside these cold, hard walls.

I see him before his hollow eyes can spot me. Dark circles surround those dead eyes, and his face has sunken in from weight loss. He looks lost. He looks fragile and weak. The hardened criminals surrounding him are a contrast to the hollowed man. When he catches eyes with me, his face lights up. I'm here to tell him that he can rot in hell and I'm not holding his name any longer. John is looking for the last chance of a friend, and I'm not bringing it.

"Oh my god, Medeia, I'm so happy you came. I'd hug you, but that guard would knock my teeth out for touching you," he exclaims as he rushes to the table.

"That's fine, John. I don't think a hug is appropriate, anyway." He misses what I'm saying. The tone isn't set. He doesn't bother to listen to the fact that I'm hinting that nothing is right between us, that the time that's passed hasn't brought us closer. He chooses to dismiss me as if I have a tiny voice that human ears can't hear. He needs control over the situation, and for him to gain it, he pretends that it's all going his way until everything around him conforms to the notion.

We sit across from each other, papers in my lap waiting to take their place on the small rickety wooden table between us—the words *Decree of Divorce* in calligraphy on top. The weight of them bores holes into my lap as we sit across from each other, tension thick.

"John, we need to talk," I start, but as per usual, John can't wait to interrupt me.

"You look well, Medeia. I'm so happy to see you. Everything that the police are saying is just crazy. I'm glad you aren't buying any of it. I knew you wouldn't leave me, my sweet girl. You know the real me. You know I would never do such a thing or dare try to harm you in any way. I only look out for what's best for you."

There it is. Like a shoe that you just took off the night before, slipping into it feels just the same in the morning. I'm being drawn back in with his smooth talk, his unique pet names and the way he makes me feel like he's dripping me in attention when the reality is that John is painting an illusion in front of my face so he can steal something from me.

"John, I do know the real you. That's what you always forget." I am exasperated. I am mad at him for even trying it again, but can I sincerely blame him? It's all he has left. He's in prison with an insurmountable amount of evidence against him in a crime that will put him away for a long time. He has nothing left to grab at but straws. I don't want to be the last thing he grabs for when he makes the fall down the rabbit hole. He won't take me along for this ride.

"Yes, babe, you do." He drums the table when he realizes that the conversation isn't going his way and chooses to switch tactics. "I can't believe the trial is postponed. It's ridiculous. I'm innocent."

"It's the holidays, John, people who didn't kill their mistresses deserve to be at home opening gifts with their children." I roll my eyes.

"I didn't kill her. She wasn't my mistress." He spits the words behind clenched teeth to keep the truth from falling out along with them.

"That's right. Anna was your girlfriend."

He shakes his head and allows his attention to fall on the girl who is delivering the speech to her father, ignoring me.

"John, I filed for a divorce." I calmly set down the papers between us.

"What?" The guard shushes him, reminding him to keep his voice down or his visit will end. "You did what?" he hisses.

"I filed for divorce." I grab the papers and push them closer to him. He jolts back like they're going to bite him. "I believe under the circumstances that it isn't that far-fetched of an idea, that someone wouldn't want to be attached to a murderer who was plotting to have them committed to a mental facility."

He gasps.

"What John, do you think because I'm not personally involved in your case with the lawyers that I don't hear the stories and the gossip? That I don't read Anna's friend's comments on all the news posts on Facebook? Or the articles that show the text messages for the whole world to see?"

"I – "

"Save it." I tap the papers. "I'm here to serve you."

"What are you hoping to get?" I watch the guilt shift to manipulation on John's face. "You already signed a prenup." The devil smiles at me. I smile back.

"Which is nulled when not signed with equal legal representation. I never had a lawyer look over it when I signed it, so my lawyer is working to have it thrown out. Also, thanks for not being honest about your previous arrest records, I'm sure that will benefit the case. Shit, John, I almost forgot the best part about that prenup."

"What?" He's scared.

"You get everything; it's lopsided. My lawyer said he works hard to get those thrown out, and it typically works." I wink. "So, I want my share. Half."

"Half?" He squeezes the table edge.

"Half," I confirm.

"Why do you deserve that? You don't even work."

"I didn't. I do now. But, you're correct in the marriage you did support me financially, making me a dependent. I get a least three year's worth of alimony, I believe."

"What?"

"Or half of everything, and I leave you alone."

"I'll fight it." His jaw pops in frustration.

"I suspected as much, so we will just get together in court when we can." I point around the room. "I know you are rather tied up these days."

"You bitch," he spits.

"Murderer," I correct, but he assumes that I accuse him.

"I am innocent."

"Slit her throat," I state without the presence of who.

"I did not." He looks around nervously as other visitors and inmates are taking an interest in us. John's an embarrassment, and it infuriates him to feel like others are witnessing him in this state.

"Dumped her body," I continue, only this time I do direct the accusation at John.

"I won't give you the divorce. Do you know what is happening to me in here? I haven't slept for days. I was raped by two guys the first night I was in here, and they keep trying to hunt me down again and get me alone. And now you want to come in here and ask me for a divorce? What happened to for better or for worse?"

"I'm not asking you, John. I'm telling you. I filed for a divorce. If you fight it, I'll wait it out until it goes through. I won't have your name attached to me anymore. And the guys who raped you? Let them have you. It wouldn't be the first time that you stepped out on our marriage, would it? You want to come at me for the line 'for better or for worse,' then how about forsaking all others?" I feel a small burst in my heart to know that the universe has a funny bone, and it's somewhere in John's stolen asshole virginity. "You always did want to try anal." I laugh.

"Goddammit, Medeia." He slams his fist on the table. The guard starts to walk over.

"Goodbye, John. Take your papers with you, won't you, dear?" I stand to leave. The guard takes John by the arm.

"I warned you, tough guy. Not in my visiting room, back to your bunk." He lifts John off the chair by just one arm. There's no way that John can fight him back.

"Sir, will you kindly make sure he takes these with him?" I tap the papers on the desk. After looking down at them, the guard smiles at me as he plucks them up with ease and delight.

"Certainly, ma'am. And good for you." He has a wide grin, and I return the gesture.

"Goodbye, John." I look into his eyes. It's at that moment that I confess through that look that I put him there. I tell him with my eyes that I'm the reason he got it up the ass by some bullies in the big house. I'm the reason he has no friends who want to associate with him anymore. I am the reason he won't be coming home.

But, just like John, he doesn't listen when I talk.

Medeia's Journal

DEAR ANNA,

You got what you wanted. I'm leaving John. How does it feel? I wish you could tell me.

Medeia's Journal

DEAR ANNA,

Did you realize that John had isolated me from everyone I loved? If you had known, would you have stopped him? Was the act just part of your plan to get me prepped and ready for the life of solitude in a mental facility?

I am curious about your part in the plan to have me committed to the mental hospital. Were you just the motivation behind it, or did you have a hand in plotting the whole thing?

Medeia's Journal

DEAR ANNA,

Christmas is over now, and you didn't thank me for your gift. Manners, my dear.

Medeia's Journal

DEAR ANNA,

I live a whole new life now, but you're still here. Our redemption is coming up fast — John's trial. There are riots in the street for your justice. I think about telling them that it has already been served, but they would never listen.

I watch as your mother gains glory in her fame from your demise. Would you like me to take her out?

She smiles for the camera and puts that GoFundMe cash she raised for a search party to find you to good use on her vanity. At least you were someone else's cash cow, instead of always being the one to milk the teat.

Medeia's Journal

DEAR ANNA,

The trial is tomorrow, and this will be the longest letter that I write to you. The more I talk to you here the closer I feel, but honestly, who knew you better than me?

Your mother wants justice for her 'precious little princess,' but she didn't want to be near you when you were alive. I watch the moment she slammed the door in your face over and over in my mind every time I see her on TV screaming for your justice. How could she be so cold? You would have benefited from the kind of love that my mother gave to me, but it didn't save her in the end, either.

We're on a rollercoaster with the men we have chosen in this life—your mother, mine, you, and me. Your mother never stuck with anyone long, but never gave up hope that the next guy coming was going to be the one to save her. You were a product of a one-night stand that she didn't want to be reminded of. You weighed her down when it came to her future. She couldn't get far with a baby around, so to please the man in her life at the time, she relinquished you to her mother. Your grandmother fought for you, at least.

My mother was too far into a bad situation to turn around and admit she made a mistake. Call it foolish pride that she clung to, but she chose us instead of herself. She believed staying was better than being on her own. She didn't think she could provide us any better life on her own. She was different than your mother, yet her fate was worse. She laid cold in a puddle of her blood because the lover who was supposed to protect her got mad.

John told you about my mother, you helped him plan little things to say to spark instability in my recovery, but I won't hold it against you. You didn't know her. She was everything. Things you couldn't dream of being, and things I'm too far gone from achieving myself. You judged solely on your love for John, and that emotion is beyond itself a powerful thing. You turned yourself into a calculating person to satisfy the itch to be with him.

I changed once for his love as well, so I can understand that part of you.

Then there's you and me; tangled with the same man, but our relationships were so different. John adored you. He didn't batter and berate your self-esteem until you molded into a lifeless doll. No, he championed you, adapted to your evil, manipulative ways, meshing them with the ability he already possessed. You were both on your way to becoming a powerful entity together. You were made for each other in a sick way, but like all the others before us, I didn't want to play the tragic part in your love story.

I broke the pattern.

I'm free, but you still chain me.

I see you in my sleep. Jane shakes me awake to silence my screams. Sometimes she sits with me for hours before I fall asleep again, constantly telling me that it gets better. Can I tell you about Jane?

She's wonderful. The strength she has. She also broke her pattern, took justice into her own hands from her abuser. You wouldn't like her. You didn't have the backbone to take down your torturous mother, you became her, instead — a whore.

I hope you find peace where you are. For me, I will roam the rest of my life with the cross attached to my back, and you tucked into my pocket safe from the world's knowledge.

Forty-Five

THE TRIAL DAY HAS FINALLY arrived. I make my way to the courthouse after debating all night about coming at all. I refuse to be on the witness stand. John's lawyer, Dennis, believed it best I didn't as well. John may have started the whole situation, but I was the catalyst moving its direction, and now I need to see the ending.

Jane flanks my side. I don't know if I would be able to make it through this moment without her. We park in the parking garage and walk toward the front of the building with our arms linked. When we come around the corner, we see the protestors with their signs and hear their chants of justice for Anna.

In a world that was once John's playground, he is despised by all who lay eyes on him now. Strangers spit toward him as he is escorted inside for his judgment to begin. They shout and wave their homemade signs in his direction.

"Why don't you slit your own throat?"

"You should get the death penalty."

"Look at her face, John, I hope she haunts your dreams."

Their brutality causes me to wince. If the police had looked harder for another suspect instead of closing the case so quickly, they would have found me, and those would be the words ringing inside my ears as my hands are clasped together in cuffs.

"Come on." Jane nudges me forward. We are not without our own judgment as we walk up. An older lady decides to shout my identity to the crowd, and they gather around to offer me their opinions on my life.

"If you could have fucked your husband better maybe she'd be alive."

"Excuse me?" Jane screams.

"Maybe if she paid attention to what her husband was doing, she could have saved this girl's life." The old lady looks at me as if I'm a pile of shit. I want to smile and kiss her cheek and tell her that I am the monster that lives under the bed waiting to grab you in your sleep. I'm the face in the morning of every mistake you've ever committed. I am the one who took her life. I passed judgment on them and punished how I saw fit.

I stare her down, and she bustles away out of my sight. I wish her death and pray that I have the powers bestowed in my dead heart to cast such a spell.

Jane pulls me forward. "Ignore the old bat."

We make our way through the entrance and the metal detectors, then we are directed to the courtroom. I lean on Jane while we walk, feeling my legs begin to give way underneath me.

"Oh god, Jane," I sputter at the door. "Where do we sit?"

There is a John side, and there is an Anna side. There is no I-hate-both-of-them side.

Jane hesitates, as well. "Uh. I'm not sure. Is it like a wedding? Do they each have sides?" she whispers as people push past us, annoyed that we are in their way of seeing the show.

"Well, Anna's side is insane. Let's sit on the other side—" she doesn't say John's side— "to stay away from the crowd."

"Toward the back, please," I add weakly.

Among the audience in attendance to this shit show stands a crew of Anna's Angels, each decked out with their own personalized printed photo t-shirt. I laugh inside my head. The group is led by Anna's mother, who didn't give a damn about her child when she was alive. She's eating up every second of this fame. Each time I see her on the news she has something new in the way of a makeover. She finally got veneers to cover the immense gaps in her teeth—years of drug use, no doubt, and their consequences. Her wig is off-centered as I watch her raise her hands high above her head holding an 8x10 framed picture of Anna. Nails, freshly done. Had to look stunning for all the cameras.

I take note of the picture in her hands; it's Anna's senior picture from nearly five years ago. Her mother couldn't even bother to have a more recent photo. How can anyone believe this woman's story? How does she have an entire three rows of pews donning this ridiculous apparel? It's amazing what a human being will do for attention, even a few minutes of it.

As I scan down the line, I meet Samantha's face four rows up. She's rolling her eyes at Anna's mother. I watch her shake her head, filled with abhorrence, as she turns back around in her seat. Thank you. Someone else understands. She catches my eye when she turns. I stare with my mouth open.

Could she place me from the trinket shop? She lends me a half smile — an apology for having such a shitty friend. I bow my head.

"What was that?"

"I'm not sure," I tell Jane. "I think I was just given some weird apology from Anna's best friend."

"How can that be Anna's best friend? I thought Anna was all looks." She glances back at Anna's mother to confirm the vanity trait.

"That's not what she looked like before," I answer her mind's questions.

I gaze upon the jury perched in their judgment box, higher than everyone else. There are a plethora of middle-aged women who read their Bibles front to back every year. John doesn't stand a chance in hell at winning this case. They don't like adulterers or the kind that approve of the activity under any circumstance.

"Anna was a model human being who volunteered at many organizations..." While the attorney describes her to everyone, I lose count of the groups she participated in. Funny, in all the time I followed her she didn't once reach out to the poor and needy aside from taking her mom some overpriced groceries. I did some digging of my own into Anna's background when it was finally free from suspicion and found that the first married man that she had an affair with was a pastor. Instead of thumping people with Bibles, they thumped on it like rabbits. She may have presented herself as a model citizen on the outside, but inside lingered a pure evil.

John's lawyer's opening statement sets out to slander Anna's name.

"Miss Trayor had a history of manipulating married men into getting things she wanted from them. Whether it be a car, money, or some other material item, she made a lot of enemies that way, but John wasn't one of them. My client is innocent. Miss Trayor's seedy past led to her demise. Someone framed John to get back at her for the past."

It might make a little headway with some of the overly stuffy broads behind that box, but to me, it was just plain tacky. The prosecutor shakes his head, he has seen it all before in his line of work, but I bet this tactic was just a little too much for even the strongest of hearts. John's lawyer continues.

"We don't have the evidence to prove the allegations, but enough of Miss Trayor's past on record to give reasonable doubt to Mr. Moore's involvement in the crime." I bow my head into my hand and shake side to side. John found the most expensive idiot known to man.

The first witnesses that the prosecution calls to the stand are his strongest on the list, professionals who can explain the evidence found at the crime scene and the drop-off site in extensive detail and layman's terms. They are poetically versed in their science, impressing all the people in the room. Even John is impressed by the way they speak.

"The body was found near the woods by the warehouse, after investigating some tire marks and finding Miss Trayor's car still at the warehouse, we decided to gain a search warrant for the building. Upon entering, we found a mattress stained with blood. That blood proved to be Anna Trayor's.

"The blood splatter on the cardboard boxes and floor surrounding the mattress, show that the assailant was above her at the time of the attack and sliced her neck from left to right in a quick swipe."

"The toxicology reports indicate that Anna Trayor was drugged with prescription anti-depressants acting as a sleep aid, the same brand that was readily available to Mr. Moore through his wife's medicine cabinet."

"Rigor Mortis began to set in at approximately two hours after Miss Trayor's demise, and this allowed us to take in account how her body was positioned during the attack. It was a neutral position. There was no struggle. She knew the person above her. And it was indicated, in my professional opinion, that the killer was a lover because of the proximity of secondary blood splatter from the attacker's face dripping back onto Miss Trayor's."

"The DNA samplings on the knife and the semen found inside Miss Trayor's body came back a perfect match for Mr. Moore."

"It was found and noted that Mr. Moore did have a violent past, having spent three months in prison for an aggravated assault charge. On the day of his arrest, his wife was there with a bruise on her face that she did confirm came from Mr. Moore striking her. He was also found with a gun that he legally cannot own."

I bounce my foot off the ground; to an innocent by-stander it merely looks like a nervous tick, but inside I'm finally bouncing like Anna with joy as all the scientists hammer the nails into John's coffin. *Without a single doubt, these were John Moore's fingerprints. The fingerprints found in a perfect grip formation on the knife.* They even hold the knife up and demonstrate how a killer would use it. Some of the ladies on the jury gasp as they watch in horror as the forensic expert explains how her throat was slit. I love how close they come to the truth; science is a marvel. The only part they are missing is me.

John's lawyer flailed at cross-examining the forensic experts and going so far as to insult one when he questioned his background.

"I beg your pardon, sir, but I've been in this field for a near forty years now, before all of the advancements in science. I can confirm without a doubt that it is your client's fingerprints holding the knife in the exact position it would take to create such a wound upon the victim's neck."

John sank in his chair with each testimony, but he got even lower when the witnesses were brought up to provide the motive.

Forty-Six

"I WANT TO CALL SAMANTHA Davis to the stand, please." I sit up straighter at the sound of her name, and Jane follows suit.

After being sworn in, Samantha begins to give the jury and judge something that the forensic experts couldn't provide—the story of Anna and John's relationship. I love this girl's high morals. I hope for great things in her life. Probably not friends, because she's on the stand singing her dead friend's sins like a canary, but great things, nonetheless.

Samantha sits on the stand without an ounce of fear haunting her.

"Miss Samantha Davis, can you kindly tell us about the relationship your friend, Anna Trayor, had with the accused?"

"Yes, she was his mistress so to speak. She liked saying that she was his girlfriend, but he was married, so I think that falls under a mistress title."

"Did Anna work for Mr. Moore?"

"Yes, sir, she did. That's how they met." She nods her head like a period at the end of each statement.

"That was going to be my next question." The lawyer smiles at her. "Was Anna known for manipulating material things out of men like the defense claimed in their opening statement?"

"Yes. It was the second married guy she was fooling around with, I think his name was Bill, but anyway, she blackmailed him with photos of themselves in compromising positions if he didn't give her his wife's Mercedes Benz." Samantha doesn't flinch.

"Did she continue and follow through with this plan?" The prosecutor casually leans against his desk now; his case is in the bag.

"Well, up until her death she drove a white Mercedes Benz SUV, so what do you think?" Some of the crowd laugh.

"I'm sorry, Miss Davis, but we have to be clear for the record here with no speculation."

"Oh, I'm sorry. Yes, Anna did follow through with the plan and ended up having the vehicle transferred into her name." Samantha smooths her hair down, feeling a little uneasy that she slipped up.

"Did she ever mention a plan to manipulate Mr. Moore?"

"No, sir. She always told me she loved John." She glares over at John.

"Yet, they couldn't be together."

"No."

"And why is that?"

"Because he is married, and he didn't want his wife to be able to gain access to any part of his money if they divorced." She looks toward me apologetically — I breathe out a sigh. The lawyer follows her sight and offers me a sad smile.

"Did Anna come up with any plans to have John to herself?"

"No, but John did." The crowd gasps as she stares him down. "He told Anna one night that his wife was taking anti-depressants because her father murdered her mother. In my mind, it was reasonable for Mrs. Moore to be upset over that, but Anna said that John wanted to use it to get rid of her."

"Get rid of her; how?"

"He told Anna that he had contacted a place out of curiosity asking about the facility to see if it would be a good fit for his wife. They told him what the base level of acceptance was and John decided to try to get his wife committed. Anna got on board with it because it meant she got to be with John."

"What kind of place was this?"

"A home for the mentally ill, sir." She shies away from his gaze.

"That seems like a pretty nasty thing to do to a person, did you try to stop her?"

"Yes, sir. I told her at every turn that it was a terrible idea and she needed to realize she was the mistress."

The lawyer walks over to his desk and retrieves an audio device. "If you will, Miss Davis, listen to this recording and tell me what you make of it."

Over the scratchy audio of the recorder, the courtroom hears Samantha's voice. *"Listen, Anna. I'm done. You and John are sick for what you're trying to do to his wife. If you don't like the fact that I told you the truth, then I'm done with it. You deserve John if you're going to be that nasty of a human being. His wife deserves nothing but all of his money in the divorce, and I hope she gets it. You're proving yourself to be no better than your mother."*

When it's done, Samantha grabs a tissue and dabs her eyes.

"That's me," she chokes out. "I left that voicemail for Anna. I didn't know she stood me up because she was dead."

"Your tone is nothing but of a concerned friend," the lawyer attempts to soothe her. "Did she ever mention to you that John had a violent temper?"

"Not in an angry way. In the bedroom sense, she did make mention that he was into some crazy aggressive stuff." Samantha glances toward John and wills his death with those eyes. I bite my tongue to suppress a giggle. Jane grips my hand, trying to hold her own laughter in.

"Like what?" The prosecutor looks over at John. No fear. Ballsy.

"Oh, gosh ... this is embarrassing to talk about, but she said he liked to choke her and scream names at her in role-playing."

"What kind of names?" The prosecutor continues to stare straight at John as he questions Samantha. John squirms.

"Whore. Bitch. Cunt. He had a colorful vocabulary."

"John wasn't the only person that Anna was seeing at the time of her murder, was he?"

"She was dating Thomas, a guy I set her up with hoping she would forget all the foolishness of being with a married man, but she never left John."

"Do you think Thomas could be the one who killed Anna?" he questions with his head tilted toward the crowd.

"No, things weren't that serious between them, and besides he left for vacation the day before she was murdered.

He wasn't even in town." Samantha shrugs. She knows it was John, no doubt in her mind.

"How was her relationship with Thomas?"

"She didn't love him as much as John, but she clung to him more each time John ran back to his wife. She wanted better for herself. She and John had a huge fight after his birthday party, and I thought John was out of the picture, until one day when she confessed that he kept texting her and she might meet with him to see what he wanted. I told her it was a bad idea, but she went anyway. The next thing I know, she winds up with her throat slit." Samantha slams her hand on the railing of the witness box, boring holes into John's head.

"Thank you. I have no further questions."

Now it's time for John's attorney to question Samantha. He's been messing up every time he's up there, and you can feel everyone in the room cringe when he clears his throat for questioning. What kind of a disaster are we going to watch this time? John places his head in his hand and hides his face.

"Miss Davis, would you say you were great friends with Miss Anna Trayor?"

"Yes, I would." She shakes her head; he doesn't meet her level.

"How can you be such great friends if you are telling her deepest secrets?" He leans in toward her, and she leans back. I imagine he has terrible breath.

"Secrets don't count when your friend ends up murdered, sir." She holds back an eye-roll so hard I think she may need an exorcist.

"What do you mean? Aren't secrets the true bonds of friendship?" He leans in onto the witness stand as best he can at his short stature; it ends up being more comical than intimidating.

"No, the true bonds of friendship are honesty. Anna was my friend because she appreciated how blunt I could be about things. And I didn't mind how blunt she could be at times. We balanced each other and didn't want either to fail. No one around her took the time to tell her when she was making a mistake or that she was worth more than the paths she kept choosing. I did that for her. I told her the truth no matter if it hurt because I wanted the best for her,"

"Did you want to hurt your friend, then?"

"No, sir. I wanted her to know the truth. I told her John wouldn't leave his wife for her, not to hurt her feelings, but to give her a push in the direction of leaving him so she could start fresh with someone who didn't have strings attached." Samantha smacks her hand down on the banister close to the lawyer's hand.

"So, John wasn't the only man that could have killed Anna in a jealous rage?"

"Excuse me?"

"You mentioned she had a boyfriend. What was his temper like?"

"Just how I said it was earlier in my testimony. Thomas is a nice guy." Samantha is getting annoyed. She isn't the only person in the room that wishes the gavel would fall on his whole charade of playing lawyer. I'm glad I refused to research a better lawyer for John's defense. This is what happens when you have limited resources behind bars.

"Are you sure he was? What if he was mean and cold? Did you set up their meeting because you were jealous of Anna and wanted her gone?"

"Oh, my god. Are you delusional?"

"Objection, your Honor. Accusing the witness." The prosecutor jumps out of his seat to a standing position.

"Sustained. That's enough, counselor," the judge booms.

Samantha answers anyway. "No, I wasn't jealous of Anna. I didn't want that lifestyle. I don't condone being an adulterer. It doesn't mean that I wanted Anna punished for it. I wanted her to choose better in her life, to quit giving in to people who just wanted to use her. That's why I introduced her to Thomas. Whatever kind of painting you're trying to make won't work."

The judge almost claps. No more objections are yelled out because she shut them all down. John's lawyer has no further questions. Samantha loves the truth as I love clinging to lies. I adore every twist I can make out of them and the lives I have ruined because of the redemption I have found. She finds her safety in the truth; I find mine along with my freedom in the lies.

The next to the stand is my therapist, Dr. Janson. He is here to prove that his notes during our discussions led him to believe in John's ability to gaslight me. Hearing his professional opinion of what was being done to me in my home, under my nose, is hard to swallow. I almost walk out for fresh air.

"She had reported several times that her husband felt she needed to increase her medication. She would also make mention of the oppression in her household, not being allowed to

have a job or friends because of her husband's rules. Hiding her friendship and feeling the need to hide her job as well. When it came to light that she was working, Mr. Moore immediately told her to quit."

"So, in your professional opinion, does the motive that Mr. Moore was attempting to create mental instability in his wife hold water?"

"Yes."

They call one of the arresting officers to discuss John's previous arrest record that includes a history of violence and the bruise on my cheek at the time of the arrest. He speaks of my confession on how it got there, and also the gun in John's possession which because of his past he was not legally allowed to own — driving the nail in deeper.

John throws his head down on the table before him. It's over for him.

Medeia's Journal

DEAR ANNA,

Your friend Samantha loves you even though you are nothing but a wreck inside. I admire her, and I wish to be more like her. She gave you the answers to your problems, but you chose to ignore them. On some level, I think you liked playing dangerous games with your life, hoping for someone to save you.

I did that for you.

It wasn't in the way that you were hoping for or imagined that you deserved, but I cut you free from John. I created this attention that you're receiving. I made your mother love you even if it is just a show for the cameras desperately grasping to get the behind the scenes story. They all want to hear your name and story. They all want justice for your death. You are the innocent victim to them no matter your contribution in all of this.

I did that for you.

You're welcome.

Forty-Seven

AS THE JURY DELIBERATES, Jane and I take a walk around the block. The February air is frigid and threatens to seize our lungs, but the air inside the building is too stifling, making the outside feel welcoming.

"I should confess."

"What?" Jane is shocked. "Absolutely not."

"I did all of that. I made that scene in there. I'm a monster, Jane. I am the reason they're tearing him apart." I kick some snow piled off the curb.

"Then what, Medeia? What does jail hold for you? Better yet, if they can go with the psych story you might get sent to one of those places instead, then John wins," she taunts.

"Shut up," I hiss.

She kicks the snow next to me and tightens the scarf around her neck. "You can't have everything in black and white; there is gray floating all around us. It's what makes up most of our soul. You were drowning and found a life raft. You can't just throw it back because other people might drown. You need to save yourself sometimes."

"Yeah, except I'm making someone drown so that I can float." I walk down the street. One more block might do it. "I'm no better than John or Anna."

Jane falls into step next to me. "My ex-husband struck me one time they had to take out an ovary. An ovary. Can you believe it? Can you imagine hitting someone repeatedly with such force that they lose an ovary?" Jane talks to the cement and not to me.

"Jesus, Jane. That's awful."

"Not as awful as the fact that I lost my right ovary to an ectopic pregnancy years before that day." Silence falls on our lips, nothing but the busy hustle of people not involved in this case or our lives going about their day around us, driving in their cars, and living far removed from two murderers talking on the sidewalk.

"His mistress got pregnant. I was so pissed. He took away my last chance at ever becoming a mom, and he gave it to *her*." I watch the tears sting Jane's eyes as she fights them away. "Then he took away where I lived because he had a baby on the way, and he took away my right to any money because he needed it for the child."

"He was a monster."

"So, I took it back." She stamps her foot and forces me to look into her eye. "Should I tell the world my sin? I'm just as awful as he was."

"No. Jesus, no. He deserved it."

"John deserves this."

I deflate. "Jane."

"No, you can't see it because you're the one right in it, so let me tell you on the outside you aren't the one who is alone in the fault. You didn't start this. He should clean it up." She grabs my arm and steers me toward the building again. "And now we are going to watch him get his judgment, and then we will drink tonight until we are drunker than we have ever been because even though we've committed the worst of sins, it doesn't mean we don't feel."

Back inside, the jury has finished deliberating. It only took them an hour to decide John's fate.

"We, the jury, find the defendant, John Moore, to be guilty of the charge of first-degree murder."

Cheers are surrounding us in the back row. John's mother cries in the front row behind him. I can't see John anymore. His head has bowed too low, and I'm no longer in the position back here to see his reaction. I watch Anna's mother hoot and holler her joy, bouncing up and down. I look for an honest response — something that describes the weight.

Samantha.

She's bowed her head in graceful prayer, shedding a tear that she quickly wipes away. She's talking to Anna and telling her the results and that she misses her. Justice doesn't take away what was done here. It doesn't bring Anna back or replace the last ten years of my life.

I head toward the door to the courthouse. I can't breathe anymore. Hands all around me, touching my arms. Some cruel with their touch accusing me of not being a good enough wife. Others offer comfort telling me they're sorry for what I'm going through. It doesn't matter what side of the fence you stand on someone will disagree.

I burst through the front doors and slam my body into one of the concrete pillars at the front of the building. My body shakes with tears. I'm free.

Medeia's Journal

DEAR ANNA,
    The end.

Epilogue

JOHN WAS SENTENCED to life in prison, a decision he didn't take lying down, and he set out for an appeal.

Our court date for the divorce proved to be another loss for him. His assets are now all mine. He's left with nothing because what is a man without the possibility of parole going to do with anything outside the walls of a prison? Nothing. So, the judge granted everything to me.

I put the house up for sale immediately and sold everything that I could. Jane and I spent one night there when we were boxing things up to ship to buyers. The house no longer felt anything more than cold. Nothing like the life I am living now, and Jane agreed.

Jane put her house on the market at the same time, and when they both sold, we used the money to move to Louisiana. New Orleans. A fresh start for two girls who needed to have new memories to scare away the demons of the past. We took turns waking and comforting each other from our nightmares, but the incidents lessened when we finally made a move.

Word from Pittsburgh still travels down this way. I clutch the newspaper article in my hand as I search for Jane out on the back deck.

"Jane?"

"Yeah?" She brushes the dirt off her hands from flowers she was tending. "What's that?"

"He's dead."

"Who's dead?" I watch the dirt smear on the corners of her mouth when her hand comes up to it. "No. Give me that." She rips the paper from my hands and begins to read out loud. "John Moore was found in his cell dead of an apparent suicide by hanging. Mr. Moore's appeal in the murder case of mistress Anna Trayor was recently denied. It is led to believe that this was the reasoning behind Mr. Moore's ultimate decision to end his life."

"Jesus," I say. Hearing it out loud feels weirder than in my head.

Jane grabs my arm and leads me into the house, tracking mud and dirt all over the wood floor until we finally reach our small kitchen. She lets go of me and reaches for the shelf above the fridge and grabs a bottle of tequila, twisting the cap off and taking a shot before handing it to me. I follow suit.

"He's dead," I say as I drink from the bottle, a large chug that burns my throat but does nothing to wake the new numbness inside. I've killed again.

"What do we do? Celebrate? That feels wrong," she says, grabbing for the bottle to take her turn.

"Commemorate?" I offer.

She shakes her head. "Even worse." She chugs the bottle.

"I know," I say, taking another large chug. "Get a shower and those weird voodoo things you picked up the other day. Cancel dinner with my brother and sister." One bonus of New Orleans was that I found my siblings. They missed me as much as I did them. After one awkward minute, we synced again. They loved Jane and accepted her as another sister.

"What are you going to do?" she calls.

"I have to grab something!" I shout as I run to my room on the top floor. We bought this house because both of our bedrooms have balconies; naturally, mine was the perfect side for the sun to rise, and Jane's the sunsets. In the corner of my room, I have my dresser. It has a special secret compartment in the top drawer. I throw my socks and underwear on the floor so that I can get to it.

"What's that?" Jane finds me an hour later in our backyard stoking the firepit.

I hesitate to answer, so she grabs the book from my hand.

"Dear Anna..." Jane reads. "Medeia, you wrote to her."

"I never sent them. Journaling was just something that always helped me work out my feelings." She nods and notes the firepit.

"I'll go grab more tequila," she replies.

We sit and burn the pages one by one, never reading a single letter. Jane told me that the stones she bought from a psychic store in town would help clear the energy, but I know I'll never be released of the thoughts.

I can convince myself that I am justified in what I have done, but it doesn't take away the sin. I have stolen a human life. I am no better than my father, nor do I deserve the best in life. I can't trust anyone but Jane with my secrets, and for the most part, Anna is the only secret she knows. What I did was despicable, and I should rot in jail for it. Like my father, I am free when I don't belong amongst society. I'm just better at planning my lies than most.

When we've set the last note ablaze, I toss the cover of the journal on top of the fire and watch the worst time of my life reduce itself to nothing but ashes. It's unimaginable that it could ever be this far behind me. Only on the surface, does it look like it is.

"I'm going to bed." I stumble out of my chair around the firepit. Jane waves a goodnight. She wants to stay out and watch the sunset, anyway.

When I make it upstairs, I fall on the bed without shedding my clothing or shoes. Before my eyes fall in sleep, I see Anna in the corner laughing at me.

Sneak Peek

IF YOU ENJOYED READING Medeia's story, turn the page to read the first chapter of Jane's story. Available November 12th, 2019.

One

"YOU HAVEN'T BEEN GONE one day, and I already have a new stray."

I hear the cans in the pantry slam on the shelf as Ramona grumbles once again about my leaving. She's in her early sixties, bare minimum, though I'd wager she has a few more years behind that famous scowl of hers than I think. I have never asked. We've known each other for months, but I'm still terrified to bring out her bark. With Ramona, it's worse than her bite at times.

"See? You don't need me," I call over my shoulder. I'm met with a grumble echoing in the pantry as a response.

I look behind me to see her short auburn curls bouncing next to the door of the kitchen cabinet. The mask of hairspray on her head is no match for the sweat of helping me move, and the curls, fried from a cheap curling iron, are beginning to deflate. She turns her head out toward me, catching me spying on her. Her lipstick bleeds out onto her crepe skin, and when I stare at the crimson running into her frown line, it only gets deeper.

"Quit looking at me and get to work. We still have rooms to clean at the motel," she shouts, slamming her wrinkled hands down on her hips for an intimidation factor. I almost laugh because of her tiny stature, but I know better.

I look about the living room where I'm sitting on the floor, filling the bookshelf. There are two cardboard boxes in the middle of the floor. That's all I have to my name. All my possessions fit into two medium-sized boxes. We'll be done in an hour if that. I sigh. It's not much, but it's finally mine. It wasn't long ago that I was sitting in a mansion with thousands of things around me, but now my life has been reduced to two cardboard boxes, all thanks to Stewart and his whore.

"I can't believe you came to help me. Who's running the place?" Ramona owns a motel just outside of Pittsburgh. It's a cheap little place, with a few sketchy clients scattered about, but mostly it's a haven for women, the strays, that Ramona helps. Women like me, that got kicked out on their ass and have no place to call their home, and nowhere and nobody to run to for shelter. Now, I have that place— this apartment.

"Hannah. She's a stray from years back. I asked for a favor." Ramona never leaves the motel. I'm touched to know that under her hard exterior, I've wormed my way in enough for her to consider it.

"Oh." I tap on the trunk next to me. It's the only thing here in this apartment that I didn't acquire within the last couple of months. It's been with me since childhood. It was my mother's, and I wasn't about to let Stewart keep it even if it meant going to the house and facing his pregnant mistress to get it.

"Where's that boy of yours? Shouldn't he be helping us move all this shit?" Ramona dismounts from the two-step ladder in the kitchen to glare at me over the tiny island that completes the kitchen section of the ample open space.

"Billy? He's not my boy, and you know it." I glare. "Besides, he had to work. Something about an undercover job." I shrug. Billy, a part of my old life that transferred over into my new, was not the romantic hero that Ramona was begging for him to be, and her constant reference to Billy being more than what he is annoys me.

"He likes you. I can see it in his eyes, Jane." She waddles out of the kitchen, satisfied with the completion of her task, and rips open one of the cardboard boxes on the floor. I shuffle over from my spot to mirror her image with the other box, having completed my task at the bookshelf.

"I don't feel like arguing with you," I groan. There will be other days and other times that I can take up this argument with Ramona, but today isn't one of those times that I have the energy for it.

"Then don't," she cackles, and it immediately breaks out into a cough — too many cigarettes.

"Let's just finish this, huh?" I raise my eyebrow at her. "Before your lungs give out." She frowns at my own annoying tick— reminding her that the cigarettes will give her cancer.

"Looks like we'll make it back before lunchtime." She surveys the contents of the boxes and realizes her morning off wasn't worth it. I feel guilty that Ramona's first day off in as long as I've known her is for nothing.

"Yea," I whisper. "Thanks for coming, Ramona. I know it's not much to unpack." I hold my right elbow in the opposite arm, itching the back of it in embarrassment, suddenly aware of the little bit that I have to claim as my own.

"No problem, kid. Too bad they never found your stuff in that car." She pats my shoulder — *that car*. A shiver of ice runs down my spine and sends me clinging my arms around my body tightly for warmth — *that car.*

"Well, at least everything is fresh for your new life." She tosses a throw pillow onto my secondhand couch, unaware that I'm struggling to breathe in the encompassing feeling of that night flashing back into my mind.

"Yeah. My new life." I exhale, and the apartment comes back into view.

"Quit your moaning. It's better than it was. Now you have me." She digs her wrinkled hands into the box and gathers up a few more living room items that I bought to make the space feel homey. Useless purchases as Ramona called them, but they bring a certain level of peace to me. Those items represent that I'm not just surviving, living day to day only satisfying my means, but that I'm breathing in a life all my own and thriving. At least I hope to someday.

"That it is." I kick the other box into my bedroom because the only things inside are my clothes.

My life before coming to Ramona's motel may have looked glamorous on the outside, but inside I wore the marks of Stewart's frustration with my inability to fit in with his crowd. Still, I never left— believing the punishments would stop as soon as I mastered the skills that he desperately thought I lacked. I lived every day thinking that I would reach that level and suddenly my husband's hand would drop and never land on me again. That level, that day, never came. There is no such spot.

I start to hang my consignment store purchased clothing in my small closet. The entire apartment is smaller than my closet when I was married to Stewart. Still, I'm happier here than I was in that big old mansion. If only my new life came without the nagging feeling of being found by that maniac driver, the owner of *that car.*

"Well, I'm done with my box." Ramona plunks down on my bed and begins placing shirts in the box on hangers for me. She doesn't even need to be asked. We have become in sync the last couple of months, working like a well-oiled machine knowing the other one's actions and what needs to be done. We immediately jump in to help and get the job done without a single word being said

"Ramona, maybe this is stupid," I blurt. "It's safe at the motel with you." I grip the edge of the last shirt I've hung. This move, leaving that haven, could expose me. He could find me here. He never found me at the motel. I was hidden well there.

"Nonsense. Your boy toy told you this is the safest complex. He's a cop; he should know which places see the most crime." She hands me a group of shirts to hang and starts work getting my khakis on pants hangers, prompting me to continue working.

"You're right, but do I really need my own space?" I wish there were a concrete answer letting me know if this apartment is going to work out or not, there's too much at stake in the unknown.

"Kid," Ramona sighs, "this is a new step, and it's all your own. I know it feels scary, but you can do this."

"Okay."

"Besides, I don't want your ass living near me anymore." I chuckle.

"Ramona!"

"I'm serious. Your snoring can be heard through the walls." I know she's dramatic on purpose to ease the fear in my chest. She knows what people need, sensing their emotions, and hands it over. Even with her sarcastic mannerisms, she can't hide her empathetic golden heart. I see it.

"Thank you."

"Don't thank me for that. Thank me for not warning your neighbors." I hum in response.

What would I do without Ramona? One thing is for sure; I would have died that night if it weren't for her help.

Keep reading here[1].

---

1.   https://www.amazon.com/dp/B07ZG69NJW

Author's Note

THANK YOU SO MUCH FOR reading Dear Anna. I have been living with Medeia inside my head for months now, and it feels so good to finally get her story out. This is my first psychological thriller, and I'm happy to say that it won't be my last.

If this is my first book that you've read, please consider moving on to Pressing Flowers[1], it's a women's fiction novel dealing with the heavy subject of grief.

Thank you so much for purchasing this book and taking the journey inside Medeia's mind. I would love to hear your thoughts, email me with them at authorkatieblanchard@yahoo.com . Reviews help authors get exposure, so please leave one when you're done as well.

Thank you again for your support!

Katie Blanchard

---

1.   https://www.books2read.com/PressingFlowersKB

About the Author

KATIE BLANCHARD IS an avid reader and kid wrangler. She lives in Southwestern, Pennsylvania with her two children and husband. Katie is also the author of the women's fiction novel, *Pressing Flowers*. When she isn't writing characters out on her keyboard, she's putting her hands to good use crocheting blankets.

To find out more about Katie Blanchard, go to www.authorkatieblanchard.com[1]

Or if social media is more your thing and you want to keep up on my writing progress, photos from my crazy life with two kids, or chat books and coffee?

Follow me here: Facebook[2] – Twitter[3] – Instagram[4]

I'm also on Goodreads[5]! Follow me and join my reader group here[6]!

---

1.   http://www.authorkatieblanchard.com

2.   http://bit.ly/KBlanchardFBPage

3.   http://bit.ly/KBlanchardTwitter

4.   http://bit.ly/KBlanchardIG

5.   http://bit.ly/KBlanchardGoodreads

6.   http://bit.ly/KBlanchardReaderGroupFB

Thank Yous

THIS BOOK WOULD NOT have been possible without the help of an entire village of folks. I am forever grateful for them and in no order, I want to give them their shout-outs!

To my husband, Brian, for EVERYTHING! For the snacks while I wrote, the wine that was brought to me, for never looking at me like I'm crazy when I talk about my characters as if they're real, for helping me when I get stuck, for making the kids stay away when I'm writing, for loving me selflessly and believing in my dreams as if they were your own. You are the most amazing human being, and after 17 years of knowing you, I love you still. I'd choose you again, EVERY. DAMN. DAY.

Special shout-out to my kids, Blaine and Lila, you challenge Mommy's multitasking skills every day and make her better. Not only that, every day I think about making a good example for you and making you proud. I hope I accomplished that.

To my sister, Christa, for inspiring me and championing me. For reading pages repeatedly without complaint. How can a person be so selfless? You amaze me with your love and support. I'm blessed to not only call you my sister, my blood, my ride-or-die, my soulmate, but my friend in this life.

To my parents, for never following the norm. For always telling me that I can do anything I set my mind to. So many people say that's a bad thing for a child to hear because it gives them false hope, well, I'm glad you don't listen to that nonsense. Thanks for always building me up. My self-esteem is 100% your fault and I thank you.

To my beta readers, Melissa, Carol, Stephanie, Jasmine, Carrie, Monica, Shannon, Danielle, Mary, and Debbie. Thank you for taking in the roughest of rough drafts and giving me your feedback.

Which brings me to Traci Finlay. Girl. There wouldn't be a *Dear Anna* without you. Hands down, you are amazing. Thank you for your brainstorming, your eagle eye, your dedication, and your commentary. I am forever grateful that I met you. And someday, I am going to fight the demon lizards and visit you. I swear.

To Bex, the editing ninja, thank you for proofreading and cleaning up the edges of this book for me. I was going cross-eyed and needed you.

To Teddi, for the cover, for the teasers, for your hard work and positive energy. I have said it before, but the world needs to know that you are an amazing person to have in my corner. I am thankful for you.

To everyone along the way that has shared a post, made a comment, or cheered for me in the writing process, thank you thank you thank you thank you. I can't say it enough. Thank you from the bottom of my heart.

Made in the USA
Las Vegas, NV
15 December 2020